HIT MAN

"PAGE-TURNER OF THE WEEK . . .
Macabre charm . . . In what amounts to a series
of interlocking short stories with more plot twists
than the current White House imbroglio,
Keller proves the perfect observer of life—
clear-eyed, ironic and always dead-on."

People

"A collection of stories that reads like the flowing
memoir of a man who is letting it all out for
the first time . . . The ironic tone and confessional
content make these intimate tales so funny and
full of rue . . . [Keller] may have no ethics,
but he definitely has a way about him."

The New York Times Book Review

"A brilliant writer . . . superb entertainment."

Booklist

"Block's ravenous fans [will be]
delighted to see at least three masterpieces
gathered in one volume."

Kirkus Reviews

"Block, one of the genre's finest practitioners,
is in fine form here. Anyone looking
for a disturbing detour from the mainstream
will want to pick up *Hit Man*."

Chicago Tribune

LAWRENCE BLOCK

"One of the very best writers now working the beat."

The Wall Street Journal

LAWRENCE BLOCK

HIT MAN

HarperTorch
An Imprint of **HarperCollins***Publishers*

"Answers to Soldier," "Keller's Therapy," "Dogs Walked, Plants Watered," "Keller's Karma," "Keller in Shining Armor," "Keller on the Spot," and "Keller's Last Refuge" originally appeared in *Playboy* magazine.

HARPERTORCH
An Imprint of HarperCollins*Publishers*
195 Broadway
New York, NY, 10007

Copyright © 1998 by Lawrence Block
Excerpt from *Hit Man* copyright © 2000 by Lawrence Block
Inside cover author photo by Sigrid Estrada
Library of Congress Catalog Card Number: 97-20272
ISBN: 0-380-72541-X

First HarperTorch paperback printing: July 2002
First Avon Books paperback printing: February 1999
First William Morrow hardcover printing: February 1998

HarperCollins®, HarperTorch™, and ◆™ are trademarks of HarperCollins Publishers Inc.
Avon Trademark Reg. U.S. Pat. Off. and in Other Countries, Marca Registrada, Hecho en U.S.A.

Printed in the United States of America

Visit HarperTorch on the World Wide Web at
www.harpercollins.com

23 24 25 26 27 LBC 28 27 26 25 24

for EVAN HUNTER

ACKNOWLEDGMENTS

Keller gets around a great deal, and it is perhaps fitting that the author was similarly peripatetic while chronicling his adventures. He is thus pleased to acknowledge the following venues, where various sections of this book were written: the Virginia Center for the Creative Arts, in Sweet Briar, Virginia; the Ragdale Foundation, in Lake Forest, Illinois; the Park Plaza Motor Lodge, in Johnson City, New York; the SS *Nordlys*, in Norwegian coastal waters; Emilie Poe Wood's house, in Lucedale, Mississippi; Continental Airlines flight 214 from Houston to Newark; and, in New York City, the Writers Room (Waverly Place), the Writers Room (Astor Place), the Peacock Caffè (Greenwich Avenue), Caffè Lucca (Bleecker Street), and the Donnell branch of the New York Public Library.

Grateful acknowledgment is also due to those publications in which some of Keller's adventures appeared in a slightly different form: *Murder on the Run*, a collection of stories by members of the Adams Round Table; *Murder Is My Business*, an anthology edited by Mickey Spillane and Max Allan Collins; and, of course, *Playboy*.

Answers to Soldier

Keller flew United to Portland. He read a magazine on the leg from JFK to O'Hare, ate lunch on the ground, and watched the movie on the nonstop flight from Chicago to Portland. It was a quarter to three local time when he carried his hand luggage off the plane, and then he had only an hour's wait before his connecting flight to Roseburg.

But when he got a look at the size of the plane he walked over to the Hertz desk and told them he wanted a car for a few days. He showed them a driver's license and a credit card and they let him have a Ford Taurus with thirty-two hundred miles on the clock. He didn't bother trying to refund his Portland-to-Roseburg ticket.

The Hertz clerk showed him how to get on I-5. Keller pointed the car in the right direction and set the cruise control three miles an hour over the posted speed limit. Everybody else was going a few miles an hour faster than that, but he was in no hurry, and he didn't want to invite a close look at his driver's license. It was probably all right, but why ask for trouble?

It was still light out when he took the off ramp for the second Roseburg exit. He had a reservation at the Douglas Inn, a Best Western on Stephens Street. He found it without any trouble. They had him in a ground-floor room in the front, and he had them change it to one a flight up in the rear.

He unpacked, showered. The phone book had a street map of downtown Roseburg, and he studied it, getting his bearings, then tore it out and took it with him when he went out for a walk. The little print shop was only a few blocks away on Jackson, two doors in from the corner, between a tobacconist and a photographer with his window full of wedding pictures. A sign in Quik Print's window offered a special on wedding invitations, perhaps to catch the eye of bridal couples making arrangements with the photographer.

Quik Print was closed, of course, as were the tobacconist and the photographer and the credit jeweler next door to the photographer and, as far as Keller could tell, everybody else in the neighborhood. He didn't stick around long. Two blocks away he found a Mexican restaurant that looked dingy enough to be authentic. He bought a local paper from the coin box out front and read it while he ate his chicken enchiladas. The food was good, and ridiculously inexpensive. If the place were in New York, he thought, everything would be three or four times as much and there'd be a line in front.

The waitress was a slender blonde, not Mexican at all. She had short hair and granny glasses and an overbite, and she sported an engagement ring on the appropriate finger, a diamond solitaire with a tiny stone. Maybe she and her fiancé had picked it out at the credit jeweler's, Keller thought. Maybe the photographer next door would take their wedding pictures. Maybe they'd get Burt Engleman to print their wedding invitations. Quality printing, reasonable rates, service you can count on.

In the morning he returned to Quik Print and looked in the window. A woman with brown hair was sitting at a gray metal desk, talking on the telephone. A man in shirtsleeves stood at a copying machine. He wore horn-rimmed glasses with round lenses and his hair was cropped short on his egg-shaped head. He was balding, and that made him look older, but Keller knew he was only thirty-eight.

Keller stood in front of the jeweler's and pictured the waitress and her fiancé picking out rings. They'd have a double-ring ceremony, of course, and there would be something engraved on the inside of each of their wedding bands, something no one else would ever see. Would they live in an apartment? For a while, he decided, until they saved the down payment for a starter home. That was the phrase you saw in real estate ads and Keller liked it. A starter home, something to practice on until you got the hang of it.

At a drugstore on the next block, he bought an unlined paper tablet and a black felt-tipped pen. He used four sheets of paper before he was pleased with the result. Back at Quik Print, he showed his work to the brown-haired woman.

"My dog ran off," he explained. "I thought I'd get some flyers printed, post them around town."

LOST DOG, he'd printed. PART GER. SHEPHERD. ANSWERS TO SOLDIER. CALL 555-1904.

"I hope you get him back," the woman said. "Is it a him? Soldier sounds like a male dog, but it doesn't say."

"It's a male," Keller said. "Maybe I should have specified."

"It's probably not important. Did you want to offer a reward? People usually do, though I don't know if it makes any difference. If I found somebody's dog, I wouldn't care about a reward. I'd just want to get him back with his owner."

"Everybody's not as decent as you are," Keller said. "Maybe I should say something about a reward. I didn't even think of that." He put his palms on the desk and leaned forward, looking down at the sheet of paper. "I don't know," he said. "It looks kind of homemade, doesn't it? Maybe I should have you set it in type, do it right. What do you think?"

"I don't know," she said. "Ed? Would you come and take a look at this, please?"

The man in the horn-rims came over and said he thought a hand-lettered look was best for a lost-dog notice. "It makes it more personal," he said. "I could do it in type for you, but I think people would respond to it better as it is. Assuming somebody finds the dog, that is."

"I don't suppose it's a matter of national importance, anyway," Keller said. "My wife's attached to the animal and I'd like to recover him if it's possible, but I've a feeling he's not to be found. My name's Gordon, by the way. Al Gordon."

"Ed Vandermeer," the man said. "And this is my wife, Betty."

"A pleasure," Keller said. "I guess fifty of these ought to be enough. More than enough, but I'll take fifty. Will it take you long to run them?"

"I'll do it right now. Take about three minutes, set you back three-fifty."

"Can't beat that," Keller said. He uncapped the

felt-tipped pen. "Just let me put in something about a reward."

Back in his motel room, he put through a call to a number in White Plains. When a woman answered he said, "Dot, let me speak to him, will you?" It took a few minutes, and then he said, "Yeah, I got here. It's him, all right. He's calling himself Vandermeer now. His wife's still going by Betty."

The man in White Plains asked when he'd be back.

"What's today, Tuesday? I've got a flight booked Friday, but I might take a little longer. No point rushing things. I found a good place to eat. Mexican joint, and the motel set gets HBO. I figure I'll take my time, do it right. Engleman's not going anywhere."

He had lunch at the Mexican café. This time he ordered the combination plate. The waitress asked if he wanted the red or green chili.

"Whichever's hotter," he said.

Maybe a mobile home, he thought. You could buy one cheap, a nice double-wide, make a nice starter home for her and her fellow. Or maybe the best thing for them was to buy a duplex and rent out half, then rent out the other half when they were ready for something nicer for themselves. No time at all you're in real estate, making a nice return, watching your holdings appreciate. No more waiting on tables for her, and pretty soon her husband could quit slaving at the lumber mill, quit worrying about layoffs when the industry hit one of its slumps.

How you do go on, he thought.

He spent the afternoon walking around town. In a gun shop, the proprietor, a man named McLarendon, took some rifles and shotguns off the wall and let him get the feel of them. A sign on the wall read GUNS DON'T KILL PEOPLE UNLESS YOU AIM REAL GOOD. Keller talked politics with McLarendon, and socioeconomics. It wasn't that tricky to figure out his position and to adopt it as one's own.

"What I really been meaning to buy," Keller said, "is a handgun."

"You want to protect yourself and your property," McLarendon said.

"That's the idea."

"And your loved ones."

"Sure."

He let the man sell him a gun. There was, locally, a cooling-off period. You picked out your gun, filled out a form, and four days later you could come back and pick it up.

"You a hothead?" McLarendon asked him. "You fixing to lean out the car window, bag a state trooper on the way home?"

"It doesn't seem likely."

"Then I'll show you a trick. We just backdate this form and you've already had your cooling-off period. I'd say you look cool enough to me."

"You're a good judge of character."

The man grinned. "This business," he said, "a man's got to be."

It was nice, a town that size. You got into your car and drove for ten minutes and you were way out in the country.

Keller stopped the Taurus at the side of the road, cut the ignition, rolled down the window. He took the gun from one pocket and the box of shells from the other. The gun—McLarendon had kept calling it a weapon—was a .38-caliber revolver with a two-inch barrel. McLarendon would have liked to sell him something heavier and more powerful. If Keller had wanted, he probably would have been thrilled to sell him a bazooka.

Keller loaded the gun and got out of the car. There was a beer can lying on its side perhaps twenty yards off. He aimed at it, holding the gun in one hand. A few years ago they started firing two-handed in cop shows on TV, and nowadays that was all you saw, television cops leaping through doorways and spinning around corners, gun gripped rigidly in both hands, held out in front of their bodies like a fire hose. Keller thought it looked silly. He'd feel self-conscious, holding a gun like that.

He squeezed the trigger. The gun bucked in his hand, and he missed the beer can by several feet. The report of the gunshot echoed for a long time.

He took aim at other things—at a tree, at a flower, at a white rock the size of a clenched fist. But he couldn't bring himself to fire the gun again, to break the stillness with another gunshot. What was the point, anyway? If he used the gun, he'd be too close to miss. You got in close, you pointed, you fired. It wasn't rocket science, for God's sake. It wasn't neurosurgery. Anyone could do it.

He replaced the spent cartridge and put the loaded gun in the car's glove compartment. He spilled the rest of the shells into his hand and walked a few yards from the road's edge, then hurled them with a sweeping sidearm motion. He gave the empty box a toss and got back into the car.

Traveling light, he thought.

*   *   *

Back in town, he drove past Quik Print to make sure it was still open. Then, following the route he'd traced on the map, he found his way to 1411 Cowslip Lane, a Dutch Colonial house on the north edge of town. The lawn was neatly trimmed and fiercely green, and there was a bed of rosebushes on either side of the path leading from the sidewalk to the front door.

One of the leaflets at the motel had told how roses were a local specialty. But the town had been named not for the flower but for Aaron Rose, an early settler.

He wondered if Engleman knew that.

He circled the block, parked two doors away on the other side of the street from the Engleman residence. "Vandermeer, Edward," the white pages listing had read. It struck Keller as an unusual alias. He wondered if Engleman had picked it out for himself, or if the feds had selected it for him. Probably the latter, he decided. "Here's your new name," they would tell you, "and here's where you're going to live and what you're going to be." There was an arbitrariness about it that somehow appealed to Keller, as if they relieved you of the burden of decision. Here's your new name, and here's your new driver's license with your new name already on it. You like scalloped potatoes in your new life, and you're allergic to bee stings, and your favorite color is cobalt blue.

Betty Engleman was now Betty Vandermeer. Keller wondered why her first name had remained the same. Didn't they trust Engleman to get it right? Did they figure him for a bumbler, apt to blurt out "Betty" at an inopportune moment? Or was it sheer coincidence or sloppiness on their part?

Around six-thirty the Englemans came home from

work. They rode in a Honda Civic hatchback with local plates. They had evidently stopped to shop for groceries on the way home. Engleman parked in the driveway while his wife got a bag of groceries from the back. Then he put the car in the garage and followed her into the house.

Keller watched lights go on inside the house. He stayed where he was. It was starting to get dark by the time he drove back to the Douglas Inn.

On HBO, Keller watched a movie about a gang of criminals who had come to a town in Texas to rob the bank. One of the criminals was a woman, married to one of the other gang members and having an affair with another. Keller thought that was a pretty good recipe for disaster. There was a prolonged shoot-out at the end, with everybody dying in slow motion.

When the movie ended he went over to switch off the set. His eye was caught by the stack of flyers Engleman had run off for him. LOST DOG. PART GER. SHEPHERD. ANSWERS TO SOLDIER. CALL 555-1904. REWARD.

Excellent watchdog, he thought. Good with children.

He didn't get up until almost noon. He went to the Mexican place and ordered huevos rancheros and put a lot of hot sauce on them. He watched the waitress's hands as she served the food and again when she took his empty plate away. Light glinted off the little diamond. Maybe she and her husband would wind up in Cowslip Lane, he thought. Not right away, of course; they'd have to start out in the duplex, but that's what they could aspire to, a Dutch Colonial with that odd kind of pitched roof. What did they call it, anyway? Was that a mansard roof, or did that word describe something else? Was it a gambrel, maybe?

He thought he ought to learn these things. You saw the words and didn't know what they meant, saw the houses and couldn't describe them properly.

He had bought a paper on his way into the café, and now he turned to the classified ads and read through the real estate listings. Houses seemed very inexpensive. You could actually buy a low-priced home here for twice what he would be paid for the week's work.

There was a safe deposit box no one knew about, rented under a name he'd never used for another purpose, and in it he had enough currency to buy a nice home here outright for cash.

Assuming you could still do that. People were funny about cash these days, leery of letting themselves be used to launder drug money.

Anyway, what difference did it make? He wasn't going to live here. The waitress could live here, in a nice little house with mansards and gambrels.

Engleman was leaning over his wife's desk when Keller walked into Quik Print. "Why, hello," he said. "Have you had any luck finding Soldier?"

He remembered the name, Keller noticed.

"As a matter of fact," he said, "the dog came back on his own. I guess he wanted the reward."

Betty Engleman laughed.

"You see how fast your flyers worked," he went on. "They brought the dog back before I even got the chance to post them. I'll get some use out of them eventually, though. Old Soldier's got itchy feet, he'll take off again one of these days."

"Just so he keeps coming back," she said.

"Reason I stopped by," Keller said, "I'm new in town, as you might have gathered, and I've got a business venture I'm getting ready to kick into gear. I'm going to need a printer, and I thought maybe we could sit down and talk. You got time for a cup of coffee?"

Engleman's eyes were hard to read behind the glasses. "Sure," he said. "Why not?"

They walked down to the corner, Keller talking about what a nice day it was, Engleman saying little beyond agreeing with him. At the corner Keller said, "Well, Burt, where should we go for coffee?"

Engleman just froze. Then he said, "I knew."

"I know you did. I could tell the minute I walked in there. How?"

"The phone number on the flyer. I tried it last night. They never heard of a Mr. Gordon."

"So you knew last night. Of course you could have made a mistake on the number."

Engleman shook his head. "I wasn't going on memory. I kept an extra copy of the flyer and dialed the number right off it. No Mr. Gordon and no lost dog. Anyway, I think I knew before then. I think I knew the minute you walked in the door."

"Let's get that coffee," Keller said.

They went into a place called the Rainbow Diner and had coffee at a table on the side. Engleman added artificial sweetener to his and stirred it long enough to dissolve marble chips. He had been an accountant back east, working for the man Keller had called in White Plains. When the feds were trying to make a RICO case against Engleman's boss, Engleman was a logical place to apply pressure. He wasn't really a criminal, he hadn't done much of anything, and they told him he was going to prison unless he rolled over and testified. If he did what they said, they'd give him a new name and move him someplace safe. If not, he could talk to his wife once a month through a wire screen and have ten years to get used to it.

"How did you find me?" he wanted to know. "Somebody leaked it in Washington?"

Keller shook his head. "Freak thing," he said. "Somebody saw you on the street, recognized you, followed you home."

"Here in Roseburg?"

"I don't think so. Were you out of town a week or so ago?"

"Oh, God," Engleman said. "We went down to San Francisco for the weekend."

"That sounds right."

"I thought it was safe. I don't even know anybody in San Francisco, I was never there in my life. It was her birthday, we figured nothing could be safer. I don't know a soul there."

"Somebody knew you."

"And followed me back here?"

"I don't even know. Maybe they got your plate and had somebody run it. Maybe they checked your registration at the hotel. What's the difference?"

"No difference."

Engleman picked up his coffee and stared into the cup. Keller said, "You knew last night. You're in that program. Isn't there someone you're supposed to call?"

"There's someone," Engleman said. He put his cup down. "It's not that great a program," he said. "It's great when they're telling you about it, but the execution leaves a lot to be desired."

"I've heard that," Keller said.

"Anyway, I didn't call anybody. What are they going to do? Say they stake my place out, the house and the print shop, and they pick you up. Even if they make something stick against you, what good does it do me? We'll still have to move again because the guy'll just send somebody else, right?"

"I suppose so."

"Well, I'm not moving anymore. They moved us three times and I don't even know why. I think it's automatic, part of the program, they move you a few times during the first year or two. This is the first place we've really settled in since we left, and we're starting to make money at Quik Print, and I like it. I like the town and I like the business. I don't want to move."

"The town seems nice."

"It is," Engleman said. "It's better than I thought it would be."

"And you didn't want to develop another accounting practice?"

"Never," Engleman said. "I had enough of that, believe me. Look what it got me."

"You wouldn't necessarily have to work for crooks."

"How do you know who's a crook and who isn't? Anyway, I don't want any kind of work where I'm always looking at the inside of somebody else's business. I'd rather have my own little business, work there side by side with my wife. We're right there on the street and you can look in the front window and see us. You need stationery, you need business cards, you need invoice forms, I'll print 'em for you."

"How did you learn the business?"

"It's a franchise kind of thing, a turnkey operation. Anybody could learn it in twenty minutes."

"No kidding?"

"Oh, yeah. Anybody."

Keller drank some of his coffee. He asked if Engleman had said anything to his wife and learned that he hadn't. "That's good," he said. "Don't say anything. I'm this guy, weighing some business ventures, needs a printer, has to have, you know, arrangements so there's no cash-flow problem. And I'm shy talking business in front of women, so the two of us go off and have coffee from time to time."

"Whatever you say," Engleman said.

Poor scared bastard, Keller thought. He said, "See, I don't want to hurt you, Burt. I wanted to, we wouldn't be having this conversation. I'd put a gun to your head, do what I'm supposed to do. You see a gun?"

"No."

"The thing is, I don't do it, they send somebody else. I come back empty, they want to know why. What I have to do, I have to figure something out. You're positive you don't want to run?"

"No. The hell with running."

"Swell, I'll figure something out," Keller said. "I've got a few days. I'll think of something."

After breakfast the next morning, Keller drove to the office of one of the real estate agents whose ads he'd been reading. A woman about the same age as Betty Engleman took him around and showed him three houses. They were modest homes but decent and comfortable, and they ranged between forty and sixty thousand dollars.

He could buy any of them out of his safe deposit box.

"Here's your kitchen," the woman said. "Here's your half-bath. Here's your fenced yard."

"I'll be in touch," he told her, taking her card. "I have a business deal pending and a lot depends on the outcome."

He and Engleman had lunch the next day. They went to the Mexican place and Engleman wanted everything very mild. "Remember," he told Keller, "I used to be an accountant."

"You're a printer now," Keller said. "Printers can handle hot food."

"Not this printer. Not this printer's stomach."

They each drank a bottle of Carta Blanca with the meal. Keller had another bottle afterward. Engleman had a cup of coffee.

"If I had a house with a fenced yard," Keller said, "I could have a dog and not worry about him running off."

"I guess you could," Engleman said.

"I had a dog when I was a kid," Keller said. "Just the once. I had him for about two years when I was eleven, twelve years old. His name was Soldier."

"I was wondering about that."

"He wasn't part shepherd. He was a little thing. I suppose he must have been some kind of terrier cross."

"Did he run off?"

"No, he got hit by a car. He was stupid about cars, he just ran out into the street. The driver couldn't help it."

"How did you happen to call him Soldier?"

"I forget. Then, when I did the flyer, I don't know,

I had to put 'Answers to something.' All I could think of were names like Fido and Rover and Spot. Be like signing John Smith on a hotel register, you know? Then it came to me. Soldier. Been years since I thought about that dog.''

After lunch Engleman went back to the shop and Keller returned to the motel for his car. He drove out of town on the same road he'd taken the day he bought the gun. This time he drove a few miles farther before pulling over and cutting the engine.

He got the gun from the glove box and opened the cylinder, spilling the shells into his palm. He tossed them underhand, then weighed the gun in his hand for a moment before hurling it into a patch of brush.

McLarendon would be horrified, he thought. Mistreating a weapon in that fashion. Showed what an astute judge of character the man was.

He got back into his car and drove back to town.

He called White Plains. When the woman answered, he said, "You don't have to disturb him, Dot. Just tell him I didn't make my flight today. I changed the reservation, I moved it ahead to Tuesday. Tell him everything's okay, only it's taking a little longer, like I thought it might.'' She asked how the weather was. "It's real nice,'' he said. "Very pleasant. Listen, don't you think that's part of it? If it was raining I'd probably have it all taken care of, I'd be home by now.''

Quik Print was closed Saturdays and Sundays. Saturday afternoon Keller called Engleman at home and asked him if he felt like going for a ride. "I'll pick you up,'' he offered.

When he got there Engleman was waiting out in

front. He got in and fastened his seat belt. "Nice car," he said.

"It's a rental."

"I didn't figure you drove your own car all the way out here. You know, it gave me a turn. When you said, 'How about going for a ride?' You know, going for a ride. Like there's a connotation."

"Actually," Keller said, "we probably should have taken your car. I figured you could show me the area."

"You like it here, huh?"

"Very much," Keller said. "I've been thinking. Suppose I just stayed here."

"Wouldn't he send somebody?"

"You think he would? I don't know. He wasn't knocking himself out trying to find you. At first, sure, but then he forgot about it. Then some eager beaver in San Francisco happens to spot you, and sure, he tells me to go out and handle it. But if I just don't come back—"

"Caught up in the lure of Roseburg," Engleman said.

"I don't know, Burt, it's not a bad place. You know, I'm going to stop that."

"What?"

"Calling you Burt. Your name's Ed now, so why don't I call you Ed? What do you think, Ed? That sound good to you, Ed, old buddy?"

"And what do I call you?"

"Al's fine," Keller said. "What should I do, take a left here?"

"No, go another block or two," Engleman said. "There's a nice back road, leads through some very pretty scenery."

A while later Keller said, "You miss it much, Ed?"

"Working for him, you mean?"

"No, not that. The city."

"New York? I never lived in the city, not really. We were up in Westchester."

"Still, the whole area. You miss it?"

"No."

"I wonder if I would." They fell silent, and after perhaps five minutes Keller said, "My father was a soldier, he was killed in the war when I was just a baby. That's why I named the dog Soldier."

Engleman didn't say anything.

"Except I think my mother was lying," he went on. "I don't think she was married, and I have a feeling she didn't know who my father was. But I didn't know that when I named the dog. When you think about it, it's a stupid name anyway for a dog, Soldier. It's probably stupid to name a dog after your father, as far as that goes."

Sunday he stayed in the room and watched sports on television. The Mexican place was closed; he had lunch at Wendy's and dinner at a Pizza Hut. Monday at noon he was back at the Mexican café. He had the newspaper with him, and he ordered the same thing he'd ordered the first time, chicken enchiladas.

When the waitress brought coffee afterward, he asked her, "When's the wedding?"

She looked utterly blank. "The wedding," he repeated, and pointed at the ring on her finger.

"Oh," she said. "Oh, I'm not engaged or anything. The ring was my mom's from her first marriage. She never wears it, so I asked could I wear it, and she said it was all right. I used to wear it on the other hand, but it fits better here."

He felt curiously angry, as though she'd betrayed

the fantasy he'd spun out about her. He left the same tip he always left and took a long walk around town, gazing in windows, wandering up one street and down the next.

He thought, Well, *you* could marry her. She's already got the engagement ring. Ed'll print the invitations, except who would you invite?

And the two of you could get a house with a fenced yard, and buy a dog.

Ridiculous, he thought. The whole thing was ridiculous.

At dinnertime he didn't know what to do. He didn't want to go back to the Mexican café but he felt perversely disinclined to go anywhere else. One more Mexican meal, he thought, and he'd wish he had that gun back, so he could shoot himself.

He called Engleman at home. "Look," he said, "this is important. Could you meet me at your shop?"

"When?"

"As soon as you can."

"We just sat down to dinner."

"Well, don't ruin your meal," Keller said. "What is it, seven-thirty? How about if you meet me in an hour?"

He was waiting in the photographer's doorway when Engleman parked the Honda in front of his shop. "I didn't want to disturb you," he said, "but I had an idea. Can you open up? I want to see something inside."

Engleman unlocked the door and they went in. Keller kept talking to him, saying he'd figured out a way he could stay in Roseburg and not worry about the man in White Plains. "This machine you've got," he said, pointing to one of the copiers. "How does it work?"

"How does it work?"

"What does that switch do?"

"This one?"

Engleman leaned forward and Keller drew the loop of wire from his pocket and whipped it around the other man's neck. The garrote was fast, silent, effective. Keller made sure Engleman's body was where you couldn't see it from the street, made sure to wipe his own prints off any surfaces he might have touched. He turned off the lights, closed the door behind him.

He had already checked out of the Douglas Inn, and now he drove straight to Portland, with the Ford's cruise control set just below the speed limit. He drove half an hour in silence, then turned on the radio and tried to find a station he could stand. Nothing pleased him and he gave up and switched it off.

Somewhere north of Eugene he said, "Jesus, Ed, what else was I going to do?"

He drove straight through to Portland and got a room at the ExecuLodge near the airport. In the morning he turned in the Hertz car and dawdled over coffee until his flight was called.

He called White Plains as soon as he was on the ground at JFK. "It's all taken care of," he said. "I'll come by sometime tomorrow. Right now I just want to get home, get some sleep."

The following afternoon in White Plains, Dot asked him how he had liked Roseburg.

"Really nice," he said. "Pretty town, nice people. I wanted to stay there."

"Oh, Keller," she said. "What did you do, look at houses?"

"Not exactly."

"Every place you go," she said, "you want to live there."

"It's nice," he insisted. "And living's cheap compared to here. They don't even have a sales tax in the state, if you can believe that."

"Is sales tax a big problem for you, Keller?"

"A person could have a decent life there," he said.

"For a week," she said. "Then you'd go nuts."

"You really think so?"

"Come *on*," she said. "Roseburg, Oregon? Give me a break."

"I guess you're right," he said. "I guess a week's about as much as I could handle."

A few days later he was going through his pockets before taking some clothes to the cleaners. He found the Roseburg street map and pored over it, remembering where everything was. Quik Print, the Douglas Inn, the house on Cowslip Lane. The Mexican café, the other places he'd eaten. The gun shop. The houses he'd looked at.

Seemed so long ago, he thought. So long ago, so far away.

2

Keller on Horseback

At the airport newsstand, Keller picked up a paper-back western. The cover was pretty much generic, showing a standard-issue Marlboro man, long and lean, walking down the dusty streets of a western town with a gun riding his hip. Neither the title nor the author's name meant anything to Keller. What drew him was a line that seemed to leap out from the cover.

"He rode a thousand miles," Keller read, "to kill a man he never met."

Keller paid for the book and tucked it into his carry-on bag. When the plane was in the air he dug it out and looked at the cover, wondering why he'd bought it. He didn't read much, and when he did he never chose westerns.

Maybe he wasn't supposed to read this book. Maybe he was supposed to keep it as a talisman.

All for that one sentence. Imagine riding a thousand miles on a horse for any purpose, let alone the killing of a stranger. How long would it take, a thousand-mile journey on horseback? A thoroughbred got around a racecourse in something like two minutes, but it couldn't go all day at that pace any more than a human being could string together twenty-six four-minute miles and call it a marathon.

What could you manage on a horse, fifty miles a day? A hundred miles in two days, a thousand miles in twenty? Three weeks, say, at the conclusion of which a man would probably be eager to kill anybody, stranger or blood kin.

Was Ol' Sweat 'n' Leather getting paid for his thousand miles? Was he in the trade? Keller turned the book over in his hands, read the paragraph on the back cover. It did not sound promising. Something about a drifter in the Arizona territory, a saddle tramp, looking to avenge an old Civil War grievance.

Forgive and forget, Keller advised him.

Keller, riding substantially more than a thousand miles, albeit on a plane instead of a horse, was similarly charged with killing a man as yet unmet. And he was drifting into the Old West to do it, first to Denver, then to Casper, Wyoming, and finally to a town called Martingale. That had been reason enough to pick up the book, but was it reason enough to read it?

He gave it a try. He read a few pages before they came down the aisle with the drink cart, read a couple more while he sipped his V-8 and ate the salted nuts. Then he evidently dozed off, because the next thing he knew the stewardess was waking him to apologize for not having the fruit plate he'd ordered. He told her it didn't matter, he'd have the regular dinner.

"Or there's a Hindu meal that's going begging," she said.

His mind filled with a vision of an airline tray wrapped in one of those saffron-colored robes, extending itself beseechingly and demanding alms. He had the regular dinner instead and ate most of it, except for the mystery meat. He dozed off afterward and didn't wake up until they were making their descent into Stapleton Airport.

Earlier, he'd tucked the book into the seat pocket in front of him, and he'd intended to let it ride off into the sunset wedged between the air-sickness bag and the plastic card with the emergency exit diagrams. At the last minute he changed his mind and brought the book along.

He spent an hour on the ground in Denver, another hour in the air flying to Casper. The cheerful young man at the Avis counter had a car reserved for Dale Whitlock. Keller showed him a Connecticut driver's license and an American Express card and the young man gave him a set of keys and told him to have a nice day.

The keys fit a white Chevy Caprice. Cruising north on the interstate, Keller decided he liked everything about the car but its name. There was nothing capricious about his mission. Riding a thousand miles to kill a man you hadn't met was not something one undertook on a whim.

Ideally, he thought, he'd be bouncing along on a rutted two-lane blacktop in a Mustang, say, or maybe a Bronco. Even a Pinto sounded like a better match for a rawboned, leathery desperado like Dale Whitlock than a Caprice.

It was comfortable, though, and he liked the way it handled. And the color was okay. But forget white. As far as he was concerned, the car was a palomino.

It took about an hour to drive to Martingale, a town of around ten thousand midway between Casper and

Sheridan on I-25. Just looking around, you knew right away that you'd left the East Coast far behind. Mountains in the distance, a great expanse of sky overhead. And, right in front of you, frame buildings that could have been false fronts in a Randolph Scott film. A feed store, a western wear emporium, a run-down hotel where you'd expect to find Wild Bill Hickok holding aces and eights at a table in the saloon, or Doc Holliday coughing his lungs out in a bedroom on the second floor.

Of course there were also a couple of supermarkets and gas stations, a two-screen movie house and a Toyota dealership, a Pizza Hut and a Taco John's, so it wasn't too hard to keep track of what century you were in. He saw a man walk out of the Taco John's looking a lot like the young Randolph Scott, from his boots to his Stetson, but he spoiled the illusion by climbing into a pickup truck.

The hotel that inspired Hickok-Holliday fantasies was the Martingale, located right in the center of things on the wide main street. Keller imagined himself walking in, slapping a credit card on the counter. Then the desk clerk—Henry Jones always played him in the movie—would say that they didn't take plastic. "Or p-p-paper either," he'd say, eyes darting, looking for a place to duck when the shooting started.

And Keller would set a silver dollar spinning on the counter. "I'll be here a few days," he'd announce. "If I have any change coming, buy yourself a new pair of suspenders."

And Henry Jones would glance down at his suspenders, to see what was wrong with them.

He sighed, shook his head, and drove to the Holiday Inn near the interstate exit. They had plenty of rooms, and gave him what he asked for, a nonsmoking room on the third floor in the rear. The desk clerk was a woman, very young, very blond, very perky, with nothing about her to remind you of Henry Jones. She said, "Enjoy your stay with us, Mr. Whitlock." Not stammering, eyes steady.

He unpacked, showered, and went to the window to look at the sunset. It was the sort of sunset a hero would ride off into, leaving a slender blonde to bite back tears while calling after him, "I hope you enjoyed your stay with us, Mr. Whitlock."

Stop it, he told himself. Stay with reality. You've flown a couple of thousand miles to kill a man you never met. Just get it done. The sunset can wait.

He hadn't met the man, but he knew his name. Even if he wasn't sure how to pronounce it.

The man in White Plains had handed Keller an index card with two lines of block capitals hand-printed.

"Lyman Crowder," he read, as if it rhymed with *louder*. "Or should that be Crowder?" As if it rhymed with *loader*.

A shrug in response.

"Martingale, WY," Keller went on. "Why indeed? And where, besides Wyoming? Is Martingale near anything?"

Another shrug, accompanied by a photograph. Or a part of one; it had apparently been cropped from a larger photo, and showed the upper half of a middle-aged man who looked to have spent a lot of time outdoors. A big man, too. Keller wasn't sure how he knew that. You couldn't see the man's legs and there was nothing else in the photo to give you an idea of scale. But somehow he could tell.

"What did he do?"

Again a shrug, but one that conveyed information to Keller. If the other man didn't know what Crowder had done, he had evidently done it to somebody else. Which meant the man in White Plains had no personal interest in the matter. It was strictly business.

"So who's the client?"

A shake of the head. Meaning that he didn't know who was picking up the tab, or that he knew but wasn't saying? Hard to tell. The man in White Plains was a man of few words and master of none.

"What's the time frame?"

"The time frame," the man said, evidently enjoying the phrase. "No big hurry. One week, two weeks." He leaned forward, patted Keller on the knee. "Take your time," he said. "Enjoy yourself."

On the way out he'd shown the index card to Dot. He said, "How would you pronounce this? As in *crow* or as in *crowd*?"

Dot shrugged.

"Jesus," he said, "you're as bad as he is."

"Nobody's as bad as he is," Dot said. "Keller, what difference does it make how Lyman pronounces his last name?"

"I just wondered."

"Well, stick around for the funeral," she suggested. "See what the minister says."

"You're a big help," Keller said.

There was only one Crowder listed in the Martingale phone book. Lyman Crowder, with a telephone number but no address. About a third of the book's listings were like that. Keller wondered why. Did these people assume everybody knew where they lived in a town this size? Or were they saddle tramps with cellular phones and no fixed abode?

Probably rural, he decided. Lived out of town on some unnamed road, picked up their mail at the post office, so why list an address in the phone book?

Great. His quarry lived in the boondocks outside of a town that wasn't big enough to have boondocks, and Keller didn't even have an address for him. He had a phone number, but what good was that? What was he supposed to do, call him up and ask directions? "Hi, this here's Dale Whitlock, we haven't met, but I just rode a thousand miles and—"

Scratch that.

He drove around and ate at a downtown café called the Singletree. It was housed in a weathered frame building just down the street from the Martingale Hotel. The café's name was spelled out in rope nailed to the vertical clapboards. For Keller the name brought a vision of a solitary pine or oak set out in the middle of vast grasslands, a landmark for herdsmen, a rare bit of shade from the relentless sun.

From the menu, he learned that a singletree was some kind of apparatus used in hitching up a horse, or a team of horses. It was a little unclear to him just what it was or how it functioned, but it certainly didn't spread its branches in the middle of the prairie.

Keller had the special, a chicken-fried steak and some French fries that came smothered in gravy. He was hungry enough to eat everything in spite of the way it tasted.

You don't want to live here, he told himself.

It was a relief to know this. Driving around Martingale, Keller had found himself reminded of Roseburg, Oregon. Roseburg was larger, with none of the Old West feel of Martingale, but they were both small western towns of a sort Keller rarely got to. In Roseburg Keller had allowed his imagination to get away from him for a little while, and he wouldn't want to let that happen again.

Still, crossing the threshold of the Singletree, he had been unable to avoid remembering the little Mexican place in Roseburg. If the food and service here turned out to be on that level—

Forget it. He was safe.

After his meal Keller strode out through the bat-wing doors and walked up one side of the street and down the other. It seemed to him that there was something unusual about the way he was walking, that his gait was that of a man who had just climbed down from a horse.

Keller had been on a horse once in his life, and he couldn't remember how he'd walked after he got off of it. So this walk he was doing now wasn't coming from his own past. It must have been something he'd learned unconsciously from movies and TV, a synthesis of all those riders of the purple sage and the silver screen.

No need to worry about yearning to settle here, he knew now. Because his fantasy now was not of someone settling in but passing through, the saddle tramp, the shootist, the flint-eyed loner who does his business and moves on.

That was a good fantasy, he decided. You wouldn't get into any trouble with a fantasy like that.

Back in his room, Keller tried the book again but couldn't keep his mind on what he was reading. He turned on the TV and worked his way through the channels, using the remote control bolted to the nightstand. Westerns, he decided, were like cops and cabs, never around when you wanted them. It seemed to him that he never made a trip around the cable circuit without running into John Wayne or Randolph Scott or Joel McCrea or a rerun of *Gunsmoke* or *Rawhide* or one of those spaghetti westerns with Eastwood or Lee Van Cleef. Or the great villains—Jack Elam, Strother Martin, the young Lee Marvin in *The Man Who Shot Liberty Valance*.

It probably said something about you, Keller thought, when your favorite actor was Jack Elam.

He switched off the set and looked up Lyman Crowder's phone number. He could dial it, and when someone picked up and said, "Crowder residence," he'd know how the name was pronounced. "Just checking," he could say, cradling the phone and giving them something to think about.

Of course he wouldn't say that, he'd mutter something harmless about a wrong number, but was even that much contact a good idea? Maybe it would put Crowder on his guard. Maybe Crowder was already on his guard, as far as that went. That was the trouble with going in blind like this, knowing nothing about either the target or the client.

If he called Crowder's house from the motel, there might be a record of the call, a link between Lyman Crowder and Dale Whitlock. That wouldn't matter much to Keller, who would shed the Whitlock identity on his way out of town, but there was no reason to create more grief for the real Dale Whitlock.

Because there was a real Dale Whitlock, and Keller was giving him grief enough without making him a murder suspect.

It was pretty slick the way the man in White Plains worked it. He knew a man who had a machine with which he could make flawless American Express cards. He knew someone else who could obtain the names and account numbers of bona fide American Express cardholders. Then he had cards made that were essentially duplicates of existing cards. You didn't have to worry that the cardholder had reported his card as stolen, because it hadn't been stolen, it was still sitting in his wallet. You were off somewhere charging the earth, and he didn't have a clue until the charges turned up on his monthly statement.

The driver's license was real, too. Well, technically it was a counterfeit, of course, and the photograph on it showed Keller, not Whitlock. But someone had managed to access the Connecticut Bureau of Motor Vehicles computer, and thus the counterfeit license showed the same number as Whitlock's, and gave the same address.

In the old days, Keller thought, it had been a lot more straightforward. You didn't need a license to ride a horse or a credit card to rent one. You bought or stole one, and when you rode into town on it nobody asked to see your ID. They might not even come right out and ask your name, and if they did they wouldn't expect a detailed reply. "Call me Tex," you'd say, and that's what they'd call you as you rode off into the sunset.

"Goodbye, Tex," the blonde would call out. "I hope you enjoyed your stay with us."

The lounge downstairs turned out to be the hot spot in Martingale. Restless, Keller had gone downstairs to have a quiet drink. He walked into a thickly carpeted room with soft lighting and a good sound system. There were fifteen or twenty people in the place, all of them either having a good time or looking for one.

Keller ordered a Coors at the bar. On the jukebox, Barbara Mandrell sang a song about cheating. When she was done, a duo he didn't recognize sang a song about cheating. Then came Hank Williams's oldie, "Your Cheatin' Heart."

A subtle pattern was beginning to emerge.

"I love this song," the blonde said.

A different blonde, not the perky young thing from the front desk. This woman was taller, older, and fuller-figured. She wore a skirt and a sort of cowgirl blouse with piping and embroidery on it.

"Old Hank," Keller said, to say something.

"I'm June."

"Call me Tex."

"Tex!" Her laughter came in a sort of yelp. "When did anybody ever call you Tex, tell me that?"

"Well, nobody has," he admitted, "but that's not to say they never will."

"Where are you from, Tex? No, I'm sorry, I can't call you that, it sticks in my throat. If you want me to call you Tex you're going to have to start wearing boots."

"You see by my outfit that I'm not a cowboy."

"Your outfit, your accent, your haircut. If you're not an easterner, then I'm a virgin."

"I'm from Connecticut."

"I knew it."

"My name's Dale."

"Well, you could keep that. If you were fixing to be a cowboy, I mean. You'd have to change the way you dress and talk and comb your hair, but you could hang on to Dale. There another name that goes with it?"

In for a penny, in for a pound. "Whitlock," he said.

"Dale Whitlock. Shoot, that's pretty close to perfect. You tell 'em a name like that, you got credit down at the Agway in a New York minute. Wouldn't even have to fill out a form. You married, Dale?"

What was the right answer? She was wearing a ring herself, and the jukebox was now playing yet another cheating song.

"Not in Martingale," he said.

"Oh, I like that," she said, eyes sparkling. "I like the whole idea of regional marriage. I *am* married in Martingale, but we're not *in* Martingale. The town line's Front Street."

"In that case," he said, "maybe I could buy you a drink."

"You easterners," she said. "You're just so damn fast."

There had to be a catch.

Keller didn't do too badly with women. He got lucky once in a while. But he didn't have the sort of looks that made heads turn, nor had he made seduction his life's work. Some years ago he'd read a book called *How to Pick Up Girls*, filled with opening lines that were guaranteed to work. Keller thought they were silly. He was willing to believe they would work, but he was not able to believe they would work for him.

This woman, though, had hit on him before he'd had time to become aware of her presence. This sort of thing happened, especially when you were dealing with a married woman in a bar where all they played were cheating songs. Everybody knew what everybody else was there for, and nobody had time to dawdle. So this sort of thing happened, but it never seemed to happen to him, and he didn't trust it.

Something would go wrong. She'd call home and find out her kid was running a fever. Her husband would walk in the door just as the jukebox gave out with "You Picked a Fine Time to Leave Me, Lucille." She'd be overcome by conscience, or rendered unconscious by the drink Keller had just bought her.

"I'd say my place or yours," she said, "but we both know the answer to that one. What's your room number?" Keller told her. "You go on up," she said. "I won't be a minute. Don't start without me."

He brushed his teeth, splashed on a little aftershave. She wouldn't show, he told himself. Or she'd expect to be paid, which would take a little of the frost off the pumpkin. Or her husband would turn up and they'd try to work some variation of the badger game.

Or she'd be sloppy drunk, or he'd be impotent. Or something.

"Whew," she said. "I don't guess you need boots after all. I'll call you Tex or Slim or any damn thing you want me to, just so you come when you're called. How long are you in town for, Dale?"

"I'm not sure. A few days."

"Business, I suppose. What sort of business are you in?"

"I work for a big corporation," he said. "They fly me over to look into situations."

"Sounds like you can't talk about it."

"Well, we do a lot of government work," he said. "So I'm really not supposed to."

"Say no more," she said. "Oh, Lord, look at the time!"

While she showered, he picked up the paperback and rewrote the blurb. He killed a thousand miles, he thought, to ride a woman he never met. Well, sometimes you got lucky. The stars were in the right place, the forces that ruled the universe decided you deserved a present. There didn't always have to be a catch to it, did there?

She turned off the shower, and he heard the last line of the song she'd been singing. " 'And Celia's at the Jackson Park Inn,' " she sang, and moments later she emerged from the bathroom and began dressing.

"What's this?" she said. " 'He rode a thousand miles to kill a man he never met.' You know, that's funny, because I just had the darnedest thought while I was running the soap over my pink and tender flesh."

"Oh?"

"I just said that last to remind you what's under this here skirt and blouse. Oh, the thought I had? Well, something you said, government work. I thought maybe this man's CIA, maybe he's some old soldier of fortune, maybe he's the answer to this maiden's prayers."

"What do you mean?"

"Just that it was already a real fine evening, Dale, but it would be heaven on earth if what you came to Martingale for was to kill my damn husband."

Christ. Was *she* the client? Was the pickup downstairs a cute way for them to meet? Could she actually be that stupid, coming on in a public place to a man she was hiring to kill her husband?

For that matter, how had she recognized him? Only Dot and the man in White Plains had known the name he was using. They'd have kept it to themselves. And she'd made her move before she knew his name. Had she been able to recognize him? *I see by your outfit that you are a hit man? Something along those lines?*

"Yarnell," she was saying. "Hobart Lee Yarnell, and what he'd like is for people to call him Bart, and what everybody calls him is Hobie. Now what does that tell you about the man?"

That he's not the man I came here to kill, Keller thought. This was comforting to realize, but left her waiting for an answer to her question. "That's he's not used to getting his own way," Keller said.

She laughed. "He's not," she said, "but it's not for lack of trying. You know, I like you, Dale. You're a nice fellow. But if it wasn't you tonight it would have been somebody else."

"And here I thought it was my aftershave."

"I'll just bet you did. No, the kind of marriage I got, I come around here a lot. I've put a lot of quarters in that jukebox the last year or so."

"And played a lot of cheating songs?"

"And done a fair amount of cheating. But it doesn't really work. I still wake up the next day married to that bastard."

"Why don't you divorce him?"

"I've thought about it."

"And?"

"I was brought up not to believe in it," she said. "But I don't guess that's it. I wasn't raised to believe in cheating, either." She frowned. "Money's part of it," she admitted. "I won't bore you with the details, but I'd get gored pretty bad in a divorce."

"That's a problem."

"I guess, except what do I care about money any-way? Enough's as much as a person needs, and my daddy's got pots of money. He's not about to let me starve."

"Well, then—"

"But he thinks the world of Hobie," she said, glar-ing at Keller as if it were his fault. "Hunts elk with him, goes after trout and salmon with him, thinks he's just the best thing ever came over the pass. And he doesn't even want to hear the word *divorce*. You know that Tammy Wynette song where she spells it out a letter at a time? I swear he'd leave the room before you got past *R*. I say it'd about break Lyman Crowder's heart if his little girl ever got herself divorced."

Well, it was true. If you kept your mouth shut and your ears open, you learned things. What he had learned was that Crowder rhymed with powder.

Now what?

After her departure, after his own shower, he paced back and forth trying to sort it all out. In the few hours since his arrival in Martingale, he'd slept with a woman who turned out to be the loving daughter of the target and, in all likelihood, the un-loving wife of the client.

Well, maybe not. Lyman Crowder was a rich man, lived north of town on a good-sized ranch that he ran pretty much as a hobby. He'd made his real money in oil, and nobody ever made a small amount of money that way. You either went broke or got rich. Rich men had enemies. People they'd crossed in business, people who stood to profit from their death.

But it figured that Yarnell was the client. There

was a kind of poetic inevitability about it. She picks him up in the lounge, it's not enough that she's the target's daughter. She also ought to be the client's wife. Round things out, tie up all the loose ends.

The thing to do . . . well, he knew the thing to do. The thing to do was get a few hours' sleep and then, bright and early, reverse the usual order of affairs by riding off into the sunrise. Get on a plane, get off in New York, and write off Martingale as a happy little romantic adventure. Men, after all, had been known to travel farther than that in the hope of getting laid.

He'd tell the man in White Plains to find somebody else. Sometimes you had to do that. No blame attached, as long as you didn't make a habit of it. He'd say he was blown.

Which, come to think of it, he was. Quite expertly, as a matter of fact.

In the morning he got up and packed his carry-on. He'd call White Plains from the airport, or wait until he was back in New York. He didn't want to phone from the room. When the real Dale Whitlock had a fit and called American Express, they'd look over things like the Holiday Inn statement. No sense leaving anything that led anywhere.

He thought about June, and the memory made him playful. He checked the time. Eight o'clock, two hours later in the East, not an uncivil time to call.

He called Whitlock's home in Rowayton, Connecticut. A woman answered. He identified himself as a representative of a political polling organization, using a name she would recognize. By asking questions that encouraged lengthy responses, he had no trouble keeping her on the phone. "Well, thank you very much," he said at length. "And have a nice day."

Now let Whitlock explain that one to American Express. He finished packing and was almost out the door when his eye caught the paperback western. Take it along? Leave it for the maid? What?

He picked it up, read the cover line, sighed. Was this what Randolph Scott would do? Or John Wayne, or Clint Eastwood? How about Jack Elam?

No, of course not.

Because then there'd be no movie. A man rides into town, starts to have a look at the situation, meets a woman, gets it on with her, then just backs out and rides off? You put something like that on the screen, it wouldn't even play in the art houses.

Still, this wasn't a movie.

Still . . .

He looked at the book and wanted to heave it across the room. But all he heaved was a sigh. Then he unpacked.

He was having a cup of coffee in town when a pickup pulled up across the street and two men got out of it. One of them was Lyman Crowder. The other, not quite as tall, was twenty pounds lighter and twenty years younger. Crowder's son, by the looks of him.

His son-in-law, as it turned out. Keller followed the two men into a store where the fellow behind the counter greeted them as Lyman and Hobie. Crowder had a lengthy shopping list composed largely of items Keller would have been hard put to find a use for.

While the owner filled the order, Keller had a look at the display of hand-tooled boots. The pointed toes would be handy in New York, he thought, for killing cockroaches in corners. The heels would add better than an inch to his height. He wondered if he'd feel awkward in the boots, like a teenager in her first pair of high heels. Lyman and Hobie looked comfortable enough in their boots, as pointy in the toes and as elevated in the heels as any on display, but they also looked comfortable in their string ties and ten-gallon hats, and Keller was sure he'd feel ridiculous dressed like that.

They were a pair, he thought. They looked alike, they talked alike, they dressed alike, and they seemed uncommonly fond of one another.

Back in his room, Keller stood at the window and looked down at the parking lot, then across the way at a pair of mountains. A few years ago his work had taken him to Miami, where he'd met a Cuban who'd cautioned him against ever taking a hotel room above the second floor. "Suppose you got to leave in a hurry?" the man said. "Ground floor, no problem. Second floor, no problem. Third floor, break your fockeen leg."

The logic of this had impressed Keller, and for a while he had made a point of taking the man's advice. Then he happened to learn that the Cuban not only shunned the higher floors of hotels but also refused to enter an elevator or fly in an airplane. What had looked like tradecraft now appeared to be nothing more than phobia.

It struck Keller that he had never in his life had to leave a hotel room, or any other sort of room, by the window. This was not to say that it would never happen, but he'd decided it was a risk he was prepared to run. He liked high floors. Maybe he even liked running risks.

He picked up the phone, made a call. When she answered he said, "This is Tex. Would you believe my business appointment canceled? Left me with the whole afternoon to myself."

"Are you where I left you?"

"I've barely moved since then."

"Well, don't move now," she said. "I'll be right on over."

Around nine that night Keller wanted a drink, but he didn't want to have it in the company of adulterers and their favorite music. He drove around in his palomino Caprice until he found a place on the edge of town that looked promising. It called itself Joe's Bar. Outside it was nondescript. Inside it smelled of stale beer and casual plumbing. The lights were low. There was sawdust on the floor and the heads of dead animals on the walls. The clientele was exclusively male, and for a moment this gave Keller pause. There were gay bars in New York that tried hard to look like this place, though it was hard for Keller to imagine why. But Joe's, he realized, was not a gay bar, not in any sense of the word.

He sat on a wobbly stool and ordered a beer. The other drinkers left him alone, even as they left each other alone. The jukebox played intermittently, with men dropping in quarters when they could no longer bear the silence.

The songs, Keller noted, ran to type. There were the tryin'-to-drink-that-woman-off-of-my-mind songs and the if-it-wasn't-for-bad-luck-I-wouldn't-have-no-luck-at-all songs. Nothing about Celia in the Jackson Park Inn, nothing about heaven being just a sin away.

These songs were for drinking and feeling really rotten about it.

"'Nother damn day," said a voice at Keller's elbow.

He knew who it was without turning. He supposed he might have recognized the voice, but he didn't think that was it. No, it was more a recognition of the inevitability of it all. Of course it would be Yarnell, making conversation with him in this bar where no one made conversation with anyone. Who else could it be?

"'Nother damn day," Keller agreed.

"Don't believe I've seen you around."

"I'm just passing through."

"Well, you got the right idea," Yarnell said. "Name's Bart."

In for a pound, in for a ton. "Dale," Keller said.

"Good to know you, Dale."

"Same here, Bart."

The bartender loomed before them. "Hey, Hobie," he said. "The usual?"

Yarnell nodded. "And another of those for Dale here." The bartender poured Yarnell's usual, which turned out to be bourbon with water back, and uncapped another beer for Keller. Somebody broke down and fed the jukebox a quarter and played "There Stands the Glass."

Yarnell said, "You hear what he called me?"

"I wasn't paying attention."

"Called me Hobie," Yarnell said. "Everybody does. You'll be doing the same, won't be able to help yourself."

"The world is a terrible place," Keller said.

"By God, you got that right," Yarnell said. "No one ever said it better. You a married man, Dale?"

"Not at the moment."

" 'Not at the moment.' I swear I'd give a lot if I could say the same."

"Troubles?"

"Married to one woman and in love with another one. I guess you could call that trouble."

"I guess you could."

"Sweetest, gentlest, darlingest, lovingest creature God ever made," Yarnell said. "When she whispers 'Bart' it don't matter if the whole rest of the world shouts 'Hobie.' "

"This isn't your wife you're talking about," Keller guessed.

"God, no! My wife's a round-heeled, mean-spirited, hard-hearted tramp. I hate my damn wife. I love my girlfriend."

They were silent for a moment, and so was the whole room. Then someone played "The Last Word in Lonesome Is Me."

"They don't write songs like that anymore," Yarnell said.

The hell they didn't. "I'm sure I'm not the first person to suggest this," Keller said, "but have you thought about—"

"Leaving June," Yarnell said. "Running off with Edith. Getting a divorce."

"Something like that."

"Never an hour that I don't think about it, Dale. Night and goddam day I think about it. I think about it and I drink about it, but the one thing I can't do is do it."

"Why's that?"

"There is a man," Yarnell said, "who is a father and a best friend to me all rolled into one. Finest man I ever met in my life, and the only wrong thing he ever did in his life was have a daughter, and the biggest mistake I ever made was marrying her. And if there's one thing that man believes in it's the sanctity of marriage. Why, he thinks *divorce* is the dirtiest word in the language."

So Yarnell couldn't even let on to his father-in-law that his marriage was hell on earth, let alone take steps to end it. He had to keep his affair with Edith very much Back Street. The only person he could talk to was Edith, and she was out of town for the next week or so, which left him dying of loneliness and ready to pour out his heart to the first stranger he could find. For which he apologized, but—

"Hey, that's all right, Bart," Keller said. "A man can't keep it all locked up inside."

"Calling me Bart, I appreciate that. I truly do. Even Lyman calls me Hobie and he's the best friend any man ever had. Hell, he can't help it. Everybody calls me Hobie sooner or later."

"Well," Keller said. "I'll hold out as long as I can."

Alone, Keller reviewed his options.

He could kill Lyman Crowder. He'd be keeping it simple, carrying out the mission as it had been given to him. And it would solve everybody's problems. June and Hobie could get the divorce they both so desperately wanted.

On the downside, they'd both be losing the man each regarded as the greatest thing since microwave popcorn.

He could toss a coin and take out either June or her husband, thus serving as a sort of divorce court of last resort. If it came up heads, June could spend the rest of her life cheating on a ghost. If it was tails, Yarnell could have his cake and Edith, too. Only a question of time until she stopped calling him Bart and took to calling him Hobie, of course, and next thing you knew she would turn up at the Holiday Inn, dropping her quarter in the slot to play "Third-Rate Romance, Low-Rent Rendezvous."

It struck Keller that there ought to be some sort of solution that didn't involve lowering the population. But he knew he was the person least likely to come up with it.

If you had a medical problem, the treatment you got depended on the sort of person you went to. You didn't expect a surgeon to manipulate your spine, or prescribe herbs and enemas, or kneel down and pray with you. Whatever the problem was, the first thing the surgeon would do was look around for something to cut. That's how he'd been trained, that's how he saw the world, that's what he did.

Keller, too, was predisposed to a surgical approach. While others might push counseling or 12-step programs, Keller reached for a scalpel. But sometimes it was difficult to tell where to make the incision.

Kill 'em all, he thought savagely, and let God sort 'em out. Or ride off into the sunset with your tail between your legs.

First thing in the morning. Keller drove to Sheridan and caught a plane to Salt Lake City. He paid cash for his ticket, and used the name John Richards. At the TWA counter in Salt Lake City he bought a one-way ticket to Las Vegas and again paid cash, this time using the name Alan Johnson.

At the Las Vegas airport he walked around the long-term parking lot as if looking for his car. He'd been doing this for five minutes or so when a balding man wearing a glen plaid sportcoat parked a two-year-old Plymouth and removed several large suitcases from its trunk, affixing them to one of those aluminum luggage carriers. Wherever he was headed, he'd packed enough to stay there for a while.

As soon as he was out of sight, Keller dropped to a knee and groped the undercarriage until he found the magnetized Hide-A-Key. He always looked before breaking into a car, and he got lucky about one time in five. As usual, he was elated. It was a good omen, finding a key. It boded well.

Keller had been to Vegas frequently over the years. He didn't like the place, but he knew his way around. He drove to Caesars Palace and left his borrowed Plymouth for the attendant to park. He knocked on the door of an eighth-floor room until its occupant protested that she was trying to sleep.

He said, "It's news from Martingale, Miss Bodine. For Christ's sake, open the door."

She opened the door a crack but kept the chain fastened. She was about the same age as June but looked older, her black hair a mess, her eyes bleary, her face still bearing traces of yesterday's makeup.

"Crowder's dead," he said.

Keller could think of any number of things she might have said, ranging from "What happened?" to "Who cares?" This woman cut to the chase. "You idiot," she said. "What are you doing here?"

Mistake.

"Let me in," he said, and she did.

Another mistake.

The attendant brought Keller's Plymouth and seemed happy with the tip Keller gave him. At the airport, someone else had left a Toyota Camry in the spot

where the balding man had originally parked the
Plymouth, and the best Keller could do was wedge
it into a spot one aisle over and a dozen spaces off
to the side. He figured the owner would find it, and
hoped he wouldn't worry that he was in the early
stages of Alzheimer's.

Keller flew to Denver as Richard Hill, to Sheridan
as David Edwards. En route he thought about Edith
Bodine, who'd evidently slipped on a wet tile in the
bathroom of her room at Caesars, cracking her skull
on the side of the big tub. With the DO NOT DISTURB
sign hanging from the doorknob and the air condi-
tioner at its highest setting, there was no telling how
long she might remain undisturbed.

He'd figured she had to be the client. It wasn't June
or Hobie, both of whom thought the world revolved
around Lyman Crowder, so who did that leave?
Crowder himself, turned sneakily suicidal? Some old
enemy, some business rival?

No, Edith was the best prospect. A client would
either want to meet Keller—not obliquely, as both
Yarnells had done, but by arrangement. Or the client
would contrive to be demonstrably off the scene
when it all happened. Thus the trip to Las Vegas.

Why? The Crowder fortune, of course. She had
Hobie Yarnell crazy about her, but he wouldn't leave
June for fear of breaking Crowder's heart, and even
if he did he'd go empty-handed. Having June killed
wouldn't work either, because she didn't have any
real money of her own. But June would inherit if the
old man died, and later on something could always
happen to June.

Anyway, that's how he figured it. If he'd wanted
to know Edith's exact reasoning he'd have had to ask
her, and that had struck him as a waste of time. More

to the point, the last thing he'd wanted was a chance to get to know her. That just screwed everything up, when you got to know these people.

If you were going to ride a thousand miles to kill a man you'd never met, you were really well advised to be the tight-lipped stranger every step of the way. No point in talking to anybody, not the target, not the client, and not anybody else, either. If you had anything to say, you could whisper it to your horse.

He got off the fourth plane of the day at Sheridan, picked up his Caprice—the name was seeming more appropriate with every passing hour—and drove back to Martingale. He kept it right around the speed limit, then slowed down along with everyone else five miles outside of Martingale. They were clearing a wreck out of the northbound lane. That shouldn't have slowed things down in the southbound lane, but of course it did; everybody had to slow down to see what everyone else was slowing down to look at.

Back in his room, he had his bag packed before he realized that he couldn't go anywhere. The client was dead, but that didn't change anything; since he had no way of knowing that she was the client or that she was dead, his mission remained unchanged. He could go home and admit an inability to get the job done, waiting for the news to seep through that there was no longer any job to be done. That would get him off the hook after the fact, but he wouldn't have covered himself with glory, nor would he get paid. The client had almost certainly paid in advance, and if there'd been a middleman between the client and the man in White Plains he had almost certainly passed the money on, and there was very little likelihood that the man in White Plains would even consider the notion of refunding a fee to a dead client, not that anyone would raise the subject. But neither would the man in White Plains pay Keller for work he'd failed to perform. The man in White Plains would just keep everything.

Keller thought about it. It looked to him as though his best course lay in playing a waiting game. How long could it take before a sneak thief or a chambermaid walked in on Edith Bodine? How long before news of her death found its way to White Plains?

The more he thought about it, the longer it seemed likely to take. If there were, as sometimes happened, a whole string of intermediaries involved, the message might very well never get to Garcia.

Maybe the simplest thing was to kill Crowder and be done with it.

No, he thought. He'd just made a side trip of, yes, more than a thousand miles—and at his own expense, yet—solely to keep from having to kill this legendary Man He Never Met. Damned if he was going to kill him now, after all that.

He'd wait a while, anyway. He didn't want to drive anywhere now, and he couldn't bear to look at another airplane, let alone get on board.

He stretched out on the bed, closed his eyes.

He had a frightful dream. In it he was walking at night out in the middle of the desert, lost, chilled, desperately alone. Then a horse came galloping out of nowhere, and on his back was a magnificent woman with a great mane of hair and eyes that flashed in the moonlight. She extended a hand and Keller leaped up on the horse and rode behind her. She was naked. So was Keller, although he had somehow failed to notice this before.

They fell in love. Wordless, they told each other everything, knew one another like twin souls. And then, gazing into her eyes, Keller realized who she was. She was Edith Bodine, and she was dead, he'd killed her earlier without knowing she'd turn out to be the girl of his dreams. It was done, it could never be undone, and his heart was broken for eternity.

Keller woke up shaking. For five minutes he paced the room, struggling to sort out what was a dream and what was real. He hadn't been sleeping long. The sun was setting, it was still the same endless day.

God, what a hellish dream.

He couldn't get caught up in TV, and he had no luck at all with the book. He put it down, picked up the phone, and dialed June's number.

"It's Dale," he said. "I was sitting here and—"

"Oh, Dale," she cut in, "you're so thoughtful to call. Isn't it terrible? Isn't it the most awful thing?"

"Uh," he said.

"I can't talk now," she said. "I can't even think straight. I've never been so upset in my life. Thank you, Dale, for being so thoughtful."

She hung up and left him staring at the phone. Unless she was a better actress than he would have guessed, she sounded absolutely overcome. He was surprised that news of Edith Bodine's death could have reached her so soon, but far more surprised that she could be taking it so hard. Was there more to all this than met the eye? Were Hobie's wife and mistress actually close friends? Or were they—Jesus—more than just good friends?

Things were certainly a lot simpler for Randolph Scott.

*   *   *

The same bartender was on duty at Joe's. "I don't guess your friend Hobie'll be coming around tonight," he offered. "I suppose you heard the news."

"Uh," Keller said. Some Back Street affair, he thought, if the whole town was ready to comfort Hobie before the body was cold.

"Hell of a thing," the man went on. "Terrible loss for this town. Martingale won't be the same without him."

"This news," Keller said carefully. "I think maybe I missed it. What happened, anyway?"

He called the airlines from his motel room. The next flight out of Casper wasn't until morning. Of course, if he wanted to drive to Denver—

He didn't want to drive to Denver. He booked the first flight out in the morning, using the Whitlock name and the Whitlock credit card.

No need to stick around, not with Lyman Crowder stretched out somewhere getting pumped full of embalming fluid. Dead in a car crash on I-25 North, the very accident that had slowed Keller down on his way back from Sheridan.

He wouldn't be around for the funeral, but should he send flowers? It was quite clear that he shouldn't. Still, the impulse was there.

He dialed 1-800-FLOWERS and sent a dozen roses to Mrs. Dale Whitlock in Rowayton, charging them to Whitlock's American Express account. He asked them to enclose a card reading "Just because I love you—Dale."

He felt it was the least he could do.

Two days later he was on Taunton Place in White Plains, making his report. Accidents were always good, the man told him. Accidents and natural causes, always the best. Oh, sometimes you needed a noisy hit to send a message, but the rest of the time you couldn't beat an accident.

"Good you could arrange it," the man said.

Would have taken a hell of an arranger, Keller thought. First you'd have had to arrange for Lyman Crowder to be speeding north in his pickup. Then you'd have had to get an unemployed sheepherder named Danny Vasco good and drunk and send him hurtling toward Martingale, racing his own pickup—Jesus, didn't they drive anything but pickups?—racing it at ninety-plus miles an hour, and proceeding southbound in the northbound lane. Arrange for a few near misses. Arrange for Vasco to brush a school bus and sideswipe a minivan, and then let him ram Crowder head-on.

Some arrangement.

If the man in White Plains had any idea that the client was dead as well, or even who the client was, he gave no sign to Keller. On the way out, Dot asked him how Crowder pronounced his name.

"Rhymes with *chowder*," he said.

"I knew you'd find out," she said. "Keller, are you all right? You seem different."

"Just awed by the workings of Fate," he said.

"Well," she said, "that'll do it."

On the train back to the city he thought about the workings of Fate. Earlier he'd tried to tell himself that his side trip to Las Vegas had been a waste of time and money and human life. All he'd had to do was wait a day for Danny Vasco to take the game off the boards.

Never would have happened.

Without his trip to Vegas, there would have been
no wreck on the highway. One event had opened
some channel that allowed the other to happen. He
couldn't explain this, couldn't make sense out of it,
but somehow he knew it was true.

Everything had happened exactly the way it had
had to happen. Encountering June in the Meet 'n'
Cheat, running into Hobie at the Burnout Bar. He
could no more have avoided those meetings than he
could have kept himself from buying the paperback
western novel that had set the tone for everything
that followed.

He hoped Mrs. Whitlock liked the flowers.

3

Keller's Therapy

"I had this dream," Keller said. "Matter of fact I wrote it down, as you suggested."

"Good."

Before getting on the couch Keller had removed his jacket and hung it on the back of a chair. He moved from the couch to retrieve his notebook from the jacket's inside breast pocket, then sat on the couch and found the page with the dream on it. He read through his notes rapidly, closed the book, and sat there, uncertain how to proceed.

"As you prefer," said Breen. "Sitting up or lying down, whichever is more comfortable."

"It doesn't matter?"

"Not to me."

And which was more comfortable? A seated posture seemed more natural for conversation, while lying down on the couch had the weight of tradition on its side. Keller, who felt driven to give this his best shot, decided to go with tradition. He stretched out, put his feet up.

He said, "I'm living in a house, except it's almost like a castle. Endless passageways and dozens of rooms."

"Is it your house?"

54

"No, I just live here. In fact I'm a kind of servant for the family that owns the house. They're almost like royalty."

"And you are a servant."

"Except I have very little to do, and I'm treated like an equal. I play tennis with members of the family. There's this tennis court in back of the house."

"And this is your job? To play tennis with them?"

"No, that's an example of how they treat me as an equal. And I eat at the same table with them, instead of eating downstairs with the servants. My job is the mice."

"The mice?"

The house is infested with mice. I'm having dinner with the family, I've got a plate piled high with good food, and a waiter in black tie comes in and presents a covered dish. I lift the cover and there's a note on it, and it says, 'Mice.' "

"Just the single word?"

"That's all. I get up from the table and I follow the servant down a long hallway, and I wind up in an unfinished room in the attic. There are tiny mice all over the room, there must be twenty or thirty of them, and I have to kill them."

"How?"

"By crushing them underfoot. That's the quickest and most humane way, but it bothers me and I don't want to do it. But the sooner I finish, the sooner I can get back to my dinner, and I'm very hungry."

"So you kill the mice?"

"Yes," Keller said. "One almost gets away but I stomp on it just as it's getting out the door. And then I'm back at the dinner table and everybody's eating and drinking and laughing, and my plate's been cleared away. Then there's a big fuss, and finally they bring my plate back from the kitchen, but it's not the same food as before. It's . . ."

"Yes?"

"Mice," Keller said. "They're skinned and cooked, but it's a plateful of mice."

"And you eat them?"

"That's when I woke up," Keller said. "And not a moment too soon, I'd have to say."

"Ah," Breen said. He was a tall man, long-limbed and gawky, wearing chinos and a dark green shirt and a brown corduroy jacket. He looked to Keller like someone who had been a nerd in high school, and who now managed to look distinguished, in an eccentric sort of way. He said "Ah" again, and folded his hands, and asked Keller what he thought the dream meant.

"You're the doctor," Keller said.

"You think it means that I am the doctor?"

"No, I think you're the one who can say what it means. Maybe it just means I shouldn't eat Rocky Road ice cream right before I go to bed."

"Tell me what you think the dream might mean."

"Maybe I see myself as a cat."

"Or as an exterminator?"

Keller didn't say anything.

"Let us work with this dream on a very superficial level," Breen said. "You're employed as a corporate troubleshooter, except that you used another word for it."

"They tend to call us expediters," Keller said, "but troubleshooter is what it amounts to."

"Most of the time there is nothing for you to do. You have considerable opportunity for recreation, for living the good life. For tennis, as it were, and for nourishing yourself at the table of the rich and powerful. Then mice are discovered, and it is at once clear that you are a servant with a job to do."

"I get it," Keller said.

"Go on, then. Explain it to me."

"Well, it's obvious, isn't it? There's a problem and I'm called in and I have to drop what I'm doing and go and deal with it. I have to take abrupt arbitrary action, and that can involve firing people and closing out whole departments. I have to do it, but it's like stepping on mice. And when I'm back at the table and I want my food—I suppose that's my salary?"

"Your compensation, yes."

"And I get a plate of mice." He made a face. "In other words, what? My compensation comes from the destruction of the people I have to cut adrift. My sustenance comes at their expense. So it's a guilt dream?"

"What do you think?"

"I think it's guilt. My profit derives from the misfortunes of others, from the grief I bring to others. That's it, isn't it?"

"On the surface, yes. When we go deeper, perhaps we will begin to discover other connections. With your having chosen this job in the first place, perhaps, and with some aspects of your childhood." He interlaced his fingers and sat back in his chair. "Everything is of a piece, you know. Nothing exists alone and nothing is accidental. Even your name."

"My name?"

"Peter Stone. Think about it, why don't you, between now and our next session."

"Think about my name?"

"About your name and how it suits you. And"— a reflexive glance at his wristwatch—"I'm afraid our hour is up."

*   *   *

Jerrold Breen's office was on Central Park West at Ninety-fourth Street. Keller walked to Columbus Avenue, rode a bus five blocks, crossed the street, and hailed a taxi. He had the driver go through Central Park, and by the time he got out of the cab at Fiftieth Street he was reasonably certain he hadn't been followed. He bought coffee in a deli and stood on the sidewalk, keeping an eye open while he drank it. Then he walked to the building where he lived, on First Avenue between Forty-eighth and Forty-ninth. It was a prewar high-rise, with an Art Deco lobby and an attended elevator. "Ah, Mr. Keller," the attendant said. "A beautiful day, yes?"

"Beautiful," Keller agreed.

Keller had a one-bedroom apartment on the nineteenth floor. He could look out his window and see the UN building, the East River, the borough of Queens. On the first Sunday in November he could watch the runners streaming across the Queensboro Bridge, just a couple of miles past the midpoint of the New York marathon.

It was a spectacle Keller tried not to miss. He would sit at his window for hours while thousands of them passed through his field of vision, first the world-class runners, then the middle-of-the-pack plodders, and finally the slowest of the slow, some walking, some hobbling. They started in Staten Island and finished in Central Park, and all he saw was a few hundred yards of their ordeal as they made their way over the bridge into Manhattan. Sooner or later the sight always moved him to tears, although he could not have said why.

Maybe it was something to talk about with Breen. It was a woman who had led him to the therapist's couch, an aerobics instructor named Donna. Keller had met her at the gym. They'd had a couple of dates, and had been to bed a couple of times, enough to establish their sexual incompatibility. Keller still went to the same gym two or three times a week to raise and lower heavy metal objects, and when he ran into her they were friendly.

One time, just back from a trip somewhere, he must have rattled on about what a nice town it was. "Keller," she said, "if there was ever a born New Yorker, you're it. You know that, don't you?"

"I suppose so."

"But you've always got this fantasy, living the good life in Elephant, Montana. Every place you go, you dream up a whole life to go with it."

"Is that bad?"

"Who's saying it's bad? But I bet you could have fun with it in therapy."

"You think I need to be in therapy?"

"I think you'd get a lot out of therapy," she said. "Look, you come here, right? You climb the Stair Monster, you use the Nautilus."

"Mostly free weights."

"Whatever. You don't do this because you're a physical wreck."

"I do it to stay in shape."

"And because it makes you feel good."

"So?"

"So I see you as all closed in and trying to reach out," she said. "Going all over the country and getting real estate agents to show you houses you're not going to buy."

"That was only a couple of times. And what's so bad about it, anyway? It passes the time."

"You do these things and don't know why," she

said. "You know what therapy is? It's an adventure, it's a voyage of discovery. And it's like going to the gym. It's . . . look, forget it. The whole thing's pointless anyway unless you're interested."

"Maybe I'm interested," he said.

Donna, not surprisingly, was in therapy herself. But her therapist was a woman, and they agreed he'd be more comfortable working with a man. Her exhusband had been very fond of his therapist, a West Side psychologist named Breen. Donna had never met the man herself, and she wasn't on the best of terms with her ex, but—

"That's all right," he said. "I'll call him myself."

He'd called Breen, using Donna's ex-husband's name as a reference. "But I doubt that he even knows me by name," he said. "We got to talking a while back at a party and I haven't seen him since. But something he said struck a chord with me, and, well, I thought I ought to explore it."

"Intuition is a powerful teacher," Breen said.

Keller made an appointment, giving his name as Peter Stone. In his first session he talked some about his work for a large and unnamed conglomerate. "They're a little old-fashioned when it comes to psychotherapy," he told Breen. "So I'm not going to give you an address or telephone number, and I'll pay for each session in cash."

"Your life is filled with secrets," Breen said.

"I'm afraid it is. My work demands it."

"This is a place where you can be honest and open. The idea is to uncover those secrets you've been keeping from yourself. Here you are protected by the sanctity of the confessional, but it's not my task to grant you absolution. Ultimately, you absolve yourself."

"Well," Keller said.

"Meanwhile, you have secrets to keep. I can respect that. I won't need your address or telephone number unless I'm forced to cancel an appointment. I suggest you call in to confirm your sessions an hour or two ahead of time, or you can take the chance of an occasional wasted trip. If *you* have to cancel an appointment, be sure to give me twenty-four hours' notice. Or I'll have to charge for the missed session."

"That's fair," Keller said.

He went twice a week, Mondays and Thursdays, at two in the afternoon. It was hard to tell what they were accomplishing. Sometimes Keller relaxed completely on the sofa, talking freely and honestly about his childhood. Other times he experienced the fifty-minute session as a balancing act; he was tugged in two directions at once, yearning to tell everything, compelled to keep it all a secret.

No one knew he was doing this. Once when he ran into Donna she asked if he'd ever given the shrink a call, and he'd shrugged sheepishly and said he hadn't. "I thought about it," he said, "but then somebody told me about this masseuse, she does a combination of Swedish and shiatsu, and I've got to tell you, I think it does me more good than somebody poking and probing at the inside of my head."

"Oh, Keller," she'd said, not without affection. "Don't ever change."

It was on a Monday that he recounted the dream about the mice. Wednesday morning his phone rang, and it was Dot. "He wants to see you," she said.

"Be right out," he said.

He put on a tie and jacket and caught a cab to Grand Central and a train to White Plains. There he

caught another cab and told the driver to head out
Washington Boulevard and let him off at the corner
of Norwalk. After the cab drove off he walked up
Norwalk to Taunton Place and turned left. The second house on the right was a big old Victorian with
a wrap-around porch. He rang the bell and Dot let
him in.

"The upstairs den," she said. "He's expecting
you."

He went upstairs, and forty minutes later he came
down again. A young man named Louis drove him
back to the station, and on the way they chatted
about a recent boxing match they'd both seen on
ESPN. "What I wish," Louis said, "I wish they had
like a mute button on the remote, except what it
would do is it would mute the announcers but you'd
still hear the crowd noise and the punches landing.
What you wouldn't have is the constant yammer-
yammer-yammer in your ear." Keller wondered if
they could do that. "I don't see why not," Louis said.
"They can do everything else. If you can put a man
on the moon, you ought to be able to shut up Al
Bernstein."

Keller took the train back to New York and walked
to his apartment. He made a couple of phone calls
and packed a bag. At 3:30 he went downstairs,
walked half a block, and hailed a cab to JFK, where
he picked up his boarding pass for American's 6:10
flight to Tucson.

In the departure lounge he remembered his appointment with Breen. He called and canceled the
Thursday session. Since it was less than twenty-four
hours away, Breen said, he'd have to charge him for
the missed session, unless he was able to book someone else into the slot.

"Don't worry about it," Keller told him. "I hope I'll be back in time for my Monday appointment, but it's always hard to know how long these things are going to take. If I can't make it I should at least be able to give you the twenty-four hours' notice."

He changed planes in Dallas and got to Tucson shortly before midnight. He had no luggage aside from the piece he was carrying, but he went to the baggage claim area anyway. A rail-thin man with a broad-brimmed straw hat stood there holding a hand-lettered sign that read NOSCAASI. Keller watched the man for a few minutes, and observed that no one else was watching him. He went up to him and said, "You know, I was figuring it out the whole way to Dallas. What I came up with, it's *Isaacson* spelled backwards."

"That's it," the man said. "That's exactly it." He seemed impressed, as if Keller had cracked the Japanese naval code. He said, "You didn't check a bag, did you? I didn't think so. Car's this way."

In the car the man showed him three photographs, all of the same man, heavyset, dark, with glossy black hair and a greedy pig face. Bushy mustache, bushy eyebrows. Enlarged pores on his nose.

"That's Rollie Vasquez," the man said. "Son of a bitch wouldn't exactly win a beauty contest, would he?"

"I guess not."

"Let's go," the man said. "Show you where he lives, where he eats, where he gets his ashes hauled. Rollie Vasquez, this is your life."

Two hours later the man dropped him at a Ramada Inn and gave him a room key and a car key. "You're all checked in," he said. "Car's parked at the foot of the staircase closest to your room. She's a Mitsubishi

Eclipse, pretty decent transportation. Color's supposed to be silver-blue, but she says gray on the papers. Registration's in the glove box."

"There was supposed to be something else."

"That's in the glove box, too. Locked, of course, but the one key fits the ignition and the glove box. And the doors and the trunk, too. And if you turn the key upside down it'll still fit, 'cause there's no up and down to it. You really got to hand it to those Japs."

"What'll they think of next?"

"Well, it may not seem like much," the man said, "but all the time you waste making sure you got the right key, then making sure you got it right side up."

"It adds up."

"It does," the man said. "Now, you got a full tank of gas. It takes regular, but what's in there's enough to take you upwards of four hundred miles."

"How're the tires? Never mind. Just a joke."

"And a good one," the man said. " 'How're the tires?' I like that."

The car was where it was supposed to be, and the glove box held the car's registration and a semiautomatic pistol, a .22-caliber Horstmann Sun Dog, fully loaded, with a spare clip lying alongside it. Keller slipped the gun and the spare clip into his carry-on, locked the car, and went to his room without passing the desk.

After a shower, he sat down and put his feet up on the coffee table. It was all arranged, and that made it simpler, but sometimes he liked it better the other way, when all he had was a name and address and no one on hand to smooth the way for him. This was simple, all right, but who knew what traces were being left? Who knew what kind of history the gun had, or what the string bean with the NOSCAASI sign would say if the police picked him up and shook him?

All the more reason to do it quickly. He watched enough of an old movie on cable to ready him for sleep, then slept until he woke up. When he went out to the car he had his bag with him. He expected to return to the room, but if he didn't he'd be leaving nothing behind, not even a fingerprint.

He stopped at Denny's for breakfast. Around one he had lunch at a Mexican place on Figueroa. In the late afternoon he drove up into the hills north of the city, and he was still there when the sun went down. Then he drove back to the Ramada.

That was Thursday. Friday morning the phone rang while he was shaving. He let it ring. It rang again just as he was ready to leave. He didn't answer it this time, either, but went around wiping surfaces a second time with a hand towel. Then he went out to the car.

At two that afternoon he followed Rolando Vasquez into the men's room of the Saguaro Lanes bowling alley and shot him three times in the head. The little gun didn't make much noise, not even in the confines of the tiled lavatory. Earlier he had fashioned an improvised suppressor by wrapping the barrel of the gun with a space-age insulating material that muffled most of the gun's report without adding much in the way of weight or bulk. If you could do that, he thought, you ought to be able to shut up Al Bernstein.

He left Vasquez propped in a stall, left the gun in a storm drain half a mile away, left the car in the long-term lot at the airport.

Flying home, he wondered why they had needed him in the first place. They'd supplied the car and the gun and the finger man. Why not do it all themselves? Did they really need to bring him all the way from New York to step on the mouse?

"You said to think about my name," he told Breen. "The significance of it. But I don't see how it could have any significance. It's not as if I chose it myself."

"Let me suggest something," Breen said. "There is a metaphysical principle which holds that we choose everything about our lives, that in fact we select the very parents we are born to, that everything which happens in our lives is a manifestation of our will. Thus there are no accidents, no coincidences."

"I don't know if I believe that."

"You don't have to. We'll just take it for the moment as a postulate. So, assuming that you chose the name Peter Stone, what does your choice tell us?"

Keller, stretched full length upon the couch, was not enjoying this. "Well, a peter's a penis," he said reluctantly. "A stone peter would be an erection, wouldn't it?"

"Would it?"

"So I suppose a guy who decides to call himself Peter Stone would have something to prove. Anxiety about his virility. Is that what you want me to say?"

"I want you to say whatever you wish," Breen said. "Are you anxious about your virility?"

"I never thought I was," Keller said. "Of course it's hard to say how much anxiety I might have had back before I was born, around the time I was picking my parents and deciding what name they should choose for me. At that age I probably had a certain amount of difficulty maintaining an erection, so I guess I had a lot to be anxious about."

"And now?"

"I don't have a performance problem, if that's the question. I'm not the way I was in my teens, ready to go three or four times a night, but then who in his right mind would want to? I can generally get the job done."

"You get the job done."

"Right."

"You perform."

"Is there something wrong with that?"

"What do you think?"

"Don't do that," Keller said. "Don't answer a question with a question. If I ask a question and you don't want to respond, just leave it alone. But don't turn it back on me. It's irritating."

Breen said, "You perform, you get the job done. But what do you feel, Mr. Peter Stone?"

"Feel?"

"It is unquestionably true that *peter* is a colloquialism for the penis, but it has an earlier meaning. Do you recall Christ's words to the first Peter? 'Thou art Peter, and upon this rock I shall build my church.' Because Peter *means* rock. Our Lord was making a pun. So your first name means rock and your last name is Stone. What does that give us? Rock and stone. Hard, unyielding, obdurate. Insensitive. Unfeeling."

"Stop," Keller said.

"In the dream, when you kill the mice, what do you feel?"

"Nothing. I just want to get the job done."

"Do you feel their pain? Do you feel pride in your

accomplishment, satisfaction in a job well done? Do you feel a thrill, a sexual pleasure, in their death?"

"Nothing," Keller said. "I feel nothing. Could we stop for a moment?"

"What do you feel right now?"

"Just a little sick to my stomach, that's all."

"Do you want to use the bathroom? Shall I get you a glass of water?"

"No, I'm all right. It's better when I sit up. It'll pass. It's passing already."

Sitting at his window, watching not marathoners but cars streaming over the Queensboro Bridge, Keller thought about names. What was particularly annoying, he thought, was that he didn't need to be under the care of a board-certified metaphysician to acknowledge the implications of the name Peter Stone. He had very obviously chosen it, and not in the manner of a soul deciding what parents to be born to and planting names in their heads. He had picked the name himself when he called to make his initial appointment with Jerrold Breen. *Name?* Breen had demanded. *Stone,* he had replied. *Peter Stone.*

Thing is, he wasn't stupid. Cold, unyielding, insensitive, but not stupid. If you wanted to play the name game, you didn't have to limit yourself to the alias he had selected. You could have plenty of fun with the name he'd borne all his life.

His full name was John Paul Keller, but no one called him anything but Keller, and few people even knew his first or middle names. His apartment lease and most of the cards in his wallet showed his names as J. P. Keller. Just Plain Keller was what people called him, men and women alike. ("The upstairs den, Keller. He's expecting you." "Oh, Keller, don't ever change." "I don't know how to say this, Keller, but I'm just not getting my needs met in this relationship.")

Keller. In German it meant *cellar*, or *tavern*. But the hell with that, you didn't need to know what it meant in a foreign language. Just change a vowel. Keller = Killer.

Clear enough, wasn't it?

On the couch, eyes closed, Keller said, "I guess the therapy's working."

"Why do you say that?"

"I met a girl last night, bought her a couple of drinks, went home with her. We went to bed and I couldn't do anything."

"You couldn't do anything."

"Well, if you want to be technical, there were things I could have done. I could have typed a letter, sent out for a pizza. I could have sung 'Melancholy Baby.' But I couldn't do what we'd both been hoping I would do, which was have sex with her."

"You were impotent."

"You know, you're very sharp. You never miss a trick."

"You blame me for your impotence," Breen said.

"Do I? I don't know about that. I'm not sure I even blame myself. To tell you the truth, I was more amused than devastated by the experience. And she wasn't upset, perhaps out of relief that I wasn't upset. But just so nothing like this ever happens again, I've decided I'm changing my name to Dick Hardin."

"What was your father's name?"

"My father," Keller said. "Jesus, what a question. Where did that come from?"

Breen didn't say anything.

Neither, for several minutes, did Keller. Then, eyes closed, he said, "I never knew my father. He was a soldier. He was killed in action before I was born. Or he was shipped overseas before I was born and killed when I was a few months old. Or possibly he was home when I was born, or came home on leave when I was very small, and he held me on his knee and told me he was proud of me."

"You have such a memory?"

"I have no memory," Keller said. "The only memory I have is of my mother telling me about him, and that's the source of the confusion, because she told me different things at different times. Either he was killed before I was born or shortly after, and either he died without seeing me or he saw me one time and sat me on his knee. She was a good woman but she was vague about a lot of things. The one thing she was completely clear on, he was a soldier. And he got killed over there."

"And his name—"

Was Keller, he thought. "Same as mine," he said. "But forget the name, this is more important than the name. Listen to this. She had a picture of him, a head-and-shoulders shot, this good-looking young soldier in a uniform and wearing a cap, the kind that folds flat when you take it off. The picture was in a gold frame on her dresser when I was a little kid, and she would tell me how that was my father.

"And then one day the picture wasn't there anymore. 'It's gone,' she said. And that was all she would say on the subject. I was older then, I must have been seven or eight years old.

"Couple of years later I got a dog. I named him Soldier, I called him that after my father. Years after that two things occurred to me. One, Soldier's a funny thing to call a dog. Two, whoever heard of naming a dog after your father? But at the time it didn't seem the least bit unusual to me."

"What happened to the dog?"

"He became impotent. Shut up, will you? What I'm getting to's a lot more important than the dog. When I was fourteen, fifteen years old, I used to work afternoons after school helping out this guy who did odd jobs in the neighborhood. Cleaning out basements and attics, hauling trash, that sort of thing. One time this notions store went out of business, the owner must have died, and we were cleaning out the basement for the new tenant. Boxes of junk all over the place, and we had to go through everything, because part of how this guy made his money was selling off the stuff he got paid to haul. But you couldn't go through all this crap too thoroughly or you were wasting time.

"I was checking out this one box, and what do I pull out but a framed picture of my father. The very same picture that sat on my mother's dresser, him in his uniform and his military cap, the picture that disappeared, it's even in the same frame, and what's it doing here?"

Not a word from Breen.

"I can still remember how I felt. Like stunned, like *Twilight Zone* time. Then I reach back in the box and pull out the first thing I touch, and it's the same picture in the same frame.

"The whole box is framed pictures. About half of them are the soldier and the others are a fresh-faced blonde with her hair in a page boy and a big smile on her face. What it was, it was a box of frames. They used to package inexpensive frames that way, with a photo in it for display. For all I know they still do. So what my mother must have done, she must have bought a frame in a five-and-dime and told me it was my father. Then when I got a little older she got rid of it.

"I took one of the framed photos home with me. I didn't say anything to her, I didn't show it to her, but I kept it around for a while. I found out the photo dated from World War Two. In other words, it couldn't have been a picture of my father, because he would have been wearing a different uniform.

"By this time I think I already knew that the story she told me about my father was, well, a story. I don't believe she knew who my father was. I think she got drunk and went with somebody, or maybe there were several different men. What difference does it make? She moved to another town, she told people she was married, that her husband was in the service or that he was dead, whatever she told them."

"How do you feel about it?"

"How do I feel about it?" Keller shook his head. "If I slammed my hand in a cab door, you'd ask me how I felt about it."

"And you'd be stuck for an answer," Breen said. "Here's a question for you. Who was your father?"

"I just told you—"

"But someone fathered you. Whether or not you knew him, whether or not your mother knew who he was, there was a particular man who planted the seed that grew into you. Unless you believe yourself to be the second coming of Christ."

"No," Keller said. "That's one delusion I've been spared."

"So tell me who he was, this man who spawned

you. Not on the basis of what you were told or what you've managed to figure out. I'm not asking this question of the part of you that thinks and reasons. I'm asking that part of you that simply knows. Who was your father? What was your father?"

"He was a soldier," Keller said.

Keller, walking uptown on Second Avenue, found himself standing in front of a pet shop, watching a couple of puppies cavorting in the window.

He went inside. One whole wall was given over to stacked cages of puppies and kittens. Keller felt his spirits sinking as he looked into the cages. Waves of sadness rocked him.

He turned away and looked at the other pets. Birds in cages, gerbils and snakes in dry aquariums, tanks of tropical fish. He was all right with them. It was the puppies that he couldn't bear to look at.

He left the store. The next day he went to an animal shelter and walked past cages of dogs waiting to be adopted. This time the sadness was overwhelming, and he felt it physically as pressure against his chest. Something must have shown on his face, because the young woman in charge asked him if he was all right.

"Just a dizzy spell," he said.

In the office she told him that they could probably accommodate him if he was especially interested in a particular breed. They could keep his name on file, and when a specimen of that breed became available—

"I don't think I can have a pet," he said. "I travel too much. I can't handle the responsibility." The woman didn't respond, and Keller's words echoed in her silence. "But I want to make a donation," he said. "I want to support the work you do."

He got out his wallet, pulled bills from it, handed them to her without counting them. "An anonymous donation," he said. "I don't want a receipt. I'm sorry for taking your time. I'm sorry I can't adopt a dog. Thank you. Thank you very much."

She was saying something, but he didn't listen. He hurried out of there.

"'I want to support the work you do.' That's what I told her, and then I rushed out of there because I didn't want her thanking me. Or asking me questions."

"What would she ask?"

"I don't know," Keller said. He rolled over on the couch, facing away from Breen, facing the wall. "'I want to support your work.' But I don't even know what their work is. They find homes for some animals, and what do they do with the others? Put them to sleep?"

"Perhaps."

"What do I want to support? The placement or the killing?"

"You tell me."

"I tell you too much as it is," Keller said.

"Or not enough."

Keller didn't say anything.

"Why did it sadden you to see the dogs in their cages?"

"I felt their sadness."

"One feels only one's own sadness. Why is it sad to you, a dog in a cage? Are you in a cage?"

"No."

"Your dog, Soldier. Tell me about him."

"All right," Keller said. "I guess I could do that."

A session or two later, Breen said, "You have never been married."

"No."

"I was married."

"Oh?"

"For eight years. She was my receptionist, she booked my appointments, showed clients to the waiting room until I was ready for them. Now I have no receptionist. A machine answers the phone. I check the machine between appointments, and take and return calls at that time. If I had had a machine in the first place I'd have been spared a lot of agony."

"It wasn't a good marriage?"

Breen didn't seem to have heard the question. "I wanted children. She had three abortions in eight years and never told me. Never said a word. Then one day she threw it in my face. I'd been to a doctor, I'd had tests, and all indications were that I was fertile, with a high sperm count and extremely motile sperm. So I wanted her to see a doctor. 'You fool, I've killed three of your babies already, why don't you leave me alone?' I told her I wanted a divorce. She said it would cost me."

"And?"

"We were married eight years. We've been divorced for nine. Every month I write an alimony check and put it in the mail. If it was up to me I'd rather burn the money."

Breen fell silent. After a moment Keller said, "Why are you telling me all this?"

"No reason."

"Is it supposed to relate to something in my psyche? Am I supposed to make a connection, clap my hand to my forehead, say, 'Of course, of course! I've been so blind!' "

"You confide in me," Breen said. "It seems only fitting that I confide in you."

A couple of days later Dot called. Keller took a train to White Plains, where Louis met him at the station and drove him to the house on Taunton Place. Later Louis drove him back to the train station and he returned to the city. He timed his call to Breen so that he got the man's machine. "This is Peter Stone," he said. "I'm flying to San Diego on business. I'll have to miss my next appointment, and possibly the one after that. I'll try to let you know."

Was there anything else to tell Breen? He couldn't think of anything. He hung up, packed a bag, and rode Amtrak to Philadelphia.

No one met his train. The man in White Plains had shown him a photograph and given him a slip of paper with a name and address on it. The man in question managed an adult bookstore a few blocks from Independence Hall. There was a tavern across the street, a perfect vantage point, but one look inside made it clear to Keller that he couldn't spend time there without calling attention to himself, not unless he first got rid of his tie and jacket and spent twenty minutes rolling around in the gutter.

Down the street Keller found a diner, and if he sat at the far end he could keep an eye on the bookstore's mirrored front windows. He had a cup of coffee, then walked across the street to the bookstore, where there were two men on duty. One was a dark and sad-eyed youth from India or Pakistan, the other the jowly, slightly exophthalmic fellow in the photo Keller had seen in White Plains.

Keller walked past a whole wall of videocassettes and leafed through a display of magazines. He had been there for about fifteen minutes when the kid said he was going for his dinner. The older man said, "Oh, it's that time already, huh? Okay, but make sure you're back by seven for a change, will you?"

Keller looked at his watch. It was six o'clock. The only other customers were closeted in video booths in the back. Still, the kid had had a look at him, and what was the big hurry, anyway?

He grabbed a couple of magazines at random and paid for them. The jowly man bagged them and sealed the bag with a strip of tape. Keller stowed his purchase in his carry-on and went to find himself a hotel room.

The next day he went to a museum and a movie, arriving at the bookstore at ten minutes after six. The young clerk was gone, presumably having a plate of curry somewhere. The jowly man was behind the counter, and there were three customers in the store, two checking the video selections, one looking at magazines.

Keller browsed, hoping they would decide to clear out. At one point he was standing in front of a whole wall of videocassettes and it turned into a wall of caged puppies. It was momentary, and he couldn't tell if it was a genuine hallucination or just some sort of mental flashback. Whatever it was, he didn't like it.

One customer left, but the other two lingered, and then someone new came in off the street. And in half an hour the Indian kid was due back, and who knew if he would take his full hour, anyway?

He approached the counter, trying to look a little more nervous than he felt. Shifty eyes, furtive glances. Pitching his voice low, he said, "Talk to you in private?"

"About what?"

Eyes down, shoulders drawn in, he said, "Something special."

"If it's got to do with little kids," the man said, "no disrespect intended, but I don't know nothing about it, I don't want to know nothing about it, and I wouldn't even know where to steer you."

"Nothing like that," Keller said.

They went into a room in back. The jowly man closed the door, and as he was turning around Keller hit him with the edge of his hand at the juncture of neck and shoulder. The man's knees buckled, and in an instant Keller had a loop of wire around his neck. In another minute he was out the door, and within the hour he was on the northbound Metroliner.

When he got home he realized he still had the magazines in his bag. That was sloppy, he should have discarded them the previous night, but he'd simply forgotten them altogether and never even unsealed the package.

Nor could he find a reason to unseal it now. He carried it down the hall, dropped it unopened into the incinerator. Back in his apartment, he fixed himself a weak scotch and water and watched a documentary on the Discovery Channel. The vanishing rain forest, one more goddam thing to worry about.

"Oedipus," Jerrold Breen said, holding his hands in front of his chest, his fingertips pressed together. "I presume you know the story. Unwittingly, he killed his father and married his mother."

"Two pitfalls I've thus far managed to avoid."

"Indeed," Breen said. "But have you? When you fly off somewhere in your official capacity as corporate expediter, when you shoot trouble, as it were, what exactly are you doing? You fire people, you cashier entire divisions, close plants, rearrange human lives. Is that a fair description?"

"I suppose so."

"There's an implied violence. Firing a man, terminating his career, is the symbolic equivalent of killing him. And he's a stranger, and I shouldn't doubt that the more important of these men are more often than not older than you, isn't that so?"

"What's the point?"

"When you do what you do, it's as if you are seeking out and killing your unknown father."

"I don't know," Keller said. "Isn't that a little far-fetched?"

"And your relationships with women," Breen went on, "have a strong Oedipal component. Your mother was a vague and unfocused woman, incompletely present in her own life, incapable of connection with others. Your own relationships with women are likewise blurred and out of focus. Your problems with impotence—"

"Once!"

"—are a natural consequence of this confusion. Your mother herself is dead now, isn't that so?"

"Yes."

"And your father is not to be found, and almost certainly deceased. What's called for, Peter, is an act specifically designed to reverse this entire pattern on a symbolic level."

"I don't follow you."

"It's a subtle point," Breen admitted. He crossed

his legs, propped an elbow on a knee, extended his thumb and rested his bony chin on it. Keller thought, not for the first time, that Breen must have been a stork in a prior life. "If there were a male figure in your life," Breen went on, "preferably at least a few years your senior, someone playing a faintly paternal role vis-à-vis yourself, someone to whom you turn for advice and direction."

Keller thought of the man in White Plains.

"Instead of killing this man," Breen said, "symbolically, I need hardly say—I am speaking symbolically throughout—but instead of killing him as you have done with father figures in the past, it seems to me that you might do something to nourish this man."

Cook a meal for the man in White Plains? Buy him a hamburger? Toss him a salad?

"Perhaps you could think of a way to use your particular talents to this man's benefit instead of his detriment," Breen went on. He drew a handkerchief from his breast pocket and mopped his forehead. "Perhaps there is a woman in his life—your mother, symbolically—and perhaps she is a source of great pain to your father. So, instead of making love to her and slaying him, like Oedipus, you might reverse the usual course of things by, uh, showing love to him and, uh, slaying her."

"Oh," Keller said.

"Symbolically, that is to say."

"Symbolically," Keller said.

A week later Breen handed him a photograph. "This is called the Thematic Apperception Test," Breen said. "You look at the photograph and make up a story about it."

"What kind of story?"

"Any kind at all," Breen said. "This is an exercise in imagination. You look at the subject of the photograph and imagine what sort of woman she is and what she is doing."

The photo was in color, and showed a rather elegant brunette dressed in tailored clothing. She had a dog on a leash. The dog was medium size, with a chunky body and an alert expression in its eyes. It was that color which dog people call blue, and which everyone else calls gray.

"It's a woman and a dog," Keller said.

"Very good."

Keller took a breath. "The dog can talk," he said, "but he won't do it in front of other people. The woman made a fool of herself once when she tried to show him off. Now she knows better. When they're alone he talks a blue streak, and the son of a bitch has an opinion on everything. He tells her everything from the real cause of the Thirty Years' War to the best recipe for lasagna."

"He's quite a dog," Breen said.

"Yes, and now the woman doesn't want other people to know he can talk, because she's afraid they might take him away from her. In this picture they're in the park. It looks like Central Park."

"Or perhaps Washington Square."

"It could be Washington Square," Keller agreed. "The woman is crazy about the dog. The dog's not so sure about the woman."

"And what do you think about the woman?"

"She's attractive," Keller said.

"On the surface," Breen said. "Underneath it's another story, believe me. Where do you suppose she lives?"

Keller gave it some thought. "Cleveland," he said.

"Cleveland? Why Cleveland, for God's sake?"

"Everybody's got to be someplace."

"If I were taking this test," Breen said, "I'd proba-bly imagine the woman living at the foot of Fifth Avenue, at Washington Square. I'd have her living at number one Fifth Avenue, perhaps because I'm familiar with that particular building. You see, I once lived there."

"Oh?"

"In a spacious apartment on a high floor. And once a month," he continued, "I write out an enormous check and mail it to that address, which used to be mine. So it's only natural that I would have this par-ticular building in mind, especially when I look at this particular photograph." His eyes met Keller's. "You have a question, don't you? Go ahead and ask it."

"What breed is the dog?"

"The dog?"

"I just wondered," Keller said.

"As it happens," Breen said, "it's an Australian cattle dog. Looks like a mongrel, doesn't it? Believe me, it doesn't talk. But why don't you hang on to that photograph?"

"All right."

"You're making really fine progress in therapy," Breen said. "I want to acknowledge you for the work you're doing. And I just know you'll do the right thing."

A few days later Keller was sitting on a park bench in Washington Square. He folded his newspaper and walked over to a dark-haired woman wearing a blazer and a beret. "Excuse me," he said, "but isn't that an Australian cattle dog?"

"That's right," she said.

"It's a handsome animal," he said. "You don't see many of them."

"Most people think he's a mutt. It's such an esoteric breed. Do you own one yourself?"

"I did. My ex-wife got custody."

"How sad for you."

"Sadder still for the dog. His name was Soldier. *Is* Soldier, unless she's gone and changed it."

"This fellow's name is Nelson. That's his call name. Of course the name on his papers is a real mouthful."

"Do you show him?"

"He's seen it all," she said. "You can't show him a thing."

"I went down to the Village last week," Keller said, "and the damnedest thing happened. I met a woman in the park."

"Is that the damnedest thing?"

"Well, it's unusual for me. I meet women at bars and parties, or someone introduces us. But we met and talked, and then I happened to run into her the following morning. I bought her a cappuccino."

"You just happened to run into her on two successive days."

"Yes."

"In the Village."

"It's where I live."

Breen frowned. "You shouldn't be seen with her, should you?"

"Why not?"

"Don't you think it's dangerous?"

"All it's cost me so far," Keller said, "is the price of a cappuccino."

"I thought we had an understanding."

"An understanding?"

"You don't live in the Village," Breen said. "I know where you live. Don't look so surprised. The first time you left here I watched you from the window. You behaved as though you were trying to avoid being followed. So I bided my time, and when you stopped taking precautions, that's when I followed you. It wasn't that difficult."

"Why follow me?"

"To find out who you were. Your name is Keller, you live at 865 First Avenue. I already knew *what* you were. Anybody might have known just from listening to your dreams. And paying in cash, and all of these sudden business trips. I still don't know who employs you, the crime bosses or the government, but then what difference does it make? Have you been to bed with my wife?"

"Your ex-wife."

"Answer the question."

"Yes, I have."

"Christ. And were you able to perform?"

"Yes."

"Why the smile?"

"I was just thinking," Keller said, "that it was quite a performance."

Breen was silent for a long moment, his eyes fixed on a spot above and to the right of Keller's shoulder. Then he said, "This is profoundly disappointing. I had hoped you would find the strength to transcend the Oedipal myth, not merely reenact it. You've had fun, haven't you? What a naughty little boy you've been! What a triumph you've scored over your symbolic father! You've taken his woman to bed. No doubt you have visions of getting her pregnant, so that she can give you what she so cruelly denied him. Eh?"

"Never occurred to me."

"It would, sooner or later." Breen leaned forward, concern showing on his face. "I hate to see you sabotaging your own therapeutic process this way," he said. "You were doing so *well*."

From the bedroom window you could look down at Washington Square Park. There were plenty of dogs there now, but none of them were Australian cattle dogs.

"Some view," Keller said. "Some apartment."

"Believe me," she said, "I earned it. You're getting dressed. Going somewhere?"

"Just feeling a little restless. Okay if I take Nelson for a walk?"

"You're spoiling him," she said. "You're spoiling both of us."

On a Wednesday morning, Keller took a cab to La Guardia and a plane to St. Louis. He had a cup of coffee with an associate of the man in White Plains and caught an evening flight back to New York. He caught another cab and went directly to the apartment building at the foot of Fifth Avenue.

"I'm Peter Stone," he told the doorman. "I believe Mrs. Breen is expecting me."

The doorman stared.

"Mrs. Breen," Keller said. "In Seventeen-J."

"Jesus."

"Is something the matter?"

"I guess you haven't heard," the doorman said. "I wish it wasn't me that had to tell you."

* * *

"You killed her," he said.

"That's ridiculous," Breen told him. "She killed herself. She threw herself out the window. If you want my professional opinion, she was suffering from depression."

"If you want *my* professional opinion," Keller said, "she had help."

"I wouldn't advance that argument if I were you," Breen said. "If the police were to look for a murderer, they might look long and hard at Mr. Stone-hyphen-Keller, the stone killer. And I might have to tell them how the usual process of transference went awry, how you became obsessed with me and my personal life, how I couldn't seem to dissuade you from some inane plan to reverse the Oedipal complex. And then they might ask you why you employ aliases, and just how you make your living, and . . . do you see why it might be best to let sleeping dogs lie?"

As if on cue, the dog stepped out from behind the desk. He caught sight of Keller and his tail began to wag.

"Sit," Breen said. "You see? He's well trained. You might take a seat yourself."

"I'll stand. You killed her, and then you walked off with the dog, and—"

Breen sighed. "The police found the dog in the apartment, whimpering in front of the open window. After I went down and identified the body and told them about her previous suicide attempts, I volunteered to take the dog home with me. There was no one else to look after it."

"I would have taken him," Keller said.

"But that won't be necessary, will it? You won't be called upon to walk my dog or make love to my

wife or bed down in my apartment. Your services
are no longer required." Breen seemed to recoil at
the harshness of his own words. His face softened.
"You'll be able to get back to the far more important
business of therapy. In fact"—he indicated the
couch—"why not stretch out right now?"

"That's not a bad idea. First, though, could you
put the dog in the other room?"

"Not afraid he'll interrupt, are you? Just a little
joke. He can wait for us in the outer office. There
you go, Nelson. Good dog. . . . Oh, no. How dare
you bring a gun to this office? Put that down
immediately."

"I don't think so."

"For God's sake, why kill me? I'm not your father.
I'm your therapist. It makes no sense for you to kill
me. You've got nothing to gain and everything to
lose. It's completely irrational. It's worse than that,
it's neurotically self-destructive."

"I guess I'm not cured yet."

"What's that, gallows humor? But it happens to be
true. You're a long way from cured, my friend. As
a matter of fact, I would say you're approaching a
psychotherapeutic crisis. How will you get through
it if you shoot me?"

Keller went to the window, flung it wide open.
"I'm not going to shoot you," he said.

"I've never been the least bit suicidal," Breen said,
pressing his back against a wall of bookshelves.
"Never."

"You've grown despondent over the death of your
ex-wife."

"That's sickening, just sickening. And who would
believe it?"

"We'll see," Keller told him. "As far as the therapeutic crisis is concerned, well, we'll see about that, too. I'll think of something."

The woman at the animal shelter said, "Talk about coincidence. One day you come in and put your name down for an Australian cattle dog. You know, that's a very uncommon breed in this country."

"You don't see many of them."

"And what came in this morning? A perfectly lovely Australian cattle dog. You could have knocked me over with a sledgehammer. Isn't he a beauty?"

"He certainly is."

"He's been whimpering ever since he got here. It's very sad, his owner died and there was nobody to keep him. My goodness, look how he went right to you! I think he likes you."

"I'd say we were made for each other."

"I can almost believe it. His name is Nelson, but of course you can change it."

"Nelson," he said. The dog's ears perked up. Keller reached to give him a scratch. "No, I don't think I'll have to change it. Who was Nelson, anyway? Some kind of English hero, wasn't he? A famous general or something?"

"I think an admiral. Commander of the British fleet, if I remember correctly. Remember? The Battle of Trafalgar Square?"

"It rings a muted bell," he said. "Not a soldier but a sailor. Well, that's close enough, wouldn't you say? Now I suppose there's an adoption fee to pay, and some papers to fill out."

When they'd handled that part she said, "I still can't get over it. The coincidence and all."

"I knew a man once," Keller said, "who insisted

there was no such thing as a coincidence or an accident.''

''Well, I wonder how he'd explain this.''

''I'd like to hear him try,'' Keller said. ''Let's go, Nelson. Good boy.''

4

Dogs Walked, Plants Watered

"Now here's my situation," Keller said. "Ordinarily I have plenty of free time. I take Nelson for a minimum of two long walks a day, and sometimes when the weather's nice we'll be out all afternoon. It's a pleasure for me, and he's tireless, literally tireless. He's an Australian cattle dog, and the breed was developed to drive herds of cattle vast distances. You could probably walk him to Yonkers and back and he'd still be raring to go."

"I've never been to Yonkers," the girl said.

Neither had Keller, but he had passed through it often enough on the way to and from White Plains. There was no need to mention this.

"The thing is," he went on, "I sometimes have to travel on business, and I don't get much in the way of advance warning. I get a phone call, and two hours later I'm on a plane halfway across the country, and I may not get back for two weeks. Last time I boarded Nelson, and I don't want to do that again."

"No."

"Aside from the fact that the kennels expect you to make reservations a week in advance," he said, "I think it's rotten for the dog. Last time, well, he was different when I picked him up. I don't know how to explain it, but it was days before he was his old self again."

"I know what you mean."

"So I'd like to be able call you," he said, "when I find out I have to travel. You could come in every day and feed him and give him fresh water and take him for a walk twice a day. That's the kind of thing you could do, right?"

"It's what I do," she said. "I have regular clients who don't have the time to give their pets enough attention, and I have other clients who hire me just when they go out of town, and I'll come to their houses and take care of their pets and their houseplants."

"But in the meantime," Keller said, "I thought you and Nelson ought to get to know each other, because who knows how he'll react if I just disappear one day and a few hours later you turn up and enter the apartment? He's pretty territorial."

"But if Nelson and I already knew each other—"

"That's what I was getting at," he said. "Suppose you were to walk him, I don't know, twice a week? He's not stupid, he'd get the idea right away. Then, by the time I had to leave town, you'd already be an old friend. He wouldn't go nuts when you tried to enter the apartment or resist when you tried to lead him out of it. Does that make sense to you? And what would be a fair price?"

They worked it out. She would walk Nelson for a full hour twice a week, on Tuesday mornings and Friday afternoons, and for this Keller would pay her fifty dollars a week. Then, when Keller was out of town, she would get fifty dollars a day, in return for which she would see to Nelson's food and water and walk him twice daily.

"Why don't we start now?" she suggested. "How about it, Nelson? Want to go for a walk?" The dog recognized the word but looked uncertain. "Walk, walk, walk!" she said, and his tail set to wagging.

When they were out the door Keller began to worry. Suppose she never brought the dog back? Then what?

Dogs Walked, Plants Watered, the notice had read. *Responsible Young Woman Will Provide Quality Care for Your Flora and Fauna. Call Andria.*

The notice had appeared on the community bulletin board at the neighborhood Gristede's, where Keller bought Grape-Nuts for himself and Milk-Bone for Nelson. There had been a phone number, and he had copied it down and dialed it, and now his dog was in the care and custody of this allegedly responsible young woman, and all he really knew about her was that she didn't know how to spell her own name. Suppose she let Nelson off the leash? Suppose she sold him to vivisectionists? Suppose she fell in love with him and never brought him back?

Keller went into the bathroom and stared hard at himself in the mirror. "Grow up," he said sternly.

An hour and ten minutes after they'd left, Nelson and Andria returned. "He's a pleasure to walk," she said. "No, don't pay me for today. It would be like paying an actor for an audition. You can start paying me on Tuesday. Incidentally, it's only fair to tell you that the payment you suggested is higher than my usual rates."

"That's all right."

"You're sure? Well, thanks, because I can use it. I'll see you Tuesday morning."

She showed up Tuesday morning, and again Friday afternoon. When she brought Nelson back on Friday she asked Keller if he wanted a full report.

"On what?" he wondered.

"On our walk," she said. "On what he did. You know."

"Did he bite anyone? Did he come up with a really good recipe for chili?"

"Some owners want you to give them a tree-by-tree report."

"Hey, call me irresponsible," Keller said, "but I figure there are things we're not meant to know."

After a couple of weeks he gave her a key. "Because there's no reason for me to stick around just to let you in," he said. "If I'm not going to be here I'll leave the money in an envelope on the desk." A week later he forced himself to leave the apartment half an hour before she was due to arrive. When he printed her name in block capitals on the envelope it looked strange to him, and the next time he saw her he raised the subject. "The notice you posted had your name spelled with an *I*," he said. "Is that how you spell it or was it a misprint?"

"Both," she said. "I originally spelled it with an *E*, like everybody else in the world, but people tended to give it the European pronunciation, uhn-DRAY-uh, and I hate that. This way they mostly say it right, ANN-dree-uh, although now I get the occasional person who says uhn-DRY-uh, which doesn't even sound like a name. I'd probably be better off changing my name altogether."

"That seems extreme."

"Do you think so? I've changed it every year or so since I was sixteen. I'm forever running possible names through my mind. What do you think of Hastings?''

''Distinctive.''

''Right, but is it the direction I want to go? That's what I can't decide. I've also been giving some consideration to Jane, and you can't even compare the two, can you?''

''Apples and oranges,'' Keller said.

''When the time comes,'' Andria said, ''I'll know what to do.''

One morning Keller left the house with Nelson a few minutes after nine and didn't get home until almost one. He was unhooking Nelson's leash when the phone rang. Dot said, ''Keller, I miss you, I haven't seen you in ages. I wish you'd come see me sometime.''

''One of these days,'' he said.

He filled Nelson's water dish, then went out and caught a cab to Grand Central and a train to White Plains. There was no car waiting for him, so he found a taxi to take him to the old Victorian house on Taunton Place. Dot was on the porch, wearing a floral print housedress and sipping a tall glass of iced tea. ''He's upstairs,'' she said, ''but he's got somebody with him. Sit down, pour some iced tea for yourself. It's a hot one, isn't it?''

''It's not that bad,'' he said, taking a chair, pouring from the Thermos jug into a glass with Wilma Flintstone depicted on its side. ''I think Nelson likes the heat.''

''A few months ago you were saying he liked the cold.''

''I think he likes weather,'' Keller said. ''He'd probably like an earthquake, if we had one.'' He thought about it. "I might be wrong about that," he conceded. "I don't think he'd feel very secure in an earth-quake."

"Neither would I, Keller. Am I ever going to meet Nelson the Wonder Dog? Why don't you bring him out here sometime?"

"Someday." He turned her glass so that he could see the picture on it. "Pebbles," he said. A buzzer sounded, one long and two short. "What was it Fred used to say? It's driving me crazy. I can hear him saying it but I can't remember what it was."

"Yabba dabba do?"

"Yabba dabba do, that's it. There was a song, 'Aba Daba Honeymoon,' but I don't suppose it had anything to do with Fred Flintstone."

Dot gave him a look. "That buzzer means he's ready for you," she said. "No rush, you can finish your tea. Or take it with you."

"Yabba dabba do," Keller said.

Someone drove him to the station and twenty minutes later he was on the train to New York. As soon as he got home he called Andria. He started to dial the number that had appeared on her notice at Gristede's, then remembered what she'd told him the previous Tuesday or the Friday before, whenever it was. She had moved and didn't have a new phone yet. Meanwhile she had a beeper.

"And I'll keep it even after I have a phone," she said, "because I'm out walking dogs all the time, so how could you reach me if you needed me on short notice?"

He called her beeper number and punched in his own number at the signal. She called back within five minutes.

"I figure a few days," he told her. "But it could run a week, maybe longer."

"No problem," she assured him. "I have the key. The elevator attendant knows it's all right to let me up, and Nelson thinks I'm his madcap aunt. If you run out of dog food I'll buy more. What else is there?"

"I don't know. Do you think I should leave the TV on for him?"

"Is that what you ordinarily do when you leave him alone?"

The truth of the matter was that he didn't leave Nelson alone much. More often than not lately he either took the dog along or stayed home himself. Nelson had unquestionably changed his life. He walked more than he ever used to, and he also stayed in more.

"I guess I won't leave it on," he said. "He never takes any real interest in what I'm watching."

"He's a pretty cultured guy," she said. "Have you tried him on *Masterpiece Theater*?"

Keller flew to Omaha, where the target was an executive of a telemarketing firm. The man's name was Dinsmore, and he lived with his wife and children in a nicely landscaped suburban house. He would have been a cinch to take out, but someone local had tried and missed, and the man thus knew what to expect and had changed his routine accordingly. His house had a high-tech security system, and a private security guard was posted out front from dusk to dawn. Police cruisers, marked and unmarked, drove past the house at all hours.

He had hired a personal bodyguard, too, who called for him in the morning, stayed at his side all through the day, and saw him to his door in the evening. The bodyguard was a wildly overdeveloped young man with a mane of ragged yellow hair. He looked like a professional wrestler stuffed into a business suit.

Short of leasing a plane and dive-bombing the house, Keller couldn't see an easy way to do it. Security was tight at the business premises, where access was limited to persons with photo ID badges. Even if you got past the guards, the blond bodyguard spent the whole day in a chair outside of Dinsmore's office, riffling the pages of *Iron Man* magazine.

The right move, he thought, was to go home. Come back in six weeks. By then the bodyguard would have walked off the job in steroid-inspired rage, or Dinsmore, chafing at his hulking presence, would have fired him. Failing that, the two would have relaxed their guard. The cops would be less attentive as well.

Keller would look for an opening, and it wouldn't take long to find one.

But he couldn't do that. Whoever wanted the man dead wasn't willing to wait.

"Time's what's short," his contact explained. "Soldiers, firepower, that's easy. You want a few guys in cars, somebody blocks the streets, somebody rams his car, no problem."

Wonderful. Omaha, meet Delta Force. Not too long ago Keller had imagined himself as a tight-lipped loner in the Old West, riding into town to kill a man he'd never met. Now he was Lee Marvin, leading a ragged band of losers on a commando raid.

"We'll see," he said. "I'll think of something."

*   *   *

The fourth night there he went for a walk. It was a nice night and he'd driven downtown, where a man on foot didn't arouse suspicions. But there was something wrong, and he'd been walking for fifteen minutes before he figured out what it was.

He missed the dog.

For years, Keller had been alone. He'd grown used to it, finding his own way, keeping his own counsel. Ever since childhood he'd been solitary and secretive by nature, and his line of work made these traits professional requirements.

Once, in a shop in SoHo, he'd seen a British World War II poster. It showed a man winking, his mouth a thin line. The caption read, "What I know I keep to myself," evidently the English equivalent of "Loose lips sink ships." Keller had thought about the poster for hours and returned the following day to price it. The price had been reasonable enough, but he'd realized during the negotiations that the sight of that canny face, winking forever across the room at him, would soon become oppressive. The man on the poster, advising privacy, would himself constitute an invasion of it. How could you kiss a girl with that face looking on? How could you pick your nose?

The sentiment, though, stayed with him. On the train to and from White Plains, on a flight to some distant city where his services were required, on the flight home with his mission accomplished, the Englishman's motto would sound in his mind like a mantra. What he knew he kept to himself.

In therapy he'd felt conflicted. The process wouldn't work unless he was willing to open up. But how could he tell a West Side psychologist what he wouldn't let slip to a stranger on a train, or a woman in bed? He'd wound up talking mostly of dreams and childhood memories, hoping all the while that what Dr. Jerrold Breen knew he'd keep to himself. In the end, of course, Breen had taken his knowledge to the grave, leaving Keller to resume his lifelong habit of silence.

But he'd broken that habit with Nelson.

Perhaps the best thing about dogs, it seemed to Keller, was that you could talk to them. They made much better listeners than human beings did. You didn't have to worry that you were boring them, or that they'd heard a particular story before, or that they'd think less of you for what you were revealing about yourself. You could tell them anything, secure in the knowledge that the matter would end right there. They wouldn't pass it on to somebody else, nor would they throw it back in your face in the course of an argument.

Which was not to say that they didn't listen. It was quite clear to Keller that Nelson listened. When you talked to him you didn't have the feeling that you were talking to a wall, or to a gerbil or a goldfish. Nelson didn't necessarily understand what you told him, but he damn well listened.

And Keller told him everything. The longings that had begun to stir during therapy—to open up, to divulge old secrets, to reveal oneself to oneself—now found full expression on the long walks he took with Nelson and the long evenings they spent at home.

"I never set out to do this for a living," he told Nelson one afternoon in the park. "And for a while, you know, it was just something I'd done a couple of times. It wasn't who I was.

"Except it got so it *was* who I was, and I didn't realize it. How I found out, see, I'd meet somebody who'd heard of me, and he'd show something that would surprise me, whether it was fear or respect, whatever it was. He'd be reacting to a killer, and that would puzzle me, because I didn't know that's what I was.

"I remember in high school how they did all this career counseling, showing you how to figure out what you wanted to do in life and then take steps in that direction. I think I told you how those years were sort of a blur for me. I went through them like somebody with a light concussion, I saw everything through a veil. But when they got on this career stuff I just didn't have a clue. There was this test, questions like would you rather pull weeds or sell cabbages or teach needlepoint, and I couldn't finish the test. Every question was utterly baffling.

"And then I woke up one day and realized I had a career, and it consisted of taking people out. I never had any interest in it or any aptitude for it, but it turns out you don't need any. All you need is to be able to do it. I did it once because somebody told me to, and I did it a second time because somebody told me to, and before I knew it it was what I did. Then, once I'd defined myself, I started to learn the technical aspects. Guns, other tools, unarmed techniques. How to get around people. Stuff you ought to know.

"The thing is, there's not all that much you have to know. It's not like the careers they told you about in high school. You don't prepare for it. Maybe there are things that happen to you along the way that prepare you for it, but that's not something you choose.

"What do you think? Do you want to split a hotdog? Or should we head on home?"

*   *   *

Back from his solitary walk, Keller looked at the phone and wished there was a way he could call Nelson. He'd avoided getting an answering machine, seeing great potential for disaster in such a device, but it would be useful now. He could call up and talk, and Nelson would be able to hear him.

And, if he really opened up and spoke his mind, it would all be there on the tape, where anybody could retrieve it. No, he decided, it was just as well he didn't have a machine.

At noon the following day he was in his rented car when Dinsmore and his bodyguard drove downtown and parked in front of a restaurant in the Old Market district. Keller waited outside for a few minutes, then found a parking space and went in after them. The hostess seated Keller just two tables away from Dinsmore. Keller ordered shrimp scampi and watched Dinsmore and the wrestler each put away an enormous steak.

A couple of hours later he called Dot in White Plains. "Guy's forty pounds overweight and here I just saw him tuck into a porterhouse the size of a manhole cover," he said. "Put half a shaker of salt on it first. How much of a rush are these people in? Because they shouldn't have to wait too long before a stroke or a coronary closes the account."

"There's no cause like a natural cause," Dot said. "But you know what they say about time, Keller."

"It's of the essence?"

"Yabba dabba do," Dot said.

The next day Dinsmore and his bodyguard had the same table at the same restaurant. This time a third man accompanied them. He looked to be a business associate of Dinsmore's. Keller couldn't overhear the conversation, he was seated a little farther away this time, but he could see that Dinsmore and the third man were doing the talking, while the bodyguard divided his attention between the food on his plate and the other diners in the room. Keller had brought a newspaper along and managed to have his eyes on it when the bodyguard glanced his way.

At one point Dinsmore got to his feet, and Keller's pulse quickened. Before he could react, the bodyguard was also standing, and both men walked off to the men's room. Keller stayed where he was and ate his spaghetti carbonara.

He was watching out of the corner of his eye when the two men returned to their table. The bodyguard took a moment to scan the room, while Dinsmore sat down at once and shook some more salt onto his half-eaten steak.

Almost without thinking, Keller reached out and let his hand close around his own salt cellar. It was made of glass, and fit his fist like a roll of nickels. If he were to hit someone now, the salt cellar would lend considerable authority to the blow.

Damn thing was lethal.

That night Keller had a couple of drinks after dinner. He still felt them when he got back to his motel. He walked around the block to sober up, and when he got back to his room he picked up the phone and called Nelson.

He wasn't drunk enough to expect the dog to answer. But it seemed to him that this was a way to make a minimal sort of contact. The phone would ring. The dog would hear it ring. While he could not be expected to recognize it as his master's voice, Keller would have reached out and touched him, as they said in the phone company ads.

No, of course it didn't make sense. Dialing the number, he knew it didn't make sense. But it wouldn't cost anything, and there wouldn't be a record of the call, so what harm could it do?

The line was busy.

His first reaction—and it was extremely brief, just momentary—was one of jealous paranoia. The dog was on the phone with someone else, and they were talking about Keller.

The thought came and went in an instant, leaving Keller to shake his head in wonder at the mysteries of his own mind. A flood of other explanations came to him, each of them far more probable than that first thought.

Nelson could have lurched into the end table on which the phone sat, knocking it off the hook. Andria, using the phone before or after their walk, could have replaced the receiver incorrectly. Or, most probably, the long-distance circuits were overloaded, and any call to New York would be rewarded with a busy signal.

A few minutes later he tried again and got a busy signal again.

He walked back and forth, fighting the impulse to call the operator and have her check the line. Eventually he picked up the phone and tried the number a third time, and this time it rang. He let it ring four times, and as it rang he imagined the dog's reaction—the ears pricking up, the alert gleam in the eyes.

"Good boy, Nelson," he said aloud. "I'll be home soon."

*   *   *

The next day, Friday, he spent the morning in his motel room. Around eleven he called the restaurant in the Old Market. Dinsmore had arrived at the restaurant at 12:30 on both of his previous visits. Keller booked a table for one at 12:15.

He arrived on time and ordered a cranberry juice spritzer. He looked across at Dinsmore's table, now set for two. If this went well, he thought, he could be home in time to take Nelson for a walk before bedtime.

At 12:30, Dinsmore's table remained empty. Ten minutes later a pair of businesswomen were seated at it. Keller ate his food without tasting it, drank a cup of coffee, paid the check, and left.

Saturday he went to a movie. Sunday he went to another movie and walked around the Old Market district. Sunday night he sat in his room and looked at the phone. He had already called home twice, letting the phone ring, trying to tell himself he was establishing some kind of psychic contact with his dog. He hadn't had anything to drink and he knew what he was doing didn't make any sense, but he'd gone ahead and done it anyhow.

He reached for the phone, started to dial a different number, then caught himself and left the room. He made the call from a pay phone, dialing Andria's beeper number, punching in the pay phone number after the tone sounded. He didn't know if it would work, didn't know if her beeper would receive more than a seven-number signal, didn't know if she'd be inclined to return a long-distance call. And she might be walking a dog, Nelson or some other client's, and did he really want to stand next to this phone for an hour waiting for her to call back? He couldn't call from his room, because then her call would have to come through the switchboard, and she wouldn't know whom to ask for. Even if she guessed it was him, the name Keller would mean nothing to the motel switchboard, and it was a name he didn't want anyone in Omaha to hear, anyway. So—

The phone rang almost immediately. He grabbed it and said hello, and she said, "Mr. Keller?"

"Andria," he said, and then couldn't think what to say next. He asked about the dog and she assured him that the dog was fine.

"But I think he misses you," she said. "He'll be glad when you're home."

"So will I," Keller said. "That's why I called. I had hoped to be back the day before yesterday, but things are taking longer than I thought. I'll be a few more days, maybe longer."

"No problem."

"Well, just so you know," he said. "Listen, I appreciate your calling me back. I may call again if this drags on. I'll reimburse you for the call."

"You're already paying for this one," she said. "I'm calling from your apartment. I hope that's all right?"

"Of course," he said. "But—"

"See, I was here when the beeper went off, and I figured who else would be calling me from out of town? So I figured it would be all right to use your phone, since it was probably you I'd be calling."

"Sure."

"As a matter of fact," she said, "I've been spending a lot of time here. It's nice and quiet, and Nelson seems to like the company. His ears pricked up just now when I said his name. I think he knows who I'm talking to. Do you want to say hello to him?"

"Well—"

Feeling like an idiot, he said hello to the dog and told him he was a good boy and that he'd see him soon. "He got all excited," Andria assured him. "He didn't bark, he hardly ever barks—"

"It's the dingo in him."

"—but he did a lot of panting and pawing the floor. He misses you. We're doing fine here, me and Nelson, but he'll be glad to see you."

Keller got to the restaurant at 12:15 Monday. The hostess recognized him and led him directly to the same table he'd had Friday. He looked over at Dinsmore's table and saw that it was set for four, and that there was a RESERVED card on it.

At 12:30, two men in suits were seated at Dinsmore's table. Keller didn't recognize either of them, and began to despair of his entire plan. Then Dinsmore arrived, accompanied by the wrestler.

Keller watched them while he ate his meal. Three men, drinking their drinks and wolfing their steaks, talking heartily, gesturing volubly. While the fourth man, the bodyguard, sat like a coiled spring.

Too many people, Keller thought. Give it another day.

The next day he arrived at the same time and the hostess led him to the table he'd reserved. Dinsmore's table had two places set, and a RESERVED sign in place. Keller got to his feet and went to the men's room, where he locked himself in a stall.

A few minutes later he left the men's room and threaded his way through the maze of tables, passing close to the Dinsmore table on his way, bumping into it, reaching out to steady himself.

As far as he could tell, nobody paid him any attention.

He returned to his own table, sat down, waited. At 12:30 Dinsmore's table was still unoccupied. What would he do if they gave it to somebody else? He couldn't try to undo what he'd just done, could he? He didn't see how, not with people sitting at the table.

Risky plan, he thought. Too many ways it could go wrong. If he'd been able to talk it through with Nelson first—

Get a grip on yourself, he told himself.

He was doing just that when Dinsmore and the wrestler turned up, the executive in a testy mood, the bodyguard looking sullen and bored. There was a bad moment when the hostess seemed uncertain where to seat them, but then she worked it out and led them to their usual table.

Keller longed to get out of there. He'd been picking at his veal ever since it had been placed in front of him. It tasted flat, but he figured anything would just then. Could he just put some money on the table and get the hell out? Or did he have to sit there and wait?

Fifteen minutes after his arrival, Dinsmore cried out, clutched his throat, and pitched forward onto the table. Half an hour after that, Keller turned in his rental car at the airport and booked his flight home.

In the cab from the airport, Keller had to fight the impulse to have the driver stop so he could pick up something for Nelson. He'd changed planes in St. Louis, and he'd spent most of his time between flights in the gift shop, trying to find something for the dog. But what would Nelson do with a snow shaker or a souvenir coffee mug? What did he want with a Cardinals cap, or a sweatshirt with a representation of the Gateway Arch?

"You hardly touched that," the waitress in Omaha had said of his veal. "Do you want a doggie bag?"

He'd been stuck for an answer. "Sorry," he said at length. "I'm a little rattled. That poor man . . ." he'd added, with a gesture toward the table where Dinsmore had been sitting.

"Oh, I'm sure he'll be all right," she said. "He's probably sitting up in his hospital bed right now, joking with his nurses."

Keller didn't think so.

"Hey, Mist' Keller," the elevator operator said. "Ain't seen you in a while, sir."

"It's good to be back."

"That dog be glad to see you," the man said. "That Nelson, he's a real good dog."

He was also out, a fact the attendant had neglected to mention. Keller unlocked the door and entered the apartment, calling the dog's name and getting no response. He unpacked, and decided to delay his shower until the dog was back and the girl had gone for the day.

He could have had several showers. It was fully forty minutes from the time he sat down in front of the television set until he heard Andria's key in the lock. As soon as the door was open Nelson came flying across the room, leaping up to greet Keller, tail wagging furiously.

Keller felt wonderful. A wave of contentment passed through him, and he got down on his knees to play with his dog.

* * *

"I'm sorry you had to come home to an empty house," Andria said. "If we'd known you were coming—"

"That's all right."

"Well, I'd better be going. You must be exhausted, you'll want to get to bed."

"Not for a few hours," he said, "but I'll want a shower. There's something about spending a whole day in airports and on planes—"

"I know what you mean," she said. "Well, Nelson, what's today? Tuesday? I guess I won't be seeing you until Friday." She petted the dog, then looked across at Keller. "You still want me to give him his regular walk on Friday, don't you?"

"Definitely."

"Good, because I'll be looking forward to it. He's my favorite client." She gave the dog another pat. "And thanks for paying me, and for the bonus. It's great of you. I mean, if I wind up having to get a hotel room, I can afford it."

"A hotel room?"

She lowered her eyes. "I wasn't going to mention this," she said, "but it'd give me a bad conscience not to. I don't know how you're going to feel about this, but I'll just go ahead and blurt it out, okay?"

"Okay."

"I've sort of been staying here," she said.

"You've sort of . . ."

"Sort of been living here. See, the place I was staying, it didn't work out, and there's one or two people I could call, but I thought, well, Nelson and I get along so good, and I could really spend lots of time with him if I just, like—"

"Stayed here."

"Right," she said. "So that's what I did. I didn't sleep in your bed, Mr. Keller—"

"Why not?"

"Well, I figured you might not like that. And the couch is comfortable, it really is."

She'd tried to keep her impact on his apartment minimal, she told him, stripping her bedding from the couch each morning and stowing it in the closet. And it wasn't as though she were hanging out there all the time, because when she wasn't walking Nelson she had other clients to attend to.

"Dogs to walk," he said. "Plants to water."

"And cats and fish to feed, and birds. There's this couple on Sixty-fifth Street with seventeen birds, and there's something about birds in cages. I get this urge to open the cages and open the windows and let them all fly away. But I wouldn't, partly because it would make the people really crazy, and partly because it would be terrible for the birds. I don't think they'd last long out there."

"Not in this town," Keller said.

"Just the other day one of them got out of his cage," she said, "and I just about lost it. The windows were closed so he wasn't going anywhere, but he was swooping and diving and I couldn't think how to get him back in his cage."

"What did you do?"

"What I did," she said, "is I centered all my energy in my heart chakra, and I sent this great burst of calming heart energy to the bird, and he calmed right down. Then I just held the cage door open and he flew back in."

"No kidding?"

She nodded. "I should have thought of it right

away," she said, "but when you panic you tend to overlook the obvious."

"That's the truth," he said. "Let me ask you something. Do you have a place to stay tonight?"

"Well, not yet."

"Not yet?"

"Well, I didn't know you were coming home tonight. But I know some people I can call, and—"

"You're welcome to stay here," he said.

"Oh, I couldn't do that."

"Why not?"

"Well, you're home. It wasn't really right for me to stay here when you were out of town—"

"It was fine. It meant more company for the dog."

"Anyway, you're home now. The last thing you need is a houseguest."

"One night won't hurt."

"Well," she said, "it is a little late to start looking for a place to stay."

"You'll stay here."

"But just for the one night."

"Right."

"I appreciate this," she said. "I really do."

Keller, freshly showered, stood at the sink and contemplated shaving. But whoever heard of shaving before you went to bed? You shaved in the morning, not at night.

Unless, of course, you expected to have your cheek pressed against something other than your pillow.

Cut it out, he told himself.

He got into bed and turned out the light, and Nelson sprang onto the bed beside him, turned around the compulsory three times, and lay down.

Keller slept. When he awoke the next morning, Andria was gone. The only trace of her presence was a note assuring him that she'd come walk the dog at her usual time on Friday. Keller shaved, walked the dog, and rode the train to White Plains.

It was another hot day, and this time Dot was on the porch with a pitcher of lemonade. She said, "Keller, you missed your calling. You're a great diagnostician. You gave the man a little time and he died of natural causes."

"These things happen."

"They do," she agreed. "I understand he fell in his food. Probably never get the stains out of his tie."

"It was a nice tie," Keller said.

"They said it was cardiac arrest," Dot said, "and I'll bet they're right, because it's a hell of a rare case when a man dies and his heart goes on beating. How'd you do it, Keller?"

"I centered all my energy in my heart chakra," he said, "and I sent this bolt of heart energy at him, and it was just more than his heart could handle."

She gave him a look. "If I had to guess," she said, "I'd have to say potassium cyanide."

"Good guess."

"How?"

"Switched salt shakers with him. The one I gave him had cyanide crystals mixed in with the top layer of salt. He used a lot of salt."

"They say it's bad for you. Wouldn't he taste the cyanide?"

"The amount of salt he used, I don't think he could taste the meat. I'm not sure how much taste cyanide has. Anyway, by the time it occurs to you that you don't like the way it tastes—"

"You're facedown in the lasagna. Cyanide's not traceless, is it? Won't it show up in an autopsy?"

"Only if you look for it."

"And if they look in the salt cellar?"

"When Dinsmore had his attack," he said, "a few people hurried over to see if they could help."

"Decent of them. You don't suppose one of them picked up the salt cellar?"

"It wouldn't surprise me."

"And got rid of it somewhere between the restaurant and the airport?"

"That wouldn't surprise me either."

He went upstairs to make his report. When he came downstairs again Dot said, "Keller, I'm going to start worrying about you. I think you're going soft."

"Oh?"

"There was only one reason to pick up the salt cellar."

"So they wouldn't find the cyanide," he said.

She shook her head. "If they ever start looking for cyanide, they'll find it on the uneaten food. No, you figured they wouldn't find it, and somebody else would use that salt and get poisoned accidentally."

"No point in drawing heat for no reason," he said.

"Uh-huh."

"No sense in killing people for free, either."

"Oh, I couldn't agree with you more, Keller," she said, "but I still say you're going soft. Centering in your heart choker and all."

"Chakra," he said.

"I stand corrected. What's it mean, anyway?"

"I have no idea."

"You will soon enough, now that you're centered there. Keller, you're turning human. Getting that dog was just the start of it. Next thing you know you'll be saving the whales. You'll be taking in strays, Keller. You watch.''

"That's ridiculous," he said. But on the train back to the city he found himself thinking about what she had said. Was there any truth to it?

He didn't think so, but he wasn't absolutely sure. He'd have to talk it over with Nelson.

5

Keller's Karma

In White Plains, Keller sat in the kitchen with Dot for twenty minutes. The TV was on, tuned to one of the home shopping channels. "I watch all the time," Dot said. "I never buy anything. What do I want with cubic zirconium?"

"Why do you watch?"

"That's what I ask myself, Keller. I haven't come up with the answer yet, but I think I know one of the things I like most about it. It's continuous."

"Continuous?"

"Uninterrupted. They never break the flow and go to a commercial."

"But the whole thing's a commercial," Keller said.

"That's different," she said.

A buzzer sounded. Dot picked up the intercom, listened a moment, then nodded significantly at Keller.

He went upstairs, and he was with the old man for ten or fifteen minutes. On his way out he stopped in the kitchen and got himself a glass of water. He stood at the sink and took his time drinking it. Dot was shaking her head at the television set. "It's all jewelry," she said. "Who buys all this jewelry? What do they want with it?"

"I don't know," he said. "Can I ask you something?"

"Ask away."

"Is he all right?"

"Why?"

"I just wondered."

"Did you hear something?"

"No, nothing like that. He seems tired, that's all."

"Everybody's tired," she said. "Life's a lot of work and it tires people out. But he's fine."

Keller took a train to Grand Central, a cab to his apartment. Nelson met him at the door with the leash in his mouth. Keller laughed, fastened the leash to the dog's collar. He had calls to make, a trip to schedule, but that could wait. Right now he was going to take his dog for a walk.

He headed over to the river. Nelson liked it there, but then Nelson seemed to like it everywhere. He certainly had a boundless enthusiasm for long walks. He never ran out of gas. You could exhaust yourself walking him, and he'd be ready to go again ten minutes later.

Of course you had to keep in mind that he had twice as many legs as a human being. Keller figured that had to make a difference.

"I'm going to have to take a trip," he told Nelson. "Not too long, I don't think, but that's the thing, you never really know. Sometimes I'll fly out in the morning and be back the same night, and other times it'll stretch to a week. But you don't have to worry. As soon as we get back to the house I'll call Andria."

The dog's ears pricked up at the girl's name. Keller had seen charts ranking the various breeds in intelligence, but not lately. He wasn't sure where the Australian cattle dog stood, but he figured it had to be pretty close to the top. Nelson didn't miss much.

"She's due to walk you tomorrow anyway," Keller said. "I could probably just stick a letter of instructions next to your leash, but why leave anything to chance? As soon as we get home I'll beep her."

Because Andria's living situation was still as tenuous as her career, the only number Keller had for her was that of the beeper she carried on her rounds. He called it as soon as he got home and punched in his number, and the girl called him back fifteen minutes later. "Hi," she said. "How's my favorite Australian cattle dog?"

"He's fine," Keller said, "but he's going to need company. I have to go out of town tomorrow morning."

"For how long, do you happen to know?"

"Hard to say. It might be a day, it might be a week. Is that a problem?"

She was quick to assure him that it wasn't. "In fact," she said, "the timing's perfect. I've been staying with these friends of mine, and it's not working out. I told them I'd be out of there tomorrow and I was wondering where I'd go next. Isn't it amazing the way we're always given guidance as to what to do next?"

"Amazing," he agreed.

"But that's assuming it's all right with you if I stay there while you're gone. I've done it before, but maybe you'd rather I don't this time."

"No, that's fine," Keller said. "It's more company for Nelson, so why should I object? You're not messy, you keep the place neat."

"I'm housebroken, all right. Same as Nelson." She laughed, then broke it off and said, "I really appreciate this, Mr. Keller. These friends I've been staying with, they're not getting along too well, and I'm kind of stuck in the middle. She's turned into this jealous monster, and he figures maybe he ought to give her something to be jealous about, and last night I just about walked the legs off a longhaired dachshund because I didn't want to be in their space. So it'll be a pleasure to get out of there tomorrow morning."

"Listen," he said, impulsively. "Why wait? Come over here tonight."

"But you're not leaving until tomorrow."

"So what? I've got a late evening tonight and I'll be out first thing in the morning, so we won't get in each other's way. And you'll be out of your friends' place that much sooner."

"Gee," she said, "that would be great."

When he got off the phone Keller went into the kitchen and made himself a cup of coffee. Why, he wondered, had he made the offer? It was certainly uncharacteristic behavior on his part. What did he care if she had to spend one more night suffering the dirty looks of the wife and the wandering hands of the husband?

And he'd even improvised to justify her acceptance of the offer, inventing a late evening and claiming an early flight. He hadn't booked the flight yet, and he had no plans for the evening.

Time to book the flight. Time to make plans for the evening.

The flight was booked with a single phone call, the evening planned almost as easily. Keller was dressing for it when Andria arrived, wearing striped bib overalls and bearing a forest-green backpack. Nelson made a fuss over her, and she shucked the backpack and knelt down to reciprocate.

"Well," Keller said. "You'll probably be asleep when I get home, and I'll probably leave before you wake up, so I'll say goodbye now. You know Nelson's routine, of course, and you know where everything is."

"I really appreciate this," Andria said.

Keller took a cab to the restaurant where he'd arranged to meet a woman named Yvonne, whom he'd dated three or four times since making her acquaintance at a Learning Annex class, "Deciphering the Mysteries of Baltic Cuisine." The true mystery, they'd both decided, was how anyone had the temerity to call it a cuisine. He'd since taken her to several restaurants, none of them Baltic. Tonight's choice was Italian, and they spent a good deal of time telling each other how happy they were to be eating in an Italian restaurant rather than, say, a Latvian one.

Afterward they went to a movie, and after that they took a cab to Yvonne's apartment, some eighteen blocks north of Keller's. As she fitted her key in the lock, she turned toward him. They had already reached the goodnight kiss stage, and Keller saw that Yvonne was ready to be kissed, but at the same time he sensed that she didn't really want to be kissed, nor did he really want to kiss her. They'd both had garlic, so it wasn't a reluctance to offend or be offended. He wasn't sure what it was, but he decided to honor it.

"Well," he said. "Goodnight, Yvonne."

She seemed for a moment to be surprised at being left unkissed, but she got over it quickly. "Yes, goodnight," she said, reaching for his hand, giving it a comradely squeeze. "Goodnight, John."

Goodnight forever, he thought, walking downtown on Second Avenue. He wouldn't call her again, nor would she expect his call. All they had in common was a disdain for Northern European cooking, and that wasn't much of a foundation for a relationship. The chemistry just wasn't there. She was attractive, but there was no connection between them, no spark.

That happened a lot, actually.

Halfway home, he stopped in a First Avenue bar. He'd had a little wine with dinner, and he wanted a clear head in the morning, so he didn't stay long, just nursed a beer and listened to the jukebox and looked at himself in the backbar mirror.

What a lonesome son of a bitch you are, he told his reflection.

Time to go home, when you started having thoughts like that. But he didn't want to get home until Andria had turned in for the night, and who knew what kind of hours she kept? He stayed where he was and sipped his beer, and he made another stop along the way for a cup of coffee.

When he did get home the apartment was dark. Andria was on the sofa, either asleep or faking it. Nelson, curled into a ball at her feet, got up, shook himself, and trotted silently to Keller's side. Keller went on into the bedroom, Nelson following. When Keller closed the bedroom door, the dog made an uncharacteristic sound deep in his throat. Keller didn't know what the sound meant, but he figured it had something to do with the door being closed, and Andria being on the other side of it.

He got into bed. The dog stood in front of the closed door, as if waiting for it to open. "Here, boy," Keller said. The dog turned to look at him. "Here, Nelson," he said, and the dog jumped onto the bed, turned around in a circle the ritualistic three times, and lay down in his usual spot. It seemed to Keller as though he didn't have his heart in it, but he was asleep in no time. So, eventually, was Keller.

When he woke up the dog was missing. So was Andria, and so was the leash. Keller was shaved and dressed and out the door before they returned. He got a cab to La Guardia and was there in plenty of time for his flight to St. Louis.

He rented a Ford Tempo from Hertz and let the girl trace the route to the Sheraton on the map. "It's the turn right after the mall," she said helpfully. He took the exit for the mall and found a parking place, taking careful note of where it was so he could find it again. Once, a couple of years ago, he had parked a rental car at a mall in suburban Detroit without paying attention to where he'd parked it or what it looked like. For all he knew it was still there.

He walked through the mall, looking for a sporting goods store with a selection of hunting knives. There was probably one to be found; they had everything else, including several jewelry stores to catch anyone who hadn't gotten her fill of cubic zirconium on television. But he came to a Hoffritz store first and the kitchen knives caught his eye. He picked out a boning knife with a five-inch blade.

He could have brought his own knife, but that would have meant checking a bag, and he never did that if he could help it. Easy enough to buy what you needed at the scene. The hardest part was convincing the clerk he didn't want the rest of the set, and ignoring the sales pitch assuring him the knife wouldn't need sharpening for years. He was only going to use it once, for God's sake.

*   *   *

He found the Ford, found the Sheraton, found a parking place, and left his overnight bag in the trunk. It would have been nice if the knife had come with a sheath, but kitchen knives rarely do, so he'd been moved to improvise, lifting a cardboard mailing envelope from a Federal Express drop box at the mall entrance. He walked into the hotel lobby with the mailer under his arm and the knife snug inside it.

That gave him an idea.

He checked the slip of paper in his wallet. *St. Louis, Sheraton, Rm. 314.*

"Man's a union official," the old man in White Plains had told him. "Some people are afraid he might tell what he knows."

Just recently some people at a funded drug rehabilitation project in the Bronx had been afraid their accountant might tell what she knew, so they paid a pair of teenagers $150 to kill her. The two of them picked her up leaving the office, walked down the street behind her, and after a two-block stroll the sixteen-year-old shot her in the head. Within twenty-four hours they were in custody, and two days later so was the genius who hired them.

Keller figured you got what you paid for.

He went over to the house phone and dialed 314. It rang almost long enough to convince him the room was empty. Then a man picked up and said, "Yeah?"

"FedEx," Keller said.

"Huh?"

"Federal Express. Got a delivery for you."

"That's crazy," the man said.

"Room 314, right? I'll be right up."

The man protested that he wasn't expecting anything, but Keller hung up on him in mid-sentence and got the elevator to the third floor. The halls were empty. He found room 314 and knocked briskly on the door. "FedEx," he sang out. "Delivery."

Some muffled sounds came through the door. Then silence, and he was about to knock again when the man said, "What the hell is this?"

"Parcel for you," he said. "Federal Express."

"Can't be," the man said. "You got the wrong room."

"Room 314. That's what it says, on the package and on the door."

"Well, there's a mistake. Nobody knows I'm here." That's what you think, thought Keller. "Who's it addressed to?"

Who indeed? "Can't make it out."

"Who's it from, then?"

"Can't make that out, either," Keller said. "That whole line's screwed up, sender's name and recipient's name, but it says room 314 at the Sheraton, so that's got to be you, right?"

"Ridiculous," the man said. "It's not for me and that's all there is to it."

"Well, suppose you sign for it," Keller suggested, "and you take a look what's in it, and if it's really not for you you can drop it at the desk later, or call us and we'll pick it up."

"Just leave it outside the door, will you?"

"Can't," Keller said. "It needs a signature."

"Then take it back, because I don't want it."

"You want to refuse it?"

"Very good," the man said. "You're a quick study, aren't you? Yes, by God, I want to refuse it."

"Fine with me," Keller said. "But I still need a signature. You just check where it says 'Refused' and sign by the X."

"For Christ's *sake,*" the man said, "is that the only way I'm going to get rid of you?"

He unfastened the chain, turned the knob, and opened the door a crack. "Let me show you where to sign," Keller said, displaying the envelope, and the door opened a little more to show a tall, balding man, heavyset, and unclothed but for a hotel towel wrapped around his middle. He reached out for the envelope, and Keller pushed into the room, boning knife in hand, and drove the blade in beneath the lower ribs, angling upward toward the heart.

The man fell backward and lay sprawled out on the carpet at the foot of the unmade king-size bed. The room was a mess, Keller noted, with an open bottle of scotch on the dresser and an unfinished drink on each of the bedside tables. There were clothes tossed here and there, his clothes, her clothes—

Her clothes?

Keller's eyes went to the closed bathroom door. Jesus, he thought. Time to get the hell out. Take the knife, pick up the FedEx envelope, and—

The bathroom door opened. "Harry?" she said. "What on earth is—"

And she saw Keller. Looked right at him, saw his face.

Any second now she'd scream.

"It's his heart," Keller cried. "Come here, you've got to help me."

She didn't get it, but there was Harry on the floor, and here was this nice-looking fellow in a suit, moving toward her, saying things about CPR and ambulance services, speaking reassuringly in a low and level voice. She didn't quite get it, but she didn't scream, either, and in no time at all Keller was close enough to get a hand on her.

She wasn't part of the deal, but she was there, and she couldn't have stayed in the bathroom where she belonged, oh no, not her, the silly bitch, she had to go and open the door, and she'd seen his face, and that was that.

The boning knife, washed clean of blood, wiped clean of prints, went into a storm drain a mile or two from the hotel. The FedEx mailer, torn in half and in half again, went into a trash can at the airport. The Tempo went back to Hertz, and Keller, paying cash, went on American to Chicago. He had a long late lunch at a surprisingly good restaurant in O'Hare Airport, then bought a ticket on a United flight that would put him down at La Guardia well after rush-hour traffic had subsided. He killed time in a cocktail lounge with a window from which you could watch takeoffs and landings. Keller did that for a while, sipping an Australian lager, and then he shifted his attention to the television set, where Oprah Winfrey was talking with six dwarfs. The volume was set inaudibly low, which was probably just as well. Now and then the camera panned the audience, which seemed to contain a disproportionate number of small people. Keller watched, fascinated, and refused to make any Snow White jokes, not even to himself.

He wondered if it was a mistake to go back to New York the same day. What would Andria think?

Well, he'd told her his business might not take him long. Besides, what difference did it make what she thought?

*   *   *

He had another Australian lager and watched some more planes take off. On the plane he drank coffee and ate the two little packets of peanuts. Back at La Guardia he stopped at the first phone and called White Plains.

"That was fast," Dot said.

"Piece of cake," he told her.

He caught a cab, told the driver to take the Fifty-ninth Street Bridge, and coached him on how to find it. At his apartment, he rang the bell a couple of times before using his key. Nelson and Andria were out. Perhaps they'd been out all day, he thought. Perhaps he'd gone to St. Louis and killed two people while the girl and his dog had been engaged in a single endless walk.

He made himself a sandwich and turned on the television set. Channel hopping, he wound up transfixed by an offering of sports collectibles on one of the home shopping channels. Balls, bats, helmets, caps, shirts, all of them autographed by athletes and accompanied by certificates of authenticity, the certificates themselves suitable for framing. Cubic zirconium for guys, he thought.

"When you hear the words *blue chip*," the host was saying, "what are you thinking? I'll tell you what I'm thinking. I'm thinking Mickey Mantle."

Keller wasn't sure what he thought of when he heard the words *blue chip*, but he was pretty sure it wasn't Mickey Mantle. He was working on that one when Nelson came bounding into the room, with Andria behind him.

"When I heard the TV," she said, "my first thought was I must have left it on, but I never even turned it on in the first place, so how could that be? And then I thought maybe there was a break-in, but why would a burglar turn on the television set? They don't watch them, they steal them."

"I should have called from the airport," Keller said. "I didn't think of it."

"What happened? Was your flight canceled?"

"No, I made the trip," he said. "But the business hardly took me any time at all."

"Wow," she said. "Well, Nelson and I had our usual outstanding time. He's such a pleasure to walk."

"He's well behaved," Keller agreed.

"It's not just that. He's enthusiastic."

"I know what you mean."

"He feels so good about everything," she said, "that you feel good being with him. And he really takes an interest. I took him along when I went to water the plants and feed the fish at this apartment on Park Avenue. The people are in Sardinia. Have you ever been there?"

"No."

"Neither have I, but I'd like to go sometime. Wouldn't you?"

"I never thought about it."

"Anyway, you should have seen Nelson staring at the aquarium, watching the fish swim back and forth. If you ever want to get one, I'd help you set it up. But I would recommend that you stick with freshwater. Those saltwater tanks are a real headache to maintain."

"I'll remember that."

She bent over to pet the dog, then straightened up. She said, "Can I ask you something? Is it all right if I stay here tonight?"

"Of course. I more or less figured you would."

"Well, I wasn't sure, and it's a little late to make

other arrangements. But I thought you might want
to be alone after your trip and—"

"I wasn't gone that long."

"You're sure it's all right?"

"Absolutely."

They watched television together, drinking cups of
hot chocolate that Andria made. When the program
ended Keller took Nelson for a late walk. "Do you
really want a fish tank?" he asked the dog. "If I can
have a television set, I suppose you ought to be able
to have a fish tank. But would you watch it after the
first week or so? Or would you get bored with it?"

That was the thing about dogs, he thought. They
didn't get bored the way people did.

After a couple of blocks he found himself talking
to Nelson about what had happened in St. Louis.
"They didn't say anything about a woman," he said.
"I bet she wasn't registered. I don't think she was
his wife, so I guess she wasn't officially there. That's
why he sent her to the bathroom before he opened
the door, and why he didn't want to open the door
in the first place. If she'd stayed in the bathroom
another minute—"

But suppose she had? She'd have been screaming
her head off before Keller was out of the hotel, and
she'd have been able to give a certain amount of
information to the police. How the killer had gained
access to the room, for a starter.

Just as well things had gone the way they did, he
decided. But it still rankled. They hadn't said anything at all about a woman.

There was only one bathroom. Andria used it first.
Keller heard the shower running, then nothing until
she emerged wearing a generally shapeless garment

of pink flannel that covered her from her neck to her ankles. Her toenails were painted, Keller noticed, each a different color.

Keller showered and put on a robe. Andria was on the sofa, reading a magazine. They said goodnight and he clucked to Nelson, and the dog followed him into the bedroom. When he closed the door the dog made that sound again.

He shucked the robe, got into bed, patted the bed at his side. Nelson stayed where he was, right in front of the door, and he repeated that sound in his throat, making it the least bit more insistent this time.

"You want to go out?"

Nelson wagged his tail, which Keller had to figure for a yes. He opened the door and the dog went into the other room. He closed the door and got back into bed, trying to decide if he was jealous. It struck him that he might not only be jealous of the girl, because Nelson wanted to be with her instead of with him, but he might as easily be jealous of the dog, because he got to sleep with Andria and Keller didn't.

Little pink toes, each with the nail painted a different color . . .

He was still sorting it out when the door opened and the dog trotted in. "He wants to be with you," Andria said, and she drew the door shut before Keller could frame a response.

But did he? The animal didn't seem to know what he wanted. He sprang onto Keller's bed, turned around once, twice, and then leaped onto the floor and went over to the door. He made that noise again, but this time it sounded plaintive.

Keller got up and opened the door. Nelson moved into the doorway, half in and half out of the room. Keller leaned into the doorway himself and said, "I think the closed door bothers him. Suppose I leave it open?"

"Sure."

He left the door ajar and went back to bed. Nelson seized the opportunity and went on into the living room. Moments later he was back in the bedroom. Moments after that he was on his way to the living room. Why, Keller wondered, was the dog behaving like an expectant father in a maternity ward waiting room? What was all this back-and-forth business about?

Keller closed his eyes, feeling as far from sleep as he was from Sardinia. Why, he wondered, did Andria want to go there? For the sardines? Then she could stop at Corsica for a corset, and head on to Elba for the macaroni. And Malta for the falcons, and Crete for the cretins, and—

He was just getting drifty when the dog came back.

"Nelson," he said, "what the hell's the matter with you? Huh?" He reached down and scratched the dog behind an ear. "You're a good boy," he said. "Oh yes, you're a good boy, but you're nuts."

There was a knock on the door.

He sat up in bed. It was Andria, of course, and the door was open; she had knocked to get his attention. "He just can't decide who he wants to be with," she said. "Maybe I should just pack my things and go."

"No," he said. He didn't want her to go. "No, don't go," he said.

"Then maybe I should stay."

She came on into the room. She had turned on a lamp in the living room before she came in, but the back lighting was not revealing. The pink flannel thing was opaque, and Keller couldn't tell anything about her body. Then, in a single motion, she drew the garment over her head and cast it aside, and now he could tell everything about her body.

"I have a feeling this is a big mistake," she said, "but I don't care. I just don't care. Do you know what I mean?"

"I know exactly what you mean," Keller said.

Afterward he said, "Now I suppose you'll think I put the dog up to it. I wish I could take the credit, but I swear it was all his idea. He was like that donkey in the logic problem, unable to decide between the two bales of hay. Where did he go, I wonder?"

She didn't say anything, and he looked closely and saw that she was crying. Jesus, had he said something to upset her?

He said, "Andria? Is something wrong?"

She sat up and crossed her arms beneath her breasts. "I'm just scared," she said.

"Of what?"

"Of you."

"Of me?"

"Just tell me you're not going to hurt me," she said. "Could you do that?"

"Why would I hurt you?"

"I don't know."

"Well, why would you say something like that?"

"Oh, God," she said. She put a hand to her mouth and chewed on a knuckle. Her fingernails weren't polished, just her toenails. Interesting. She said, "When I'm in a relationship I have to be completely honest."

"Huh?"

"Not that this is a relationship, I mean we just

went to bed together once, but I felt we really related, don't you think?"

Keller wondered what she was getting at.

"So I have to be honest. See, I know what you do."

"You know what I do?"

"On those trips."

That was ridiculous. How could she know anything?

"Tell me," he said.

"I'm afraid to say it."

God, maybe she did know.

"Go ahead," he said. "There's nothing to be afraid of."

"You—"

"Go ahead."

"You're an assassin."

Ooops.

He said, "What makes you think that?"

"I don't think it," she said. "I sort of know it. And I don't know how I know it. I guess I knew it the day I met you. Something about your energy, I guess. It's kind of intangible, but it's there."

"Oh."

"I sense things about people. Please don't hurt me."

"I'll never hurt you, Andria."

"I know you mean that," she said. "I hope it turns out to be true."

He thought for a moment. "If you think that about me," he said, "or know it, whatever you want to call it, and if you were afraid I might . . . hurt you—"

"Then why did I come into the bedroom?"

"Right. Why did you?"

She looked right into his eyes. "I couldn't help myself," she said.

He felt this sensation in the middle of his chest, as if there had been a steel band around his heart and it had just cracked and fallen away. He reached for her and drew her down.

On the floor at the side of the bed, Nelson slept like a lamb.

In the morning they walked Nelson together. Keller bought the paper and picked up a quart of milk. Back at the apartment, he made a pot of coffee while she put breakfast on the table.

He said, "Look, I'm not good at this, but there are some things I ought to say. The first is that you have nothing to fear from me. My work is one thing and my life is something else. I have no reason to hurt you, and even if I had a reason I wouldn't do it."

"I know that."

"Oh?"

"I was afraid last night. I'm not afraid now."

"Oh," he said. "Well, the other thing I want to say is that I know you don't have a place to stay right now, and as far as I'm concerned you can stay here as long as you want. In fact I'd like it if you stayed here. You can even sleep on the couch if you want, assuming that Nelson will allow it. I'm not sure he will, though."

She considered her reply, and the phone rang. He made a face and answered it.

It was Dot. "Young man," she said, in an old lady's quavering voice, "I think you had better pay a call on your kindly old Aunt Dorothy."

"I just did," he reminded her. "Just because it was quick and easy doesn't mean I don't need a little time off between engagements."

"Keller," she said, in her own voice, "get on the next train, will you? It's urgent."

"Urgent?"

"There's a problem."

"What do you mean?"

"Do you remember saying something about a piece of cake?"

"So?"

"So your cake fell," Dot said. "Get it?"

There was no one to meet him at the White Plains station so he took a cab to the big Victorian house on Taunton Place. Dot was waiting on the porch. "All right," she said. "Report."

"To you?"

"And then I report to him. That's how he wants it."

Keller shrugged and reported. Where he'd gone, what he'd done. It took only a few sentences. When he was done he paused for a moment, and then he said, "The woman wasn't supposed to be there."

"Neither was the man."

"How's that?"

"You killed the wrong people," she said. "Wait here, Keller, okay? I have to relay this to His Eminence. You want coffee, there's a fresh pot in the kitchen. Well, a reasonably fresh pot."

Keller stayed on the porch. There was an old-fashioned glider and he sat on that, gliding back and forth, but it seemed too frivolous for the circumstances. He switched to a chair but was too restless to stay in it. He was on his feet when Dot returned.

She said, "You said room 314."

"And that's the room I went to," he said. "That was the room I called from downstairs, and those were the numbers on the door. Room 314 at the Sheraton."

"Wrong room."

"I wrote it down," he said. "He gave me the number and I wrote it down."

"You didn't happen to save the note, did you?"

"Oh, sure," he said. "I keep everything. I have it on my coffee table, along with the boning knife and the vic's watch and wallet. No, of course I didn't keep the note."

"Of course you didn't, but it would have been nice if you'd made an exception on this particular occasion. The, uh, designated victim was in room 502."

He frowned. "That's not even close. What did he do, change his room? If I'd been given a name or a photo, you know—"

"I know. He didn't change his room."

"Dot, I can't believe I wrote it down wrong."

"Neither can I, Keller."

"If I got one digit wrong or reversed the order, well, I could almost believe that, but to turn 502 into 314—"

"You know what 314 is, Keller?" He didn't. "It's the area code for St. Louis."

"The area code? As in telephone?"

"As in telephone."

"I don't understand."

She sighed. "He's had a lot on his mind lately," she said. "He's been under a strain. So, just between you and me"—for God's sake, who was he going to tell?—"he must have looked at the wrong slip of paper and wound up giving you the area code instead of the room number."

"I thought he seemed tired. I even said something."

"And I told you life tires people out, if I remember correctly. We were both right. Meanwhile, you have to go to Tulsa."

"Tulsa?"

"That's where the target lives, and it seems he's canceling the rest of his meetings and going home this afternoon. I don't know if it's a coincidence or if the business two floors down spooked him. The client didn't want to hit him in Tulsa, but now there's no choice."

"I just did the job," Keller said, "and now I have to do it again. When she popped out of the bathroom it turned into two for the price of one, and now it's three for the price of one."

"Not exactly. He has to save face on this, Keller, so the idea is you stepped on your whatchamacallit and now you're going to correct your mistake. But when all this is history there will be a little extra in your Christmas stocking."

"Christmas?"

"A figure of speech. There'll be a bonus, and you won't have to wait for Christmas for it."

"The client's going to pay a bonus?"

"I said you'd get a bonus," she said. "I didn't say the client would be paying it. Tulsa, and you'll be met at the airport and somebody will show you around and point the finger. Have you ever been to Tulsa?"

"I don't think so."

"You'll love it. You'll want to move there."

He didn't even want to go there. Halfway down the porch stairs he turned, retraced his steps, and said, "The man and woman in 314. Who were they?"

"Who knows? They weren't Gunnar Ruthven, I can tell you that much."

"That's who I'm going to see in Tulsa?"

"Let's hope so. As far as the pair in 314, I don't know any names. He was a local businessman, owned a dry-cleaning plant or something like that. I don't know anything about her. They were married, but not to each other. What I hear, you interrupted a matinee."

"That's what it looked like."

"Rang down the curtain," Dot said. "What a world, huh?"

"His name was Harry."

"See, I told you it wasn't Gunnar Ruthven. What's it matter, Keller? You're not going to send flowers, are you?"

"I'll be gone longer this time," he told Andria. "I have to . . . go someplace and . . . take care of some business."

"I'll take care of Nelson," she said. "And we'll both be here when you get back."

His plane was leaving from Newark. He packed a bag and called a livery service for a car to the airport.

He said, "Does it bother you?"

"What you do? It would bother me if I did it, but I couldn't do it, so that's beside the point. But does it bother me that you do it? I don't think so. I mean, it's what you do."

"But don't you think it's wrong?"

She thought it over. "I don't think it's wrong for *you*," she said. "I think it's your karma."

"You mean like destiny or something?"

"Sort of. It's what you have to do in order to learn the lesson you're supposed to learn in this lifetime. We're not just here once, you know. We live many lives."

"You believe that, huh?"

"It's more a matter of knowledge than belief."

"Oh." Karma, he thought. "What about the people I go and see? It's just their karma?"

"Doesn't that make sense to you?"

"I don't know," he said. "I'll have to think about it."

He had plenty of time to think about karma. He was in Tulsa for five days before he had a chance to close the file on Gunnar Ruthven. A sad-eyed young man named Joel met his flight and gave him a tour of the city that included Ruthven's suburban home and downtown office building. Ruthven lived in a two-story mock-Tudor house on about half an acre of land and had an office in the Great Southwestern Bank building within a block of the courthouse. Then Joel drove to the All-American Inn, one of a couple of dozen motels clustered together on a strip a mile from the airport. "The reason for the name," Joel said, "is so you would know the place wasn't owned by Indians. I don't mean your Native Americans, I mean Indians from India. They own most of the motels. So this here place, the owners changed the name to the All-American, and they even had a huge sign-board announcing the place was owned and operated by hundred-percent Americans."

"Did somebody make them take the sign down?"

Joel shook his head. "After about a year," he said, "they sold out, and the new owners took the sign down."

"They didn't like the implications?"

"Not hardly. See, they're Indians. Place is decent, though, and you don't have to go through the lobby. In fact you're already registered and paid in advance for a week. I figured you'd like that. Here's your room key, and here's a set of car keys. They belong to that Toyota over there, third from the end. Paper for it's in the glove box, along with a little twenty-two automatic. If you prefer something heavier, just say so."

Keller assured him it would be fine. "Why don't you get settled," Joel said, "and get yourself something to eat if you're hungry. The Sizzler across the street on the left isn't bad. I'll pick you up in say two hours and we'll sneak a peek at the fellow you came out here to see."

Joel picked him up on schedule and they rode downtown and parked in a metered lot. They sat in the lobby of Ruthven's office building. After twenty minutes Joel said, "Getting off the elevator. Glen plaid suit, horn-rimmed glasses, carrying the aluminum briefcase. Looks space age, I guess, but I'd go for genuine leather every time, myself."

Keller took a good look. Ruthven was tall and slender, with a sharp nose and a pointed chin. Keller said, "Are you positive that's him?"

"Shit, yes, I'm positive. Why?"

"Just making sure."

Joel ran him back to the All-American and gave him a map of Tulsa with different locations marked on it—the All-American Inn, Ruthven's house, Ruthven's office, and a southside restaurant Joel said was outstanding. He also gave Keller a slip of paper with a phone number on it. "Anything you want," he said. "You want a girl, you want to get in a card game, you want to see a cockfight, just call that number and I'll take care of it. You ever been to a cockfight?"

"Never."

"You want to?"

Keller thought about it. "I don't think so," he said. "Well, if you change your mind, just let me know. Or anything else you want." Joel hesitated. "I got to say I've got a lot of respect for you," he said, averting his eyes from Keller's as he said it. "I don't guess I could do what you do. I haven't got the sand for it."

Keller went to his room and stretched out on the bed. Sand, he thought. What the hell did sand have to do with anything?

He thought about Ruthven, coming off the elevator, long and lean, and realized why he'd been bothered by the man's appearance. He wasn't what Keller had expected. He didn't look anything like Harry in 314.

Did Ruthven know he was a target? Driving around in the Toyota, keeping an eye on the man, Keller decided that he did. There was a certain wariness about him. The way to handle that, Keller decided, was to let him get over it. A few days of peace and quiet and Ruthven could revert to his usual way of thinking. He'd decide that Harry and his girlfriend had been killed by a jealous husband, and he'd drop his guard and stick his neck out, and Keller could get the job done and go home.

The gun seemed all right. The third afternoon he drove out into the country, popped a full clip into the gun, and emptied the clip at a CATTLE CROSSING sign. None of his shots hit the mark, but he didn't figure that was the gun's fault. He was fifteen yards away, for God's sake, and the sign was no more than ten inches across. Keller wasn't a particularly good shot, but he arranged his life so he didn't have to be. If you walked up behind a guy and put the gun muzzle to the back of his neck, all you had to do

was pull the trigger. You didn't have to be a marks-
man. All you needed was—

What? Karma? Sand?

He reloaded and made a real effort this time, and
two shots actually hit the sign. Remarkable what a
man could do when he put his mind to it.

The hard part was finding a way to pass the time.
He went to a movie, walked through a mall, and
watched a lot of television. He had Joel's number but
never called it. He didn't want female companion-
ship, nor did he feel like playing cards or watching
a cockfight.

He kept fighting off the urge to call New York.

On one of the home shopping channels, one
woman said earnestly to another, "Now there's one
thing we both know, and that's that you just can't
have too many earrings." Keller couldn't get the line
out of his head. Was it literally true? Suppose you
had a thousand pairs, or ten thousand. Suppose you
had a million pairs. Wouldn't that constitute a
surplus?

The woman in 314 hadn't been wearing earrings,
but there had been a pair on the bedside table. How
many other pairs had she had at home?

Finally one morning he got up at daybreak and
showered and shaved. He packed his bag and wiped
the motel room free of prints. He had done this rou-
tinely every time he left the place, so that it would
never be necessary for him to return to it, but this
morning he sensed that it was time to wind things
up. He drove to Ruthven's house and parked around
the corner at the curb. He went through the driveway
and yard of a house on the side street, scaled a four-

foot Cyclone fence, and jimmied a window in order to get into Ruthven's garage. The car inside the garage was unlocked, and he got into the back seat and waited patiently.

Eventually the garage door opened, and when that happened Keller scrunched down so that he couldn't be seen. Ruthven opened the car door and got behind the wheel.

Keller sat up slowly. Ruthven was fumbling with the key, having a hard time getting it into the ignition. But was it really Ruthven?

Jesus, get a grip. Who else could it be?

Keller stuck the gun in his ear and emptied the clip.

"These are beautiful," Andria said. "You didn't have to bring me anything."

"I know that."

"But I'm glad you did. I love them."

"I didn't know what to get you," Keller said, "because I don't know what you already have. But I figured you can never have too many earrings."

"That is absolutely true," Andria said, "and not many men realize it."

Keller tried not to smirk.

"Ever since you left," she said, "I've been thinking about what you said. That you would like it if I stayed here. But what I have to know is if you still feel that way, or if it was just, you know, how you felt that morning."

"I'd like you to stay."

"Well, I'd like it, too. I like being around your energy. I like your dog and I like your apartment and I like you."

"I missed you," Keller said.

"I missed you, too. But I liked being here while you were gone, living in your space and taking care of your dog. I have a confession to make. I slept in your bed."

"Well, for heaven's sake. Where else would you sleep?"

"On the couch."

Keller gave her a look. She colored, and he said, "While I was away I thought about your toes."

"My toes?"

"All different colors."

"Oh," she said. "Well, I had trouble deciding which color to go with, and it came to me that when God couldn't decide on a color, he created the rainbow."

"Rainbow toes," Keller said. "I think I'll take them one by one into my mouth, those pink little rainbow toes. What do you think about that?"

"Oh," she said.

Later he said, "Suppose someone got killed by mistake."

"How could that happen?"

"Say an area code turns into a room number. Human error, computer error, anything at all. Mistakes happen."

"No they don't."

"They don't?"

"People make mistakes," she said, "but there's no such thing as a mistake."

"How's that?"

"You could make a mistake," she said. "You could be swinging a dumbbell and it could sail out of the window. That would be a case of you making a mistake."

"I'll say."

"And somebody looking for an address on the next block could get out of a cab here instead, and here comes a dumbbell. The person made a mistake."

"His last one, too."

"In this lifetime," she agreed. "So you've both made a mistake, but if you look at the big picture, there was no mistake. The person got hit by a dumbbell and died."

"No mistake?"

"No mistake, because it was meant to happen."

"But if it wasn't meant to happen—"

"Then it wouldn't."

"And if it happened it was meant to."

"Right."

"Karma?"

"Karma."

"Little pink toes," Keller said. "I'm glad you're here."

6

Keller in Shining Armor

When the phone rang, Keller was finishing up the *Times* crossword puzzle. It looked as though this was going to be one of those days when he was able to fill in all the squares. That happened more often than not, but once or twice a week he'd come a cropper. A Brazilian tree in four letters would intersect with an Old World marsupial in five, and he'd be stumped. It didn't make his day when he filled in the puzzle or spoil it when he didn't, but it was something he noticed.

He put down his pencil and picked up the phone, and Dot said, "Keller, I haven't seen you in ages."

"I'll be right over," he said, and broke the connection. She was right, he thought, she hadn't seen him in ages, and it was about time he paid a visit to White Plains. The old man hadn't given him work in months, and you could get rusty, just sitting around with nothing better to do than crossword puzzles.

There was still plenty of money. Keller lived well— a good apartment on First Avenue with a view of the Queensboro Bridge, nice clothes, decent restaurants. But no one had ever taken him for a drunken sailor, and in fact he tended to squirrel money away, stuffing it in safe deposit boxes, opening savings accounts under other names. If a rainy day came along, he had an umbrella at hand.

Still, just because you had Blue Cross didn't mean you couldn't wait to get sick.

"Good boy," he told Nelson, reaching to scratch the dog behind the ears. "You wait right here. Guard the house, huh?"

He had the door open when the phone rang again. Let it ring? No, better answer it.

Dot again. "Keller," she said, "did you hang up on me?"

"I thought you were done."

"Why would you think that? I said hello, not goodbye."

"You didn't say hello. You said you hadn't seen me in ages."

"That's closer to hello than goodbye. Well, let it go. The important thing is I caught you before you left the house."

"Just," he said. "I had one foot out the door."

"I'd have called back right away," she said, "but I had a hell of a time getting quarters. You ask for change of a dollar around here, people look at you like you've got a hidden agenda."

Quarters? What did she need with quarters?

"I'll tell you what," she said. "There's this little Italian place about four blocks from you called Giuseppe Joe's. Don't ask me what street it's on."

"I know where it is."

"They've got tables set up outside under the awning. It's a beautiful spring day. Why don't you take your dog for a walk, swing by Giuseppe Joe's. See if there's anybody there you recognize."

*   *   *

"So this is the famous Nelson," Dot said. "He's a handsome devil, isn't he? I think he likes me."

"The only person he doesn't like," Keller said, "is the delivery boy for the Chinese restaurant."

"It's probably the MSG."

"He barks at him, and Nelson almost never barks. The breed's part dingo, and that makes him the silent type."

"Nelson the Wonder Dog. What's the matter, Nelson? Don't you like mu shu pork?" She gave the dog a pat. "I thought he'd be bigger. An Australian cattle dog, and you think how big sheep dogs are, and cows are bigger than sheep, et cetera, et cetera. But he's just the right size."

If he hadn't come looking for her, Keller might not have recognized Dot. He'd never seen her away from the old man's house on Taunton Place, where she'd always lounged around in a Mother Hubbard or a housedress. This afternoon she wore a tailored suit, and she'd done something to her hair. She looked like a suburban matron, Keller thought, in town on a shopping spree.

"He thinks I'm shopping for summer clothes," she said, as if reading his mind. "I shouldn't be here at all, Keller."

"Oh?"

"I've been doing things I shouldn't do," she said. "Idle hands and all that. What about you, Keller? Been a long dry spell. What have your idle hands been up to?"

Keller looked at his hands. "Nothing much," he said.

"How are you fixed for dough?"

"I'll get by."

"You wouldn't mind work, though."

"No, of course not."

"That's why you couldn't wait to hang up on me and hop on a train." She drank some iced tea and wrinkled her nose. "Two bucks a glass for this crap and they make it from a mix. You wonder why I don't come to the city often? It's nice, though, sitting at an outside table like this."

"Pleasant."

"You probably do this all the time. Walk the dog, pick up a newspaper, stop and have a cup of coffee. While away the hours. Right?"

"Sometimes."

"You're patient, Keller, I'll give you that. I take all day to come to the point and you sit there like you've got nothing better to do. But in a way that's the whole point, isn't it? You don't have anything better to do and neither do I."

"Sometimes there's no work," he said. "If nothing comes in—"

"Things have been coming in."

"Oh?"

"I'm not here, you never saw me, and we never had this conversation. Understood?"

"Understood."

"I don't know what's the matter with him, Keller. He's going through something and I don't know what it is. It's like he's lost his taste for it. There've been calls, people with work that would have been right up your alley. He tells them no. He tells them he hasn't got anybody available at the moment. He tells them to call somebody else."

"Does he say why?"

"Sure, there's always a reason. This one he doesn't want to deal with, that one won't pay enough, the other one, something doesn't sound kosher about it.

There's three jobs he turned down I know of since the first of the year."

"No kidding."

"And who knows what came in that I don't know about."

"I wonder what's wrong."

"I figure it'll pass," she said. "But who knows when? So I did something crazy."

"Oh?"

"Don't laugh, all right?"

"I won't."

"You familiar with a magazine called *Mercenary Times*?"

"Like *Soldier of Fortune*," he said.

"Like it, but more homemade and reckless." She drew a copy from her handbag, handed it to him. "Page forty-seven. It's circled, you can't miss it."

It was in the classifieds, under "Situations Wanted," circled in red Magic Marker. *Odd Jobs Wanted,* he read. *Removals a specialty. Write to Toxic Waste, PO Box 1149, Yonkers NY.*

He said, "Toxic Waste?"

"That may have been a mistake," she acknowledged. "I thought it sounded good, cold and lethal and up to here with attitude. I got a couple of letters from people with chemicals to dump and swamps to drain, wanted someone to help them do an end run around the environmentalists. Plus I managed to get myself on some damn mailing list where I get invitations to subscribe to waste-management newsletters."

"But that's not all you got."

"It's not, because I also got half a dozen letters so far from people who knew what kind of removals I had in mind. I was wondering what kind of idiot would answer a blind ad like that, and they were about what you would expect. I burned five of them."

"And the sixth?"

"Was neatly typed," she said, "on printed letterhead, if you please. And written in English, God help us. But here, read it yourself."

" 'Cressida Wallace, 411 Fairview Avenue, Muscatine, Iowa 52761. Dear Sir or—' "

"Not out loud, Keller."

Dear Sir or Madam, he read to himself. *I can only hope the removal service you provide is of the sort I require. If so, I am in urgent need of your services. My name is Cressida Wallace and I am a forty-one-year-old author and illustrator of books for children. I have been divorced for fifteen years and have no children.*

While my life was never dramatically exciting, I have always found fulfillment in my work and quiet satisfaction in my personal life. Then, four years ago, a complete stranger began to transform my life into a living hell.

Without going into detail, I will simply state that I have become the innocent target of a stalker. Why this man singled me out is quite unfathomable to me. I am neither a talk show host nor a teen-age tennis champion. While presentable, I am by no means a raving beauty. I had never met him, nor had I done anything to arouse his interest or his ill will. Yet he will not leave me alone.

He parks his car across the street and watches my house through binoculars. He follows me when I leave the house. He calls me at all hours. I have long since stopped answering the phone, but this does not stop him from leaving horribly obscene and threatening messages on my answering machine.

I was living in Missouri when this began, in a suburb of St. Louis. I have moved four times, and each time he has managed to find me. I cannot tell you how many times

*I have changed my telephone number. He always manages
to find out my new unlisted number. I don't know how.
Perhaps he has a confederate at the telephone company. . . .*

He read the letter on through to the end. There
had been a perceptible escalation in the harassment,
she reported. He had begun telling her he would kill
her, and had taken to describing the manner in which
he intended to take her life. He had on several occa-
sions broken into her house in her absence. He had
stolen some undergarments from the clothes hamper,
slashed a painting, and used her lipstick to write an
obscene message on the wall. He had performed various acts of minor vandalism on her car. After one
invasion of her home she'd bought a dog; a week
later she'd returned home to find the dog missing.
Not long afterward there was another message on
her answering machine. No human speech, just a lot
of barking and yipping and canine whimpering, end-
ing with what she took to be a gunshot.

"Jesus," Keller said.

"The dog, right? I figured that would get to you."

The police inform me there is nothing they can do, she
continued. *In two different states I obtained orders of
protection, but what good does that do? He violates them
at will and with apparent impunity. The police are power-
less to act until he commits a crime. He has committed
several, but has never left sufficient evidence for them to
proceed. The messages on my answering machine do not
constitute evidence because he uses some sort of instrument to distort his voice before leaving a message. Sometimes he changes his voice to that of a woman. The first
time he did this I picked up the phone and said hello when
I heard a female voice, sure that it was not him, and the
next thing I knew his awful voice was sounding in my*

ear, accusing me of horrible acts and promising me torture and death.

At a policeman's off-the-record suggestion, I bought myself a gun. Given the chance, I would shoot this man without a moment's hesitation. But when the attack comes, will I have the gun at hand? I doubt it. I feel certain he will choose his opportunity carefully and come upon me when I am helpless.

I know the risk I take in writing to someone who is even more a stranger to me than my tormentor is. No doubt you could use this letter as an instrument of extortion. I can say only that you would be wasting your time. I won't pay blackmail. And if you are some sort of policeman and this ad is some sort of "sting"—well, sting away! I don't care.

If you are what you imply yourself to be, please call me at the following number. . . . It is unlisted, but it is already well known to my adversary. Identify yourself with the phrase "Toxic Waste." If I'm at home, I'll pick up. If I don't, simply ring off and call back at a later time.

I am not wealthy, but I have had some success in my profession. I have saved my money and invested wisely. I will pay anything within my means to whoever will rid me forever of this diabolical man.

He folded the letter, returned it to its envelope, and handed it across the table.

"Well, Keller?"

"You call her?"

"First I went to the library," she said. "She's real. Has a whole lot of books for young readers. Writes them, draws the pictures herself. *The Bunny Who Lost His Ears*, that kind of thing."

"How did he lose his ears?"

"I didn't read the books, Keller, I just made sure they existed. Then I looked her up in a kind of *Who's*

Who they have for authors. It had her old address in Webster Groves, Missouri. Then I went home and watched him work on a jigsaw puzzle. That's his favorite thing these days, jigsaw puzzles. When he's done he glues cardboard to the back and mounts them on the wall like trophies."

"How long's he been doing that?"

"Long enough," she said. "I went downstairs and put the TV on, and the next day I went out to a pay phone and called Muscatine. I looked *that* up, too, while I was at the library. It's on the Mississippi."

"Everything's got to be someplace."

"What do you think so far, Keller? Tell me."

He reached down and scratched the dog. "I think it's asking for trouble," he said. "Guy goes down, they pick her up before the body's cold. She's got to sing like a songbird. I mean, she told us everything and we didn't even ask."

"Agreed. She'll fold the minute they knock on her door."

"So?"

"So she can't know anything," Dot said. "Can't tell what she doesn't know, right? That's the first thing I said to her, after I said 'Toxic Waste' and she picked up the phone. I laid it out for her. 'No names, no pack drill,' I said. I told her a number, said half in advance, half on completion. Cash, fifties and hundreds, wrap 'em up good and FedEx the package to John Smith at Mail Boxes Etc. in Scarsdale."

"John Smith?"

"First name that came to me. Soon as I got off the phone I went over and rented a box under that name. The owner's Afghani, he doesn't know Smith from Shinola. It's better than the post office because you can call up and find out if they've got anything for you. I called yesterday and guess what?"

"She sent the money?"

She nodded. " 'Send half the money,' I said, 'and our field operative will call when he's on the scene. He'll introduce himself and get the information he requires. You'll never meet him face-to-face, but he'll coordinate with you and take care of everything. And afterward you'll get a final call telling you where to send the balance.' "

Keller thought about it. "There's stuff they could trace," he said. "The PO box, the mailbox. Records of phone calls."

"There's always something."

"Uh-huh. What kind of a price did you set?"

"Just on the high side of standard."

"And you got half in front, and she hasn't got a clue who she sent it to."

"Meaning I could just keep it. I thought of that, obviously. If you turn it down, that's probably what I'll do."

"Just probably? You're not going to send it back."

"No, but I could call around, try and find another shooter."

"I didn't turn it down yet," he said.

"Take your time."

"The old man would have a fit. You know that, don't you?"

"Gee, I'm glad you told me that, Keller. It never would have occurred to me."

"What does that mean, anyway, 'No names, no pack drill'? I'm familiar with the expression, I get the sense of it, but what's a pack drill, do you happen to know?"

"It's just an expression, for God's sake."

"Give me the letter again," he said, and read it through rapidly. "Most of the time," he said, "the people who hire these things, there's other things they could do. They may think otherwise, but there's usually another way out."

"So?"

"So what choice has she got?"

"Nelson," Dot said, "you know what I just did? I watched your master talk himself into something."

"Muscatine," he said. "Do planes go there?"

"Not if they can help it."

"What do I do, go there and call her up? 'Toxic Waste,' and then I wait for her to pick up?"

"It's 'Toxic Shock' now," she said. "I changed the password for security reasons."

"Thank God for that," he said. "You can't be too careful."

Back at his apartment, he called Andria and made arrangements for her to care for Nelson in his absence. Then he found Muscatine on the map. You could probably fly there, or at least to Davenport, but Chicago wasn't that far. United had hourly nonstops to Chicago, and O'Hare was a nice anonymous place to rent a car.

He flew out in the morning, had a Hertz car waiting, and was in Muscatine and settled in a chain motel on the edge of the city by dinnertime. He ate right down the road at a Pizza Hut, came back and sat on the edge of his bed. He had used false identification to rent the car at O'Hare, and had registered at the motel under a different name and paid cash in advance for a week's stay. Even so, he didn't want to call the client from the motel. He was dealing with an amateur, and there were two principles to observe in dealing with amateurs. The first was to be ultra-professional yourself. The second, alas, was never to deal with an amateur.

There was a pay phone just next door; he'd noticed it coming back from the Pizza Hut. He spent a quarter and dialed the number, and after two rings the machine answered and a computer-generated voice repeated the last four numbers of the number and invited him to leave his message at the tone.

"Toxic Shock," he said.

Nothing happened. He stayed on the line for fifteen seconds and hung up.

But was that long enough? Suppose she was washing her hands, or in the kitchen making coffee. He dug out another quarter, tried again. Same story. "Toxic Shock," he said a second time, and waited for thirty seconds before hanging up.

"Great system," he said aloud, and went back to the motel.

Back at the motel, he put on the television set and watched the last half of a movie about a wife who gets her lover to kill her husband. You didn't have to have watched the first half to know what was going on, nor did you need to be a genius to know that everything was going to go wrong for them. Amateurs, he thought.

He went out and tried the number again. "Toxic Shock." Nothing.

Hell.

On the desk in his room, along with carry-out menus from half a dozen nearby fast-food outlets and a handout from the local Board of Realtors on the joys of settling in Muscatine, there was a flyer inviting him to try his luck gambling on a Mississippi riverboat. It looked appealing at first. You pictured an old paddle wheeler chunking along, heading down the river to New Orleans, with women in hoop skirts and men in frock coats and string ties, but he knew it wouldn't be anything like that. The boat wouldn't move, for one thing. It would stand at anchor, and boarding it would be like crossing the threshold of a hotel in Atlantic City.

No thanks.

Unpacking, he found the morning paper he'd read on the flight to Chicago. He hadn't finished it, and did so now, saving the crossword puzzle for last. There was a step-quote, a saying of some sort running like a flight of stairs from the upper-left to lower-right corner. He liked those, because you had the sense that solving the crossword led to a greater solution. Sometimes, too, the step-quote itself was a pearl of wisdom of the sort you found in a fortune cookie.

Often, though, the puzzles with step-quotes in them proved difficult, and this particular puzzle was one of those. There were a couple of areas he had trouble with, and they formed important parts of the step-quote, and he couldn't work it out.

There was a 900 number you could call. They printed it with the puzzle every morning, and for seventy-five cents they'd give you any three answers. You'd punch in 3-7-D on your touch-tone phone, and you'd get the answer to 37 down. He figured they used a computer. They couldn't waste an actual human being's time on that sort of thing.

But did people really call in? Obviously they did, or the service wouldn't exist. Keller found this baffling. He could see doing a crossword puzzle, it gave your mind a light workout and passed the time, but when he'd gone as far as he could he tossed the paper aside and got on with his life.

Anyway, if you were dying of curiosity, all you had to do was wait a day. They printed a filled-in version of the previous day's crossword in every paper. Why spend seventy-five cents for three answers when you could wait a few hours and get the whole thing for half a dollar?

They were immature, he decided. He'd read that the true measure of human maturity was the ability to postpone gratification.

Keller, ready to go out and try the number again, decided to postpone gratification. He took a hot shower and went to bed.

In the morning he drove into downtown Muscatine and had breakfast at a diner. The crowd was almost exclusively male and most of the men wore suits. Keller, in a suit himself, read the local paper while he ate his breakfast. There was a crossword puzzle, but he took one look at it and gave it a pass. The longest word in it was six letters: *Our northern neighbor.* The way Keller figured it, when it came to crossword puzzles it was the *Times* or nothing.

There was a pay phone at the diner, but he didn't want his conversation overheard by the movers and shakers of Greater Muscatine. Even if no one answered, he didn't want anyone to hear him say "Toxic Shock." He left the diner and found an outdoor pay phone at a gas station. He placed the call, said his two words, and in no time at all a woman cut in to say, "Hello? Hello?"

Tinny phone, he thought. Rinky-dink local phone company, what could you expect. But it was better than the computer-generated phone message. At least you knew you were talking to a person.

"It's all right," he said. "I'm here."

"I'm sorry I missed your call last night. I was out, I had to—"

"Let's not get into that," he said. "Let's not spend any more time on the phone than we have to."

"I'm sorry. Of course you're right."

"I need to know some things. The name of the person I'm supposed to meet with, first of all."

There was a pause. Then, tentatively, she said, "My understanding was that there wasn't to be a meeting."

"The other person," he said, "that I'm supposed to *meet* with, so to speak."

"Oh. I didn't . . . I'm sorry. I'm not used to this."

No kidding, he thought.

"His name is Stephen Lauderheim," she said.

"How do I find him? I don't suppose you know his address."

"No, I'm afraid not. I know the license number of his car."

He copied it down, along with the information that the car was a two-year-old white Subaru squareback. That was useful, he told her, but he couldn't cruise around town looking for a white Subaru. Where did he park this car?

"Across the street from my house," she said, "more often than I'd like."

"I don't suppose he's there now."

"No, I don't think so. Let me look. . . . No, he's not. There was a message from him last night. In between your messages. Nasty, vile."

"I wish I had a photo of him," he said. "That would help. I don't suppose—"

No photo, but she could certainly describe him. Tall, slender, light brown hair, late thirties, long face, square jaw, big white horse teeth. Oh, and he had a Kirk Douglas dimple in his chin. Oh, and she knew where he worked. At least he'd been working there the last time the police had been involved. Would that help?

Keller rolled his eyes. "It might," he said.

"The name of the firm is Loud & Clear Software," she said. "On Tyler Boulevard just beyond Five Mile Road. He's a computer programmer or technician, something like that."

"That's how he keeps getting your phone number," Keller said.

"I beg your pardon?"

"He doesn't need a confederate at the phone company. If he knows his way around computers, he can hack his way into the phone company system and get unlisted numbers that way."

"It's possible to do that?"

"So they tell me."

"Well, I'm hopelessly old-fashioned," she said. "I still do all my writing on a typewriter. But it's an electric typewriter, at least."

He had the name, the address, the car, and a precise description. Did he need anything else? He couldn't think of anything.

"This probably won't take long," he said.

He found Tyler Boulevard, found Five Mile Road, found Loud & Clear Software. The company occupied a squat concrete-block building with its own little parking lot. There were ten or a dozen cars in the lot, many of them Japanese, two of them white.

No white Subaru squareback, no plate number to match the one Cressida Wallace had given him.

If Stephen Lauderheim wasn't working today, maybe he was stalking. Keller drove back into town and got directions to Fairview Avenue. He found it in a pleasant neighborhood of prewar houses and big shade trees. Driving slowly past number 411, he looked around unsuccessfully for a white Subaru, then circled the block and parked just down the street from Cressida Wallace's house. It was a sprawling structure, three stories tall, with overgrown shrubbery obscuring the lower half of the first-floor windows. A light burned in a window on the third floor, and Keller decided that was where Cressida was, typing up happy and instructive tales of woodland creatures on her electric typewriter.

He had lunch and drove back to Loud & Clear. No white Subaru. He hung around for a while, found his way to Fairview Avenue again. No white Subaru, and no light on the third floor. He returned to his motel.

That night there was a movie he wanted to see on HBO, but the channel wasn't available on his motel TV. He was irritated, and thought about moving to another motel a few hundred yards down the road, where the signboard promised HBO, as well as waterbeds in selected units. He decided that was ridiculous, and that he was mature enough to postpone gratification in this area, even as he had to postpone the gratification of dispatching Stephen Lauderheim and getting the hell out of Muscatine.

He leafed through the phone book, looking for Lauderheim. There was no listing, which didn't surprise him. He tried Cressida Wallace, knowing she wouldn't be listed. There were several Wallaces, but none on Fairview and none named Cressida.

There were Kellers, one of them with the initial J, another with the initials JD. Either one could be John.

He did that sometimes. Looked up his name in the phone books of strange cities, as if he might actually find himself there. Not another person with the same name, that happened often enough, his was not an uncommon name. But find himself, his actual self, living an altogether different life in some other city.

It was just a thought, really. He wasn't schizophrenic, he knew it couldn't happen. He wondered, though, what that psychotherapist would have made of it. He'd had his problems with his therapist, especially toward the end, but give the devil his due; the man had guided him to some useful insights. Looking for himself in Muscatine, Iowa—Dr. Breen would have had a field day with that one.

He went out to the pay phone, fed in a slew of quarters, and called his apartment in New York. Andria answered.

"I should be home tomorrow or the next day," he said, "but it's hard to tell."

"It's a shame they never let you know exactly how long you'll be."

"Well, it's the nature of the business."

"And it must be very gratifying," she said. "Flying in, straightening everything out, turning chaos into order."

He'd told her initially that he was a corporate expediter, sent in to put things right when the local boys were stymied. Then one night it became clear that she knew what he did, and could live with it as long as he didn't do it to her. But now you'd think she'd forgotten the whole thing.

"Well, take all the time you want," she said. "Nelson and I are having a great old time."

"You know what I did?" he said abruptly. "I looked up my name in the local phone book."

"Did you find it?"

"No. But what do you figure it means?"

"Let me think about that," she said. "Okay?"

"Sure," he said. "Take all the time you want."

The next morning Keller had breakfast at the diner, swung past the house on Fairview Avenue, then drove out to the software company. This time the white Subaru was parked in the lot, and the license plate had the right letters and numbers on it. Keller parked where he could keep an eye on it and waited.

At noon, several men and women left the building and walked to their cars and drove off. None fit Stephen Lauderheim's description, and none got into the white Subaru.

At twelve-thirty, two men emerged from the building and walked along together, deep in conversation. Both wore khaki trousers and faded denim shirts and running shoes, but in other respects they looked completely different. One was short and pudgy, with dark hair combed flat across his skull. The other, well, the other just had to be Lauderheim. He fit Cressida Wallace's description to a T.

They walked together to Lauderheim's Subaru. Keller followed them to an Italian restaurant, one of a national chain. Then he drove back to Loud & Clear and parked in his old spot.

At a quarter to two, the Subaru returned and both men went back into the building. Keller drove off and found a supermarket, where he purchased a one-pound box of granulated sugar and a funnel. At a hardware store on the same small shopping plaza he bought a large screwdriver, a hammer, and a six-foot extension cord. He drove back to Loud & Clear and went to work.

The Subaru had a hatch over the gas cap. You needed a key to unlock it. He braced the screwdriver against the lock and struck it one sharp blow with the hammer, and the hatch popped. He removed the gas cap, inserted the funnel, poured in the sugar, replaced the cap, closed the hatch and wedged it shut, and went back to his own car and got behind the wheel.

Employees began to trickle out of Loud & Clear shortly after five. By six o'clock, only three cars remained in the lot. At six-twenty, Lauderheim's lunch companion came out, got into a brown Buick Century, and drove off. That left two cars, one of them the white Subaru, and they were both still there at seven.

Keller sat behind the wheel, deferring gratification. His breakfast had been light, two doughnuts and a cup of coffee, and he'd missed lunch. He was going to grab something to eat while he was in the supermarket, but it had slipped his mind. Now he was missing dinner.

Hunger made him irritable. Two cars in the lot, probably two people inside, say three at the most. They'd already stayed two hours past quitting time, and might stay until morning for all he knew. Maybe Lauderheim was waiting until the office was empty so that he could make an undisturbed phone call to Cressida.

Suppose he just went in there and did them both? Element of surprise, they'd never know what hit them. Two for the price of one, do it and let's get the hell out of here. Cops would just figure a disgruntled employee went berserk. That sort of thing happened everywhere these days, not just in post offices.

Maturity, he told himself. Maturity, deferred gratification. Above all, professionalism.

By seven-thirty he was ready to rethink his commitment to professionalism. He no longer felt hungry, but was seething with anger, all of it focused on Stephen Lauderheim.

The son of a bitch.

Why in the hell would he stalk some poor woman who spent her life in an attic writing about kitty cats and bunny rabbits? Kidnapping her dog, for God's sake, and then torturing it and killing it, and playing her a tape of the animal's death throes. Killing, Keller thought, was almost too good for the son of a bitch. Ought to stick that funnel in his mouth and pour oven cleaner down his throat.

Speak of the devil.

There he was, Stephen Fucking Lauderheim, holding the door open for a nerdy fellow wearing a lab coat and a wispy mustache. Not heading for the same car, please God? No, separate cars, with Lauderheim pausing after unlocking the Subaru to exchange a final pleasantry with the nerd in the lab coat.

Good he hadn't counted on waylaying him in the parking lot.

The nerd drove off first. Keller sat, glaring at the Subaru, until Lauderheim started it up, pulled out of the parking lot, and headed back toward town.

Keller gave him a two-block lead, then took off after him.

*   *   *

Just the other side of Four Mile Road, Keller pulled up right behind the disabled Subaru. Lauderheim already had the hood up and was frowning at the engine.

Keller got out of the car and trotted over to him.

"Heard the sound you were making," he said. "I think I know what's wrong."

"It's got to be the engine," Lauderheim said, "but I don't understand it. It never did anything like this before."

"I can fix it."

"Seriously? You mean it?"

"You got a tire iron?"

"Yeah, I suppose so," Lauderheim said, and went around to open the rear of the squareback. He found the tire iron, extended it to Keller, then drew it back. "There's nothing wrong with the tires," he said.

"No kidding," Keller said. "Give me the tire iron, will you?"

"Sure, but—"

"Say, don't I know you? You're Steve Lauderheim, aren't you?"

"That's right. Have we met?"

Keller looked at him, at the cute little chin dimple, at the big white teeth. Of course he was Lauderheim, who else could he be? But a professional made sure. Besides, it wasn't too long ago that he'd failed to make sure, and he wasn't eager to let that happen again.

"Cressida says hello," Keller said.

"Huh?"

Keller buried the tire iron in his solar plexus.

The results were encouraging. Lauderheim let out an awful sound, clapped both hands to his middle, and fell to his knees. Keller grabbed him by the front of his shirt, dragged him along the gravel until the Subaru screened the two of them from view. Then he raised the tire iron high overhead and brought it down on Lauderheim's head.

The man sprawled on the ground, still conscious, moaning softly. A few more blows to finish it?

No. Stick to the script. Keller drew the extension cord from his pocket, unwound a two-foot length of it, and looped it around Lauderheim's throat. He straddled the man, pinning him to the ground with a knee in the middle of his back, and choked the life out of him.

The Mississippi, legendary Father of Waters, swallowed the tire iron, the hammer, the screwdriver, the funnel. The empty box of sugar floated off on the current.

From a pay phone, Keller called his client. "Toxic Shock," he said, feeling like an idiot. No answer. He hung up.

He went back to his motel room, packed, carried his bag to the car. He didn't have to check out. He'd paid a week in advance, and when his week was up they'd take the room back.

He had to force himself to drive over to the Pizza Hut and get something to eat. All he wanted to do was drive straight to O'Hare and grab the first plane back to New York, but he knew he had to get some food into his system. Otherwise he'd start seeing things on the road north, swing the wheel to dodge something that wasn't there, and wind up putting the car in a ditch. Professionalism, he told himself, and ate an individual pan pizza and drank a medium Pepsi.

And placed the call again. "Toxic Shock"—and this time she was there, and picked up.

"It's all taken care of," he said.

"You mean—"

"I mean it's all taken care of."

"I can't believe it. My God, I can't believe it."

You're safe now, he wanted to say. You've got your life back.

Instead, cool and professional, he told her how to make the final payment. Cash, same as before, sent by Federal Express to Mary Jones, at another Mail Boxes Etc. location, this one in Peekskill.

"I can't thank you enough," the woman said. Keller said nothing, just smiled and rang off.

Driving north and east through Illinois, Keller went over it in his mind. He thought, *Cressida says hello.* Jesus, he couldn't believe he'd said that. What did he think he was, some kind of avenging angel? A knight in shining armor?

Jesus.

Well, nothing all day but two doughnuts and a cup of coffee. That was as far as you had to look for an explanation. Got him irritable and angry, made him take it personally.

Still, he thought, after he'd turned in the car and bought his ticket, Lauderheim was unquestionably one thoroughgoing son of a bitch. No loss to anyone.

And he could still hear her saying she couldn't thank him enough, and what was so wrong with enjoying that?

"I was thinking," Andria said. "About looking up your name in phone books?"

"And?"

"At first I thought it was a way of looking for yourself. But then I had another idea. I think it's a way of making sure there's room for you."

"Room for me?"

"Well," she said, "if you're not already there, then there's room for you."

Eight, nine days later, Dot called. Coincidentally enough, he was doing the crossword puzzle at the time.

"Keller," she said, "guess what Mary Jones didn't find in her mailbox?"

"That's strange," he said. "It's still not here? Maybe you ought to call her. Maybe FedEx lost it and it's in a back office somewhere."

"I'm way ahead of you, boy. I called her."

"And?"

"Line's been disconnected. . . . You still there, Keller?"

"I'm trying to think. You're sure that—"

"I called back, got the same recording. 'The number you have reached, blah blah blah, has been disconnected.' Leaves no room for doubt."

"No."

"The money doesn't show up, and now the line's been disconnected. Does it begin to make you wonder?"

"Maybe they arrested her," he said. "Before she could send the money."

"And stuck her in a cell and left her there? A quiet lady who writes about deaf rabbits?"

"Well—"

"Let me pull out and pass a few slow-moving vehicles," she said. "What I did, I called Information in St. Louis."

"St. Louis?"

"Webster Groves is a suburb of St. Louis."

"Webster Groves."

"Where Cressida Wallace lives, according to that reference book in the library."

"But she moved," Keller said.

"You'd think so, wouldn't you? But the Information operator had a listing for her. So I called the number. Guess what?"

"Come on, Dot."

"A woman answered. No answering machine, no computer-generated horseshit. 'Hello?' 'Cressida Wallace, please.' 'This is she.' Well, it wasn't the voice I remembered. 'Is this Cressida Wallace, the author?' 'Yes.' 'The author of *How the Bunny Lost His Ears*?' "

"And she said it was?"

"Well, how many Cressida Wallaces do you figure there are? I didn't know what the hell to say next. I told her I was from the Muscatine paper, I wanted to know her impressions of the town. Keller, she didn't know what I was talking about. I had to tell her what state Muscatine was in."

"You'd think she'd have at least heard of it," he said. "It's not that far from St. Louis."

"I don't think she gets out much. I think she sits in her house and writes her stories. I found out this much. She's lived in the same house in Webster Groves for thirty years."

He took a deep breath. He said, "Where are you, Dot?"

"Where am I? I'm at an outdoor pay phone half a mile from the house. I'm getting rained on."

"Go on home," he said. "Give me an hour or so and I'll call you back."

*   *   *

"All right," he said, closer to two hours later. "Here's how it shapes up. Stephen Lauderheim wasn't some creep, stalking some innocent woman."

"We figured that."

"He was a partner in Loud & Clear Software. He and a fellow named Randall Cleary started the firm. Lauderheim and Cleary, Loud & Clear."

"Cute."

"Lauderheim was married, father of two, bowled in a league, belonged to Rotary and the Jaycees."

"Hardly the type to kidnap a dog and torture it to death."

"You wouldn't think so."

"Who set him up? The wife?"

"I figure the partner. Company was doing great and one of the big Silicon Valley firms was looking to buy them out. My guess is one of them wanted to sell and the other didn't. Or there was some kind of partnership insurance in place. One partner dies, the other buys him out at a prearranged price, pays off the widow with the proceeds of the partnership insurance policy. Of course the company's now worth about twenty times what they agreed to."

"How'd you get all this, Keller?"

"Called the city room at the Muscatine paper, said I was covering the death for a computer magazine and could they fax me the obit and anything they'd run on the killing."

"You've got a fax?"

"The candy store around the corner's got one. All the guy in Muscatine could tell from the number I gave him was it was in New York."

"Nice."

"After the fax came in, the stuff he sent gave me

some ideas for other calls to make. I could sit on the phone for another hour and find out more, but I figure that's enough."

"More than enough," she said. "Keller, the little shit foxed us. And then she stiffed us in the bargain."

"That's what I don't get," he said. "Why stiff us? All he had to do was send the money and I'd never have thought of Iowa again unless I was flying over it. He was home free. All he had to do was pay what he owed."

"Cheap son of a bitch," Dot said.

"But where's the sense? He paid out half the money without even knowing who he was sending it to. If he could afford to do that on the come, you can imagine what kind of money was at stake here."

"It paid off."

"It paid off but he didn't. Stupid."

"Very stupid."

"I'll tell you what I think," he said. "I think the money was the least of it. I think he wanted to feel superior to us. I mean, why go through all this Cressida Wallace crap in the first place? Does he figure I'm a Boy Scout, doing my good deed for the day?"

"He figured we were amateurs, Keller. And needed to be motivated."

"Yeah, well, he figured wrong," he said. "I have to pack, I've got a flight in an hour and a half and I have to call Andria. We're getting paid, Dot. Don't worry."

"I wasn't worried," she said.

Which one, he wondered, was Cleary? The plump one who'd gone to lunch with Lauderheim? Or the nerd in the lab coat who'd walked out to the parking lot with him?

Or someone else, someone he hadn't even seen. Cleary might well have been out of town that day, providing himself with an alibi.

Didn't matter. You didn't need to know what a man looked like to get him on the phone.

Cleary, like his late partner, had an unlisted home phone number. But the firm, Loud & Clear, had a listing. Keller called from his motel room—this time he was staying at the one with HBO. He used the electronic novelty item he'd picked up at Abercrombie & Fitch, and when a woman answered he said he wanted to speak to Randall Cleary.

"Whom shall I say is calling?"

Whom, he noted. Not bad for Muscatine, Iowa.

"Cressida Wallace," he said.

She put him on hold, but he did not languish there for long. Moments later he heard a male voice, one he could not recognize. "Cleary," the man said. "Who is this?"

"Ah, Mr. Cleary," he said. "This is Miss Cressida Wallace."

"No, it's not."

"It is," Keller said, "and I understand you've been using my name, and I'm frightfully upset."

Silence from Cleary. Keller unhooked the device that had altered the pitch of his voice. "Toxic Shock," he said in his own voice. "You stupid son of a bitch."

"There was a problem," Cleary said. "I'm going to send you the money."

"Why didn't you get in touch?"

"I was going to. You can't believe how busy we've been around here."

"Why'd you disconnect your phone?"

"I thought, you know, security reasons."

"Right," Keller said.

"I'm going to pay."

"No question about it," Keller said. "Today. You're going to FedEx the money today. Overnight delivery, Mary Jones gets it tomorrow. Are we clear on that?"

"Absolutely."

"And the price went up. Remember what you were supposed to send?"

"Yes."

"Well, double it."

There was a silence. "That's impossible. It's extortion, for God's sake."

"Look," Keller said, "do yourself a favor. Think it through."

Another silence, but shorter. "All right," Cleary said.

"In cash, and it gets there tomorrow. Agreed?"

"Agreed."

He called Dot from a pay phone, had dinner, and went back to his room. This motel had HBO, so of course there was nothing on that he wanted to watch. It figured.

In the morning he skipped the diner and had a big breakfast at a Denny's on the highway. He drove up to Davenport and made two stops, at a sporting goods store and a hardware store. He went back to his motel, and around two in the afternoon he called White Plains.

"This is Cressida Wallace," he said. "Have there been any calls for me?"

"Damned if it doesn't work," Dot said. "You sound just like a woman."

"But I break just like a little girl," Keller said.

"Very funny. Quit using that thing, will you? It sounds like a woman, but it's your way of talking, your inflections underneath it all. Let me hear the Keller I know so well."

He unhooked the gadget. "Better?"

"Much better. Your pal came through."

"Got the numbers right and everything?"

"Indeed he did."

"I think the voice-change gizmo helped," he said. "It made him see we knew everything."

"Oh, he'd have paid anyway," she said. "All you had to do was yank his chain a little. You just liked using your new toy, that's all. When are you coming home, Keller?"

"Not right away."

"Well, I know that."

"No, I think I'll wait a few days," he said. "Right now he's edgy, looking over his shoulder. Beginning of next week he'll have his guard down."

"Makes sense."

"Besides," he said, "it's not a bad town."

"Oh, God, Keller."

"What's the matter?"

" 'It's not a bad town.' I bet you're the first person to say that, including the head of the chamber of commerce."

"It's not," he insisted. "The motel set gets HBO. There's a Pizza Hut down the street."

"Keep it to yourself, Keller, or everybody's going to want to move there."

"And I've got things to do."

"Like what?"

"A little metalwork project, for starters. And I want to buy something for Andria."

"Not earrings again."

"You can't have too many earrings," he said.

"Well, that's true," she agreed. "I can't argue with you there."

He hung up and used the carbide-bladed hacksaw from the hardware store to remove most of both barrels of the shotgun from the sporting goods store, then switched blades and cut away most of the stock as well. He loaded both chambers and left the gun tucked under the mattress. Then he drove along the river road until he found a good spot, and he tossed the sawed-off gun barrels, the hacksaw, and the box of shotgun shells into the Mississippi. Toxic waste, he thought, and shook his head, just imagining all the junk that wound up in the river.

He drove around for a while, just enjoying the day, and returned to the motel. Right now Randall Cleary was telling himself he was safe, he was in the clear, he had nothing to worry about. But he wasn't sure yet.

In a few days he'd be sure. He'd even think to himself that maybe he should have called Keller's bluff, or at least not agreed to pay double. But what the hell, it was only money, and money was something he had a ton of.

Stupid amateur.

Which one was he, anyway? The nerd with the wispy mustache? The plump one, the dumpling? Or someone yet unseen?

Well, he'd find out.

Keller, feeling professional, feeling mature, sat back and put his feet up. Postponing gratification was turning out to be more fun than he would have guessed.

7

Keller's Choice

Keller, behind the wheel of a rented Plymouth, kept an eye on the fat man's house. It was very grand, with columns, for heaven's sake, and a circular driveway, and one hell of a lot of lawn. Keller, who had done his share of lawn mowing as a teenager, wondered what a kid would get for mowing a lawn like that.

Hard to say. The thing was, he had no frame of reference. He seemed to remember getting a couple of bucks way back when, but the lawns he'd mowed were tiny, postage stamps in comparison to the fat man's rolling green envelope. Taking into consideration the disparity in lawn size, and the inexorable shrinkage of the dollar over the years, what was a lawn like this worth? Twenty dollars? Fifty dollars? More?

The non-answer, he suspected, was that people who had lawns like this one didn't hire kids to push a mower around. Instead they had gardeners who showed up regularly with vehicles appropriate to the season, mowing in the summer, raking leaves in the fall, plowing snow in the winter. And charging so much a month, a tidy sum that actually didn't cost the fat man anything to speak of, because he very likely billed it to his company, or took it off his taxes. Or, if his accountant was enterprising, both.

Keller, who lived in a one-bedroom apartment in midtown Manhattan, had no lawn to mow. There was a tree in front of his building, planted and diligently maintained by the Parks Department, and its leaves fell in the fall, but no one needed to rake them. The wind was pretty good about blowing them away. Snow, when it didn't melt of its own accord, was shoveled from the sidewalk by the building's superintendent, who kept the elevator running and replaced burned-out bulbs in the hall fixtures and dealt with minor plumbing emergencies. Keller had a low-maintenance life, really. All he had to do was pay the rent on time and everything else got taken care of by other people.

He liked it that way. Even so, when his work took him away from home he found himself wondering. His fantasies, by and large, centered on simpler and more modest lifestyles. A cute little house in a subdivision, an undemanding job. A manageable life.

The fat man's house, in a swank suburban community north of Cincinnati, was neither cute nor little. Keller wasn't too clear on what the fat man did, beyond the fact that it involved his playing host to a lot of visitors and spending a good deal of time in his car. He couldn't say if the work was demanding, although he suspected it might be. Nor could he tell if the man's life was manageable. What he did know, though, was that someone wanted to manage him right out of it.

Which, of course, was where Keller came in, and why he was sitting in an Avis car across the street from the fat man's estate. And was it right to call it that? Where did you draw the line between a house and an estate? What was the yardstick, size or value? He thought about it, and decided it was probably some sort of combination of the two. A brownstone on East Sixty-sixth Street was just a house, not an estate, even if it was worth five or ten times as much as the fat man's spread. On the other hand, a double-wide trailer could sit on fifteen or twenty acres of land without making the cut as an estate.

He was pondering the point when his wristwatch beeped, reminding him the security patrol was due in five minutes or so. He turned the key in the ignition, took a last wistful look at the fat man's house (or estate) across the road, and pulled away from the curb.

In his motel room, Keller put on the television set and worked his way around the dial without leaving his chair. Lately, he'd noticed, most of the decent motels had remote controls for their TV sets. For a while there you'd get the remote bolted to the top of the bedside table, but that was only handy if you happened to be sitting up in bed watching. Otherwise it was a pain in the neck. If you had to get up and walk over to the bed to change the channel or mute the commercial, you might as well just walk over to the set.

It was to prevent theft, of course. A free-floating remote could float right into a guest's suitcase, never to be seen again. Table lamps were bolted down in the same fashion, and television sets, too. But that was pretty much okay. You didn't mind being unable to move the lamp around, or the TV. The remote was something else again. You might as well bolt down the towels.

He turned off the set. It might be easy to change

channels now, but it was harder than ever to find anything he wanted to see. He picked up a magazine, thumbed through it. This was his fourth night at this particular motel, and he still hadn't figured out a good way to kill the fat man. There had to be a way, there was always a way, but he hadn't found it yet.

Suppose he had a house like the fat man's. Generally he fantasized about houses he could afford to buy, lives he could imagine himself living. He had enough money salted away so that he could buy an unassuming house somewhere and pay cash for it, but he couldn't even scrape up the down payment for a spread like the fat man's. (Could you call it that—a spread? And what exactly *was* a spread? How did it compare to an estate? Was the distinction geographical, with estates in the Northeast and spreads south and west?)

Still, say he had the money, not just to swing the deal but to cover the upkeep as well. Say he won the lottery, say he could afford the gardener and a live-in maid and whatever else you had to have. Would he enjoy it, walking from room to room, admiring the paintings on the walls, luxuriating in the depth of the carpets? Would he like strolling in the garden, listening to the birds, smelling the flowers?

Nelson might like it, he thought. Romping on a lawn like that.

He sat there for a moment, shaking his head. Then he switched chairs and reached for the phone.

He called his own number in New York, got his machine. "You. Have. Six. Messages," it told him, and played them for him. The first five turned out to be wordless hangups. The sixth was a voice he knew.

"Hey there, E.T. Call home."

*　　*　　*

He made the call from a pay phone a quarter-mile down the highway. Dot answered, and her voice brightened when she recognized his.

"There you are," she said. "I called and called."

"There was only the one message."

"I didn't want to leave one. I figured I'd tell What's-her-name."

"Andria."

"Right, and she'd pass the word to you when you called in. But she never picked up. She must be walking that dog of yours to the Bronx and back."

"I guess."

"So I left a message, and here we are, chatting away like old friends. I don't suppose you did what you went there to do."

"It's not as quick and easy as it might be," he said. "It's taking time."

"Other words, our friend's still got a pulse."

"Or else he's learned to walk around without one."

"Well," she said, "I'm glad to hear it. You know what I think you should do, Keller? I think you should check out of that motel and get on a plane."

"And come home?"

"Got it in one, Keller, but then you were always quick."

"The client canceled?"

"Not exactly."

"Then—"

"Fly home," she said, "and then catch a train to White Plains, and I'll pour you a nice glass of iced tea. And I'll explain all."

It wasn't iced tea, it was lemonade. He sat in a wicker chair on the wraparound porch of the big house on Taunton Place sipping a big glass of it. Dot, wearing a blue and white housedress and a pair of white flip-flops, perched on the wooden railing.

"I just got those the day before yesterday," she said, pointing. "Wind chimes. I was watching QVC and they caught me in a weak moment."

"It could have been a Pocket Fisherman."

"It might as well be," she said, "for all the breeze we've been getting. But how do you like this for coincidence, Keller? There you are, off doing a job in Cincinnati, and we get a call, another client with a job just down your street."

"Down my street?"

"Or up your alley. I think it's a Briticism, down your street, but we're in America, so the hell with it. It's up your alley."

"If you say so."

"And you'll never guess where this second caller lives."

"Cincinnati," he said.

"Give the man a cigar."

He frowned. "So there's two jobs in the same metropolitan area," he said. "That would be a reason to do them both in one trip, assuming it was possible. Save airfare, I suppose, if that matters. Save finding a room and settling in. Instead I'm back here with neither job done, which doesn't make sense. So there's more to it."

"Give the man a cigar and light it for him."

"Puff puff," Keller said. "The jobs are connected somehow, and I'd better know all about it up front or I might step on my own whatsit."

"And we wouldn't want anything to happen to your whatsit."

"Right. What's the connection? Same client for both jobs?"

She shook her head.

"Different clients. Same *target*? Did the fat man manage to piss off two different people to the point where they both called us within days of each other?"

"Be something, wouldn't it?"

"Well, pissing people off is like anything else," he said. "Certain people have a knack for it. But that's not it."

"No."

"Different targets."

"I'm afraid so."

"Different targets, different clients. Same time, same place, but everything else is different. So? Help me out on this, Dot. I'm not getting anywhere."

"Keller," she said, "you're doing fine."

"Four people, all of them different. The fat man and the guy who hired us to hit him, and target number two and client number two, and . . ."

"Is day beginning to break? Is light beginning to dawn?"

"The fat man wants to hire us," he said. "To kill our original client."

"Give the man an exploding cigar."

"A hires us to kill B, and B hires us to kill A."

"That's a little algebraic for me, but it makes the point."

"The contracts couldn't have come direct," he said. "They were brokered, right? Because the fat man's not a wise guy. He could be a little mobbed up, the way some businessmen are, but he wouldn't know to call here."

"He came through somebody," Dot agreed.

"And so did the other guy. Different brokers, of course."

"Of course."

"And they both called here." He raised his eyes significantly to the ceiling. "And what did he do, Dot? Say yes to both of them?"

"That's what he did."

"Why, for God's sake? We've already got a client, we can't take an assignment to kill him, especially from somebody we've already agreed to take out."

"The ethics of the situation bother you, Keller?"

"This is good," he said, brandishing the lemonade. "This from a mix or what?"

"Homemade. Real lemons, real sugar."

"Makes a difference," he said. "Ethics? What do I know about ethics? It's just no way to do business, that's all. What's the broker going to think?"

"Which broker?"

"The one whose client gets killed. What's he going to say?"

"What would you have done, Keller? If you were him, and you got the second call days after the first one."

He thought about it. "I'd say I haven't got anybody available at the moment, but I should have a good man in about two weeks, when he gets back from Aruba."

"Aruba?"

"Wherever. Then, after the fat man's toast and I've been back a week, say, you call back and ask if the contract's still open. And he says something like, 'No, the client changed his mind.' Even if he guesses who popped his guy, it's all straight and clean and businesslike. Or don't you agree?"

"No," she said. "I agree completely."

"But that's not what he did," he said, "and I'm

surprised. What was his thinking? He afraid of arousing suspicions, something like that?"

She just looked at him. He met her gaze, and read something in her face, and he got it.

"Oh, no," he said.

"I thought he was getting better," she said. "I'm not saying there wasn't a little denial operating, Keller. A little wishing-will-make-it-so."

"Understandable."

"He had that time when he gave you the wrong room number, but that worked out all right in the end."

"For us," Keller said. "Not for the guy who was in the room."

"There's that," she allowed. "Then he went into that funk and kept turning down everybody who called. I was thinking maybe a doctor could get him on Prozac."

"I don't know about Prozac. In this line of work . . ."

"Yeah, I was wondering about that. Depressed is no good, but is mellow any better? It could be counterproductive."

"It could be disastrous."

"That too," she said. "And you can't get him to go to a doctor anyway, so what difference does it make? He's in a funk, maybe it's like the weather. A low-pressure front moves in, and it's all you can do to sit on the porch with an iced tea. Then it blows over, and we get some of that good Canadian air, and it's like old times again."

"Old times."

"And yesterday he was on the phone, and then he buzzed me and I took him a cup of coffee. 'Call Keller,' he told me. 'I've got some work for him in Cincinnati.' "

"Déjà vu."

"You said it, Keller. Déjà vu like never before."

Her explanation was elaborate—what the old man said, what she thought he meant, what he really meant, di dah di dah di dah. What it boiled down to was that the original client, one Barry Moncrieff, had been elated that his problems with the fat man were soon to be over, and he'd confided as much to at least one person who couldn't keep a secret. Word reached the fat man, whose name was Arthur Strang.

While Moncrieff may have forgotten that loose lips sink ships, Strang evidently remembered that the best defense was a good offense. He made a couple of phone calls, and eventually the phone rang in the house on Taunton Place, and the old man took the call and took the contract.

When Dot pointed out the complications—i.e., that their new client was already slated for execution, with the fee paid by the man who had just become their new target—it became evident that the old man had forgotten the original deal entirely.

"He didn't know you were in Cincinnati," she explained. "Didn't have a clue he'd sent you there or anywhere else. For all he knew you were out walking the dog, assuming he remembered you had a dog."

"But when you told him . . ."

"He didn't see the problem. I kept explaining it to him, until it hit me what I was doing. I was trying to blow out a light bulb."

"Puff puff," Keller said.

"You said it. He just wasn't going to get it. 'Keller's a good boy,' he said. 'You leave it to Keller. Keller will know what to do.' "

"He said that, huh?"

"His very words. You look the least bit lost, Keller. Don't tell me he was wrong."

He thought for a moment. "The fat man knows there's a contract out on him," he said. "Well, that figures. It would explain why he was so hard to get close to."

"If you'd managed," Dot pointed out, "I'd shrug and say what's done is done, and let it go at that. But, fortunately or unfortunately, you checked your machine in time."

"Fortunately or unfortunately."

"Right, and don't ask me which is which. Easiest thing, you say the word and I call both of the middlemen and tell them we're out. Our foremost operative broke his leg in a skiing accident and you'd better call somebody else. What's the matter?"

"Skiing? This time of year?"

"In Chile, Keller. Use your imagination. Anyway, we're out of it."

"Maybe that's best."

"Not from a dollars-and-cents standpoint. No money for you, and refunds for both clients, who'll either look elsewhere or be reduced to shooting each other. I hate to give money back once it's been paid."

"What did they do, pay half in front?"

"Uh-huh. Usual system."

He frowned, trying to work it out. "Go home," she said. "Pet Andria and give Nelson a kiss, or is it the other way around? Sleep on it and let me know what you decide."

He took the train to Grand Central and walked home, rode up in the elevator, used his key in the lock. The apartment was dark and quiet, just as he'd left it.

Nelson's dish was in a corner of the kitchen. Keller looked at it and felt like a Gold Star Mother, keeping her son's room exactly as he had left it. He knew he ought to put the dish away or chuck it out altogether, but he didn't have the heart.

He unpacked and showered, then went around the corner for a beer and a burger. He took a walk afterward, but it wasn't much fun. He went back to the apartment and called the airlines. Then he packed again and caught a cab to JFK.

He phoned White Plains while he waited for them to call his flight. "On my way," he told Dot.

"You continue to surprise me, Keller," she said. "I thought for sure you'd stay the night."

"No reason to."

There was a pause. Then she said, "Keller? Is something wrong?"

"Andria left," he said, surprising himself. He hadn't intended to say anything. Eventually, sure, but not just yet.

"That's too bad," Dot said. "I thought the two of you were happy."

"So did I."

"Oh."

"She has to find herself," Keller said.

"You know, I've heard people say that, and I never know what the hell they're talking about. How would you lose yourself in the first place? And how would you know where to look for yourself?"

"I wondered that myself."

"Of course she's awfully young, Keller."

"Right."

"Too young for you, some would say."

"Some would."

"Still, you probably miss her. Not to mention Nelson."

"I miss them both," he said.

"I mean you both must miss her," Dot said. "Wait a minute. What did you just say?"

"They just called my flight," he said, and broke the connection.

Cincinnati's airport was across the river in Kentucky. Keller had turned in his Avis car that morning, and thought it might seem strange if he went back to the same counter for another one. He went to Budget instead, and got a Honda.

"It's a Japanese car," the clerk told him, "but it's actually produced right here in the US of A."

"That's a load off my mind," Keller told him.

He checked into a motel half a mile from the previous one and called in from a restaurant pay phone. He had a batch of questions, things he needed to know about Barry Moncrieff, the fellow who was at once Client #1 and Assignment #2. Dot, instead of answering, asked him a question of her own.

"What do you mean, you miss them both? Where's the dog?"

"I don't know."

"She ran off with your dog? Is that what you're saying?"

"They went off together," he said. "Nobody was running."

"Fine, she walked off with your dog. I guess she figured she needed him to help her go look for herself. What did she do, skip town while you were in Cincinnati?"

"Earlier," he said. "And she didn't skip town. We

talked about it, and she said she thought it would be best if she took Nelson with her."

"And you agreed?"

"More or less."

" 'More or less'? What does that mean?"

"I've often wondered myself. She said I don't really have time for him, and I travel a lot, and . . . I don't know."

"But he was your dog long before you even met her. You hired her to walk him when you were out of town."

"Right."

"And one thing led to another, and she wound up living there. And the next thing you know she's telling you it's best if the dog goes with her."

"Right."

"And away they go."

"Right."

"And you don't know where, and you don't know if they'll be back."

"Right."

"When did this happen, Keller?"

"About a month ago. Maybe a little longer, maybe six weeks."

"You never said anything."

"No."

"I went on about how you should pet him and kiss her, whatever I said, and you didn't say anything."

"I would have gotten around to it sooner or later."

They were both silent for a long moment. Then she asked him what he was going to do. About what, he asked.

"About what? About your dog and your girlfriend."

"I thought that's what you meant," he said, "but

you could have been talking about Moncrieff and
Strang. But it's the same answer all around. I don't
know what I'm going to do.''

What it came down to was this. He had a choice to
make. It was his decision as to which contract he
would fulfill and which he would cancel.

And how did you decide something like that? Two
people wanted his services, and only one could have
them. If he were a painting, the answer would be
obvious. You'd have an auction, and whoever was
willing to make the highest bid would have something pretty to hang over the couch. But you couldn't
have bids in the present instance because the price
had already been fixed, and both parties indepen-
dently had agreed to it. Each had paid half in advance, and when the job was done one of them
would pay the additional 50 percent and the other
would be technically entitled to a refund, but in no
position to claim it.

So in that sense the contract was potentially more
lucrative than usual, paying one and a half times the
standard rate. It came out the same no matter how
you did it. Kill Moncrieff, and Strang would pay the
rest of the money. Kill Strang, and Moncrieff would
pay it.

Which would it be?

Moncrieff, he thought, had called first. The old
man had made a deal with him, and a guarantee of
exclusivity was implicit in such an arrangement.
When you hired somebody to kill someone, you
didn't require assurance that he wouldn't hire on to
kill you as well. That went without saying.

So their initial commitment was to Moncrieff, and
any arrangements made with Strang ought to be null

and void. Money from Strang wasn't really a retainer, it came more under the heading of windfall profits, and needn't weigh in the balance. You could even argue that taking Strang's advance payment was a perfectly legitimate tactical move, designed to lull the quarry into a feeling of false security, thus making him easier to get to.

On the other hand . . .

On the other hand, if Moncrieff had just kept his damned mouth shut, Strang wouldn't have been forewarned, and consequently forearmed. It was Moncrieff, running his mouth about his plans to do the fat man in, that had induced Strang to call somebody, who called somebody else, who wound up talking to the old man in White Plains.

And it was Moncrieff's blabbing that had made Strang such an elusive target. Otherwise it would have been easy to get to the fat man, and by now Keller would have long since completed the assignment. Instead of sitting all by himself in a motel on the outskirts of Cincinnati, he could be sitting all by himself in an apartment on First Avenue.

Moncrieff, loose of lip, had sunk his own ship. Moncrieff, unable to keep a secret, had sabotaged the very contract he had been so quick to arrange. Couldn't you argue that his actions, with their unfortunate results, had served to nullify the contract? In which case the old man was more than justified in retaining his deposit while accepting a counterproposal from another interested party.

Which meant that the thing to do was regard the fat man as the bona fide client and Moncrieff (fat or lean, tall or short, Keller didn't know which) as the proper quarry.

On the other hand . . .

* * *

Moncrieff had a penthouse apartment atop a high-rise not far from Riverfront Stadium. The Reds were in town for a home stand, and Keller bought a ticket and an inexpensive pair of field glasses and went to watch them. His seat was out in right field, remote enough that he wasn't the only one with binoculars. Near him sat a father and son, both of whom had brought gloves in the hope of catching a foul ball. Neither pitcher had his stuff, and both teams hit a lot of long balls, but the kid and his father only got excited when somebody hit a long foul to right.

Keller wondered about that. If what they wanted was a baseball, wouldn't they be better off buying one at a sporting goods store? If they wanted the thrill of the chase, well, they could get the clerk to throw it up in the air, and the kid could catch it when it came down.

During breaks in the action, Keller trained the binoculars on a window of what he was pretty sure was Moncrieff's apartment. He found himself wondering whether Moncrieff was a baseball fan, and if he took advantage of his location and watched the ball games from his window. You'd need a lot more magnification than Keller was carrying, but if Moncrieff could afford the penthouse he could swing a powerful telescope as well. If he got the kind of gizmo that let you count the rings of Saturn, you ought to be able to tell whether the pitcher's curveball was breaking.

Made about as much sense as taking a glove to the game, he decided. If a man like Moncrieff wanted to watch a game, he could afford a box seat behind the Reds' dugout. Of course these days he might prefer to stay home and watch the game on television if not through a telescope, because he might figure it was safer.

And, as far as Keller could tell, Barry Moncrieff wasn't taking a lot of risks. If he hadn't guessed that the fat man might retaliate and put out a contract of his own, then he looked to be a naturally cautious man. He lived in a secure building, and he rarely left it. When he did, he never seemed to go anywhere alone.

Keller, unable to pick a target on the basis of an ethical distinction, had opted for pragmatism. His line of work, after all, was different from crapshooting. You didn't get a bonus for making your point the hard way. So, if you had to take out one of two men, why not pick the man who was easier to kill?

By the time he left the ballpark, with the Reds having lost to the Phillies in extra innings after leaving the bases loaded in the bottom of the ninth, he'd spent three full days on the question. What he'd managed to determine was that neither man was easy to kill. They both lived in fortresses, one high up in the air, the other way out in the sticks. Neither one would be impossible to hit—nobody was impossible to hit—but neither would be easy.

He'd managed to get a look at Moncrieff, managed to be in the lobby showing a misaddressed package to a concierge who was as puzzled as Keller was pretending to be, when Moncrieff entered, flanked by two young men with big shoulders and bulges under their jackets. Moncrieff was fiftyish and balding, with a downturned mouth and jowls like a basset hound.

He was fat, too. Keller might have thought of him as the fat man if he hadn't already assigned that label to Arthur Strang. Moncrieff wasn't fat the way Strang

was fat—few people were—but that still left him a
long way from being a borderline anorexic. Keller
guessed he was seventy-five to a hundred pounds
lighter than Strang. Strang waddled, while Moncrieff
strutted like a pigeon.

Back in his motel, Keller found himself watching
a newscast and looking at highlights from the game
he'd just watched. He turned off the set, picked up
the binoculars, and wondered why he'd bothered to
buy them, and what he was going to do with them
now. He caught himself thinking that Andria might
enjoy using them to watch birds in Central Park. He
told himself to stop that, and he went and took a
shower.

Neither one would be the least bit easy to kill, he
thought, but he could already see a couple of ap-
proaches to either man. The degree of difficulty, as
an Olympic diver would say, was about the same.
So, as far as he could tell, was the degree of risk.

A thought struck him. Maybe one of them deserved it.

"Arthur Strang," the woman said. "You know, he
was fat when I met him. I think he was born fat. But
he was nothing like he is now. He was just, you
know, heavy."

Her name was Marie, and she was a tall woman
with unconvincing red hair. Early thirties, Keller
figured. Big lips, big eyes. Nice shape to her, too, but
Keller's opinion, since she brought it up, was she
could stand to lose five pounds. Not that he was
going to mention it.

"When I met him he was heavy," she said, "but
he wore these well-tailored Italian suits, and he
looked okay, you know? Of course, naked, forget it."

"It's forgotten."

"Huh?" She looked confused, but a sip of her drink put her at ease. "Before we were married," she said, "he actually lost weight, believe it or not. Then we jumped over the broomstick together and he started eating with both hands. That's just an expression."

"He only ate with one hand?"

"No, silly! 'Jumped over the broomstick.' We had a regular wedding in a church. Anyway, I don't think Arthur would have been too good at jumping over anything, not even if you laid the broomstick flat on the floor. I was married to him for three years, and I'll bet he put on twenty or thirty pounds a year. Then we broke up three years ago, and have you seen him lately? He's as big as a house."

As big as a double-wide, maybe, Keller thought. But nowhere near as big as an estate.

"You know, Kevin," she said, laying a hand on Keller's arm, "it's awful smoky in here. They passed a law against it but people smoke anyway, and what are you going to do, arrest them?"

"Maybe we should get some air," he suggested, and she beamed at the notion.

Back at her place, she said, "He had preferences, Kevin."

Keller nodded encouragingly, wondering if he'd ever been called Kevin before. He sort of liked the way she said it.

"As a matter of fact," she said darkly, "he was sexually aberrant."

"Really?"

"He wanted me to do things," she said, rubbing his leg. "You wouldn't believe the things he wanted."

"Oh?"

She told him. "I thought it was disgusting," she said, "but he insisted, and it was part of what broke us up. But do you want to know something weird?"

"Sure."

"After the divorce," she said, "I sort of became more broad-minded on the subject. You might find this hard to believe, Kevin, but I'm pretty kinky."

"No kidding."

"In fact, what I just told you about Arthur? The really disgusting thing? Well, I have to admit it no longer disgusts me. In fact . . ."

"Yes?"

"Oh, Kevin," she said.

She was kinky, all right, and spirited, and afterward he decided he'd been wrong about the five pounds. She was fine just the way she was.

"I was wondering," he said on his way out the door. "Your ex-husband? How did he feel about dogs?"

"Oh, Kevin," she said. "And here I thought I was the kinky one. You're too much. Dogs?"

"I didn't mean it that way."

"I'll bet you didn't. Kevin, honey, if you don't get out of here this minute I may not let you go at all. Dogs!"

"Just as pets," he said. "Does he, you know, like dogs? Or hate them?"

"As far as I know," Marie said, "Arthur Strang has no opinion one way or the other about dogs. The subject never came up."

Laurel Moncrieff, the second of three women with whom Barry had jumped over the broomstick, had nothing to report on the ups and downs of her ex-husband's weight, or what he did or didn't like to do when the shades were drawn. She'd worked as Moncrieff's secretary, won him away from his first wife, and made sure he had a male secretary afterward.

"Then the son of a bitch joined a gym," she said, "and he wound up leaving me for his personal trainer. He wadded me up and threw me away like a used Kleenex."

She didn't look like the sort of person you'd blow your nose on. She was a slender, dark-haired woman, and she had been no harder to get acquainted with than Marie Strang, and about as easy to wind up in the hay with. She hadn't disclosed any interesting aberrations, her own or her ex-husband's, but Keller found himself with no cause to complain.

"Ah, Kevin," she said.

Maybe it was the name, he thought. Maybe he should use it more often, maybe it brought him luck.

"Living alone the way you do," he said. "You ever think about getting a dog?"

"I'm away too much," she said. "It'd be no good for me and no good for the dog."

"That's true for a lot of people," he said, "but they're used to having one around the house and they don't want to give it up."

"Whatever works," she said. "I never got used to it, and you know what they say. You don't miss what you never had."

"I guess your ex didn't have a dog."

"Not until I left and he married the bitch with the magic fingers."

"She had a dog?"

"She *was* a dog, honey. She had a face like a Rottweiler. But she's out of the picture now, and she hasn't been replaced. Serves her right, if you ask me."

"So you don't know how Barry Moncrieff felt about dogs."

"Of the canine variety, you mean? I don't think he cared much one way or the other. Hey, how'd we get on this silly subject, anyhow? Why don't you lie down and kiss me, Kevin, honey?"

They both gave money to local charities. Strang tended to support the arts, while Moncrieff donated to fight diseases and feed the homeless. They both had a reputation for ruthlessness in business. Both were childless, and presently unmarried. Neither one had a dog, or had ever had a dog, as far as he could determine. Neither had any strong prodog or antidog feelings. It would have been helpful to discover that Strang was a heavy contributor to the ASPCA and the Anti-Vivisection League, or that Moncrieff liked to go to a basement in Kentucky and watch a couple of pit bulls fight to the death, betting substantial sums on the outcome.

But he came across nothing of the sort, and the more he thought about it the less legitimate a criterion it seemed to him. Why should a matter of life and death hinge upon how a man felt about dogs? And who was Keller to care anyway? It was not as if he were a dog owner himself. Not anymore.

"Neither one's Albert Schweitzer," he told Dot, "and neither one's Hitler. They both fall somewhere in between, so making a decision on moral grounds is impossible. I'll tell you, this is murder."

"It's not," she said. "That's the whole trouble, Keller. You're in Cincinnati and the clock's running."

"I know."

"Moral decisions. This is the wrong business for moral decisions."

"You're right," he said. "And who am I to be making that kind of decision, anyway?"

"Spare me the humility," she said. "Listen, I'm as crazy as you are. I had this idea, call both brokers, have them get in touch with their clients. Explain that due to the exigencies of this particular situation, di dah di dah di dah, we need full payment in advance."

"You think they'd go for it?"

"If one of them went for it," she said, "that'd make the decision, wouldn't it? Knock him off and the other guy's left alive to pay in full, a satisfied customer."

"That's brilliant," he said, and thought a moment. "Except . . ."

"Ah, you spotted it, didn't you? The guy who cooperates, the guy who goes the extra mile to be a really good client, he's the one who gets rewarded by getting killed. I like ironic as much as the next person, Keller, but I decided that's a little too much for me."

"Besides," he said, "with our luck they'd both pay."

"And we'd be back where we started. Keller?"

"What?"

"All said and done, there's only one answer. You got a quarter?"

"Probably. Why?"

"Toss it," she said. "Heads or tails."

Heads.

Keller picked up the quarter he'd tossed, dropped it into the slot. He dialed a number, and while it rang he wondered at the wisdom of making such a decision on the basis of a coin toss. It seemed awfully arbitrary to him, but then again maybe it was the way of the world. Maybe somewhere up above the clouds there was an old man with a beard making life-and-death decisions in the very same way, tossing coins, shrugging, and passing out train wrecks and heart attacks.

"Let me talk to Mr. Strang," he told the person who answered. "Just tell him it's in reference to a recent contract."

There was a long pause, and Keller dug out another quarter in case the phone needed feeding. Then Strang came on the line. It seemed to Keller that he recognized the voice even though he had never heard it before. The voice was resonant, like an opera singer's, though hardly musical.

"I don't know who you are," Strang said without preamble, "and I don't discuss business over the phone with people I don't know."

Fat, Keller thought. The man sounded fat.

"Very wise," Keller told him. "Well, we've got business to discuss, and I agree it shouldn't be over the phone. We ought to meet, but nobody should see us together, or even know we're having the meeting." He listened for a moment. "You're the client," he said. "I was hoping you could suggest a time and a place." He listened some more. "Good," he said. "I'll be there."

"But it seems irregular," Strang said, with a whine in his voice that you would never have heard from Pavarotti. "I don't see the need for this, I really don't."

"You will," Keller told him. "I can promise you that."

He broke the connection, then opened his hand and looked at the quarter he was holding. He thought for a moment—about the old man in White Plains, and then about the old man up in the sky. The one with the long white beard, the one who tossed coins of his own and ran the universe accordingly. He thought about the turns in his own life, and the way people could walk in and out of it.

He weighed the coin in his palm—it didn't weigh very much—and he gave it a toss, caught it, slapped it down on the back of his hand.

Tails.

He reached for the phone.

"This time it's iced tea," Dot said. "Last time I promised you iced tea and gave you lemonade."

"It was good lemonade."

"Well, this is good iced tea, as far as that goes. Made with real tea."

"And real ice, I'll bet."

"You put the tea bags in a jar of cold water," she said, "and set the jar in the sun, and forget about them for a few hours. Then you put the jar in the fridge."

"You don't boil the water at all?"

"No, you don't have to. For years I thought you did but it turns out I was wrong. But I lost track of what I was getting at. Iced tea. Oh, right. This time you called and said, 'I'm on my way. Get ready to break out the lemonade.' So you were expecting lemonade this time, and here I'm giving you iced tea. Get it, Keller? Each time you get the opposite of what you expect."

"As long as it's just a question of iced tea or lemonade," he said, "I think I can ride with it."

"Well, you've always adjusted quickly to new realities," she said. "It's one of your strengths." She cocked her head and looked up at the ceiling. "Speaking of which. You were upstairs, you talked to him. What do you think?"

"He seemed all right."

"His old self?"

"Hardly that. But he listened to what I had to say and told me I'd done well. I think he was covering. I think he was clueless as to where I'd been, and he was covering."

"He does that a lot lately."

"It's got a real tea flavor, you know? And you don't boil the water at all?"

"Not unless you're in a hurry. Keller?"

He looked up from his glass of tea. She was sitting on the porch railing, her legs crossed, one flip-flop dangling from her toe.

She said, "Why both of them? If you do one, we get the final payment from the other one. This way there's nobody left to sign a check."

"He takes checks?"

"Just a manner of speaking. Point is, there's nobody left to pay up. It's not just a case of doing the second one for nothing. It cost you money to do it."

"I know."

"So explain it to me, will you?"

He took his time thinking about it. At length he said, "I didn't like the process."

"The process?"

"Making a choice. There was no way to choose, and tossing a coin didn't really help. I was still choosing, because I was choosing to accept the coin's choice, if you can follow me."

"The trail is faint," she said, "but I'm on it like a bloodhound."

"I figured they should both get the same," he said. "So I tossed twice, and got heads the first time and tails the second time, and I made appointments with both of them."

"Appointments."

"They were both good at setting up secret meetings. Strang told me how to get onto his property from the rear. There was an electric fence, but there was a place you could get over it."

"So he gave the fox the keys to the hen house."

"There wasn't any hen house, but there was a toolshed."

"And two men went into it that fateful morning and only one came out," Dot said. "And then you ran off to meet Moncrieff?"

"At the Omni downtown. He was having lunch at the restaurant, which according to him is pretty good. There's no men's room for the restaurant, you use the one off the hotel lobby. So we could meet there without ever having been in the same public space together."

"Clever."

"They were clever men, both of them. Anyway, it worked fine, same as with Strang. I used . . . well, you don't like to hear about that part of it."

"Not particularly, no."

He was silent for a time, sipping his iced tea, listening to the wind chimes when a breeze blew up. They had been still for a while when he said, "I was angry, Dot."

"I wondered about that."

"You know, I'm better off without that dog."

"Nelson."

"He was a good dog, and I liked him a lot, but they're a pain in the ass. Feed them, walk them."

"Sure."

"I liked her, too, but I'm a man who lived alone all my life. Living alone is what I'm good at."

"It's what you're used to."

"That's right. But even so, Dot. I'll walk along the street looking in windows and my eyes'll hit on a pair of earrings, and I'll be halfway in the door to buy them for her before I remember there's no point."

"All the earrings you bought for that girl."

"She liked getting them," he said, "and I liked buying them, so it worked out." He took a breath. "Anyway, I started getting angry, and I kept getting angry."

"At her."

"No, she did the right thing. I've got no reason to be angry at her." He pointed upward. "I got angry at him."

"For sending you to Cincinnati in the first place."

He shook his head. "Not him upstairs. A higher authority, the old man in the sky who flips all the coins."

"Oh, Him."

"Of course," he said, "by the time I did it, I wasn't angry. I was the way I always am. I just do what I'm there to do."

"You're a professional."

"I guess so."

"And you give value."

"Do I ever."

"Special summer rates," she said. "Murder on twofers."

Keller listened to the wind chimes, then to the silence. Eventually he would have to go back to his apartment and figure out what to do with the dog's dish. Eventually he and Dot would have to figure out what to do about the old man. For now, though, he just wanted to stay right where he was, sipping his glass of tea.

8

Keller on the Spot

Keller, drink in hand, agreed with the woman in the pink dress that it was a lovely evening. He threaded his way through a crowd of young marrieds on what he supposed you would call the patio. A waitress passed carrying a tray of drinks in stemmed glasses and he traded in his own for a fresh one. He sipped as he walked along, wondering what he was drinking. Some sort of vodka sour, he decided, and decided as well that he didn't need to narrow it down any further than that. He figured he'd have this one and one more, but he could have ten more if he wanted, because he wasn't working tonight. He could relax and cut back and have a good time.

Well, almost. He couldn't relax completely, couldn't cut back altogether. Because, while this might not be work, neither was it entirely recreational. The garden party this evening was a heaven-sent opportunity for reconnaissance, and he would use it to get a close look at his quarry. He had been handed a picture in the old man's study back in White Plains, and he had brought that picture with him to Dallas, but even the best photo wasn't the same as a glimpse of the fellow in the flesh, and in his native habitat.

And a lush habitat it was. Keller hadn't been inside the house yet, but it was clearly immense, a sprawling multilevel affair of innumerable large rooms. The grounds sprawled as well, covering an acre or two, with enough plants and shrubbery to stock an arboretum. Keller didn't know anything about flowers, but five minutes in a garden like this one had him thinking he ought to know more about the subject. Maybe they had evening classes at Hunter or NYU, maybe they'd take you on field trips to the Brooklyn Botanical Gardens. Maybe his life would be richer if he knew the names of the flowers, and whether they were annuals or perennials, and whatever else there was to know about them. Their soil requirements, say, and what bug killer to spray on their leaves, or what fertilizer to spread at their roots.

He walked along a brick path, smiling at this stranger, nodding at that one, and wound up standing alongside the swimming pool. Some twelve or fifteen people sat at poolside tables, talking and drinking, the volume of their conversation rising as they drank. In the enormous pool, a young boy swam back and forth, back and forth.

Keller felt a curious kinship with the kid. He was standing instead of swimming, but he felt as distant as the kid from everybody else around. There were two parties going on, he decided. There was the hearty social whirl of everybody else, and there was the solitude he felt in the midst of it all, identical to the solitude of the swimming boy.

Huge pool. The boy was swimming its width, but that dimension was still greater than the length of your typical backyard pool. Keller didn't know whether this was an Olympic pool, he wasn't quite

sure how big that would have to be, but he figured
you could just call it enormous and let it go at that.

Ages ago he'd heard about some college-boy stunt,
filling a swimming pool with Jell-O, and he'd wondered how many little boxes of the gelatin dessert it
would have required, and how the college boys
could have afforded it. It would cost a fortune, he
decided, to fill *this* pool with Jell-O—but if you could
afford the pool in the first place, he supposed the
Jell-O would be the least of your worries.

There were cut flowers on all the tables, and the
blooms looked like ones Keller had seen in the garden. It stood to reason. If you grew all these flowers,
you wouldn't have to order from the florist. You
could cut your own.

What good would it do, he wondered, to know the
names of all the shrubs and flowers? Wouldn't it just
leave you wanting to dig in the soil and grow your
own? And he didn't want to get into all that, for
God's sake. His apartment was all he needed or
wanted, and it was no place for a garden. He hadn't
even tried growing an avocado pit there, and he
didn't intend to. He was the only living thing in the
apartment, and that was the way he wanted to keep
it. The day that changed was the day he'd call the
exterminator.

So maybe he'd just forget about evening classes at
Hunter, and field trips to Brooklyn. If he wanted to
get close to nature he could walk in Central Park,
and if he didn't know the names of the flowers he
would just hold off on introducing himself to them.
And if—

Where was the kid?

The boy, the swimmer. Keller's companion in solitude. Where the hell did he go?

The pool was empty, its surface still. Keller saw a ripple toward the far end, saw a brace of bubbles break the surface.

He didn't react without thinking. That was how he'd always heard that sort of thing described, but that wasn't what happened, because the thoughts were there, loud and clear. *He's down there. He's in trouble. He's drowning.* And, echoing in his head in a voice that might have been Dot's, sour with exasperation: *Keller, for Christ's sake, do something!*

He set his glass on a table, shucked his coat, kicked off his shoes, dropped his pants and stepped out of them. Ages ago he'd earned a Red Cross lifesaving certificate, and the first thing they taught you was to strip before you hit the water. The six or seven seconds you spent peeling off your clothes would be repaid many times over in quickness and mobility.

But the strip show did not go unnoticed. Everybody at poolside had a comment, one more hilarious than the next. He barely heard them. In no time at all he was down to his underwear, and then he was out of range of their cleverness, hitting the water's surface in a flat racing dive, churning the water till he reached the spot where he'd seen the bubbles, then diving, eyes wide, barely noticing the burn of the chlorine.

Searching for the boy. Groping, searching, then finding him, reaching to grab hold of him. And pushing off against the bottom, lungs bursting, racing to reach the surface.

People were saying things to Keller, thanking him, congratulating him, but it wasn't really registering. A man clapped him on the back, a woman handed him a glass of brandy. He heard the word "hero" and realized that people were saying it all over the place, and applying it to him.

Hell of a note.

Keller sipped the brandy. It gave him heartburn, which assured him of its quality; good cognac always gave him heartburn. He turned to look at the boy. He was just a little fellow, twelve or thirteen years old, his hair lightened and his skin lightly bronzed by the summer sun. He was sitting up now, Keller saw, and looking none the worse for his near-death experience.

"Timothy," a woman said, "this is the man who saved your life. Do you have something to say to him?"

"Thanks," Timothy said, predictably.

"Is that all you have to say, young man?"

"It's enough," Keller said, and smiled. To the boy he said, "There's something I've always wondered. Did your whole life actually flash before your eyes?"

Timothy shook his head. "I got this cramp," he said, "and it was like my whole body turned into one big knot, and there wasn't anything I could do to untie it. And I didn't even think about drowning. I was just fighting the cramp, 'cause it hurt, and just about the next thing I knew I was up here coughing and puking up water." He made a face. "I must have swallowed half the pool. All I have to do is think about it and I can taste vomit and chlorine."

"Timothy," the woman said, and rolled her eyes.

"Something to be said for plain speech," an older man said. He had a mane of white hair and a pair of prominent white eyebrows, and his eyes were a vivid blue. He was holding a glass of brandy in one hand and a bottle in the other, and he reached with the bottle to fill Keller's glass to the brim. " 'Claret for boys, port for men,' " he said, " 'but he who would be a hero must drink brandy.' That's Samuel Johnson, although I may have gotten a word wrong."

The young woman patted his hand. "If you did, Daddy, I'm sure you just improved Mr. Johnson's wording."

"Dr. Johnson," he said, "and one could hardly do that. Improve the man's wording, that is. 'Being in a ship is being in a jail, with the chance of being drowned.' He said that as well, and I defy anyone to comment more trenchantly on the experience, or to say it better." He beamed at Keller. "I owe you more than a glass of brandy and a well-turned Johnsonian phrase. This little rascal whose life you've saved is my grandson, and the apple—nay, sir, the very nectarine—of my eye. And we'd have all stood around drinking and laughing while he drowned. You observed, and you acted, and God bless you for it."

What did you say to that? Keller wondered. *It was nothing? Well, shucks?* There had to be an apt phrase, and maybe Samuel Johnson could have found it, but he couldn't. So he said nothing, and just tried not to look po-faced.

"I don't even know your name," the white-haired man went on. "That's not remarkable in and of itself. I don't know half the people here, and I'm content to remain in my ignorance. But I ought to know your name, wouldn't you agree?"

Keller might have picked a name out of the air, but the one that leaped to mind was Boswell, and he couldn't say that to a man who quoted Samuel Johnson. So he supplied the name he'd traveled under, the one he'd signed when he checked into the hotel, the one on the driver's license and credit cards in his wallet.

"It's Michael Soderholm," he said, "and I can't even tell you the name of the fellow who brought me here. We met over drinks in the hotel bar and he said he was going to a party and it would be perfectly all right if I came along. I felt a little funny about it, but—"

"Please," the man said. "You can't possibly propose to apologize for your presence here. It's kept my grandson from a watery if chlorinated grave. And I've just told you I don't know half my guests, but that doesn't make them any the less welcome." He took a deep drink of his brandy and topped up both glasses. "Michael Soderholm," he said. "Swedish?"

"A mixture of everything," Keller said, improvising. "My great-grandfather Soderholm came over from Sweden, but my other ancestors came from all over Europe, plus I'm something like a sixteenth American Indian."

"Oh? Which tribe?"

"Cherokee," Keller said, thinking of the jazz tune.

"I'm an eighth Comanche," the man said. "So I'm afraid we're not tribal bloodbrothers. The rest's British Isles, a mix of Scots and Irish and English. Old Texas stock. But you're not Texan yourself."

"No."

"Well, it can't be helped, as the saying goes. Unless you decide to move here, and who's to say that you won't? It's a fine place for a man to live."

"Daddy thinks everybody should love Texas the way he does," the woman said.

"Everybody should," her father said. "The only thing wrong with Texans is we're a long-winded lot.

Look at the time it's taking me to introduce myself!
Mr. Soderholm, Mr. Michael Soderholm, my name's
Garrity, Wallace Penrose Garrity, and I'm your grate-
ful host this evening."

No kidding, thought Keller.

The party, lifesaving and all, took place on Saturday
night. The next day Keller sat in his hotel room and
watched the Cowboys beat the Vikings with a field
goal in the last three minutes of double overtime.
The game had seesawed back and forth, with inter-
ceptions and runbacks, and the announcers kept telling each other what a great game it was.

Keller supposed they were right. It had all the in-
gredients, and it wasn't the players' fault that he himself was entirely unmoved by their performance. He
could watch sports, and often did, but he almost
never got caught up in it. He had occasionally wondered if his work might have something to do with
it. On one level, when your job involved dealing regularly with life and death, how could you care if
some overpaid steroid abuser had a touchdown run
called back? And, on another level, you saw unortho-
dox solutions to a team's problems on the field.
When Emmitt Smith kept crashing through the Min-
nesota line, Keller found himself wondering why
they didn't deputize someone to shoot the son of a
bitch in the back of the neck, right below his star-
covered helmet.

Still, it was better than watching golf, say, which
in turn had to be better than playing golf. And he
couldn't get out and work, because there was nothing
for him to do. Last night's reconnaissance mission
had been both better and worse than he could have
hoped, and what was he supposed to do now, park

his rented Ford across the street from the Garrity mansion and clock the comings and goings?

No need for that. He could bide his time, just so he got there in time for Sunday dinner.

"Some more potatoes, Mr. Soderholm?"

"They're delicious," Keller said. "But I'm full. Really."

"And we can't keep calling you Mr. Soderholm," Garrity said. "I've only held off this long for not knowing whether you prefer Mike or Michael."

"Mike's fine," Keller said.

"Then Mike it is. And I'm Wally, Mike, or W.P., though there are those who call me 'The Walrus.' "

Timmy laughed, and clapped both hands over his mouth.

"Though never to his face," said the woman who'd offered Keller more potatoes. She was Ellen Garrity, Timmy's aunt and Garrity's daughter-in-law, and Keller was now instructed to call her Ellie. Her husband, a big-shouldered fellow who seemed to be smiling bravely through the heartbreak of male-pattern baldness, was Garrity's son Hank.

Keller remembered Timothy's mother from the night before, but hadn't got her name at the time, or her relationship to Garrity. She was Rhonda Sue Butler, as it turned out, and everybody called her Rhonda Sue, except for her husband, who called her Ronnie. His name was Doak Butler, and he looked like a college jock who'd been too light for pro ball, although he now seemed to be closing the gap.

Hank and Ellie, Doak and Rhonda Sue. And, at the far end of the table, Vanessa, who was married to Wally but who was clearly not the mother of Hank or Rhonda Sue, or anyone else. Keller supposed you could describe her as Wally's trophy wife, a sign of his success. She was young, no older than Wally's kids, and she looked to be well bred and elegant, and she even had the good grace to hide the boredom Keller was sure she felt.

And that was the lot of them. Wally and Vanessa, Hank and Ellen, Doak and Rhonda Sue. And Timothy, who he was assured had been swimming that very afternoon, the aquatic equivalent of getting right back on the horse. He'd had no cramps this time, but he'd had an attentive eye kept on him throughout.

Seven of them, then. And Keller . . . also known as Mike.

"So you're here on business," Wally said. "And stuck here over the weekend, which is the worst part of a business trip, as far as I'm concerned. More trouble than it's worth to fly back to Chicago?"

The two of them were in Wally's den, a fine room paneled in knotty pecan and trimmed out in red leather, with western doodads on the walls—here a branding iron, there a longhorn skull. Keller had accepted a brandy and declined a cigar, and the aroma of Wally's Havana was giving him second thoughts. Keller didn't smoke, but from the smell of it the cigar wasn't a mere matter of smoking. It was more along the lines of a religious experience.

"Seemed that way," Keller said. He'd supplied Chicago as Michael Soderholm's home base, though Soderholm's license placed him in Southern California. "By the time I fly there and back . . ."

"You've spent your weekend on airplanes. Well, it's our good fortune you decided to stay. Now what I'd like to do is find a way to make it your good fortune as well."

"You've already done that," Keller told him. "I crashed a great party last night and actually got to feel like a hero for a few minutes. And tonight I sit down to a fine dinner with nice people and get to top it off with a glass of outstanding brandy."

The heartburn told him how outstanding it was.

"What I had in mind," Wally said smoothly, "was to get you to work for me."

Whom did he want him to kill? Keller almost blurted out the question until he remembered that Garrity didn't know what he did for a living.

"You won't say who you work for," Garrity went on.

"I can't."

"Because the job's hush-hush for now. Well, I can respect that, and from the hints you've dropped I gather you're here scouting out something in the way of mergers and acquisitions."

"That's close."

"And I'm sure it's well paid, and you must like the work or I don't think you'd stay with it. So what do I have to do to get you to switch horses and come work for me? I'll tell you one thing—Chicago's a real nice place, but nobody who ever moved from there to Big D went around with a sour face about it. I don't know you well yet, but I can tell you're our kind of people and Dallas'll be your kind of town. And I don't know what they're paying you, but I suspect I can top it, and offer you a stake in a growing company with all sorts of attractive possibilities."

Keller listened, nodded judiciously, sipped a little brandy. It was amazing, he thought, the way things came along when you weren't looking for them. It was straight out of Horatio Alger, for God's sake— Ragged Dick stops the runaway horse and saves the daughter of the captain of industry, and the next thing you know he's president of IBM with rising expectations.

"Maybe I'll have that cigar after all," he said.

"Now, come on, Keller," Dot said. "You know the rules. I can't tell you that."

"It's sort of important," he said.

"One of the things the client buys," she said, "is confidentiality. That's what he wants and it's what we provide. Even if the agent in place—"

"The agent in place?"

"That's you," she said. "You're the agent, and Dallas is the place. Even if you get caught red-handed, the confidentiality of the client remains uncompromised. And do you know why?"

"Because the agent in place knows how to keep mum."

"Mum's the word," she agreed, "and there's no question you're the strong silent type, but even if your lip loosens you can't sink a ship if you don't know when it's sailing."

Keller thought that over. "You lost me," he said.

"Yeah, it came out a little abstruse, didn't it? Point is you can't tell what you don't know, Keller, which is why the agent doesn't get to know the client's name."

"Dot," he said, trying to sound injured. "Dot, how long have you known me?"

"Ages, Keller. Many lifetimes."

"Many lifetimes?"

"We were in Atlantis together. Look, I know nobody's going to catch you red-handed, and I know you wouldn't blab if they did. But *I* can't tell what *I* don't know."

"Oh."

"Right. I think the spies call it a double cutout. The client made arrangements with somebody we know, and that person called us. But he didn't give us the client's name, and why should he? And, come to think of it, Keller, why do you have to know, anyway?"

He had his answer ready. "It might not be a single," he said.

"Oh?"

"The target's always got people around him," he said, "and the best way to do it might be a sort of group plan, if you follow me."

"Two for the price of one."

"Or three or four," he said. "But if one of those innocent bystanders turned out to be the client, it might make things a little awkward."

"Well, I can see where we might have trouble collecting the final payment."

"If we knew for a fact that the client was fishing for trout in Montana," he said, "it's no problem. But if he's here in Dallas—"

"It would help to know his name." She sighed. "Give me an hour or two, huh? Then call me back."

If he knew who the client was, the client could have an accident.

It would have to be an artful accident too. It would have to look good not only to the police but to whoever was aware of the client's own intentions. The local go-between, the helpful fellow who'd hooked up the client to the old man in White Plains, and thus to Keller, could be expected to cast a cold eye on any suspicious death. So it would have to be a damn good accident, but Keller had managed a few of those in his day. It took a little planning, but it wasn't brain surgery. You just figured out a method and took your best shot.

It might take some doing. If, as he rather hoped, the client was some business rival in Houston or Denver or San Diego, he'd have to slip off to that city without anyone noting his absence. Then, having induced a quick attack of accidental death, he'd fly back to Dallas and hang around until someone called him off the case. He'd need different ID for Houston or Denver or San Diego—it wouldn't do to overexpose Michael Soderholm—and he'd need to mask his actions from all concerned—Garrity, his homicidal rival, and, perhaps most important, Dot and the old man.

All told, it was a great deal more complicated (if easier to stomach) than the alternative.

Which was to carry out the assignment professionally and kill Wallace Penrose Garrity the first good chance he got.

And he really didn't want to do that. He'd eaten at the man's table, he'd drunk the man's brandy, he'd smoked the man's cigars. He'd been offered not merely a job but a well-paid executive position with a future, and, later that night, light-headed from alcohol and nicotine, he'd had fantasies of taking Wally up on it.

Hell, why not? He could live out his days as Michael Soderholm, doing whatever unspecified tasks Garrity was hiring him to perform. He probably lacked the requisite experience, but how hard could it be to pick up the skills he needed as he went along? Whatever he had to do, it would be easier than flying from town to town killing people. He could learn on the job. He could pull it off.

The fantasy had about as much substance as a dream, and, like a dream, it was gone when he awoke the next morning. No one would put him on the payroll without some sort of background check, and the most cursory scan would knock him out of the box. Michael Soderholm had no more substance than the fake ID in his wallet.

Even if he somehow finessed a background check, even if the old man in White Plains let him walk out of one life and into another, he knew he couldn't really make it work. He already had a life. Misshapen though it was, it fit him like a glove.

Other lives made tempting fantasies. Running a print shop in Roseburg, Oregon, living in a cute little house with a mansard roof—it was something to tease yourself with while you went on being the person you had no choice but to be. This latest fantasy was just more of the same.

He went out for a sandwich and a cup of coffee. He got back in his car and drove around for a while. Then he found a pay phone and called White Plains.

"Do a single," Dot said.

"How's that?"

"No added extras, no free dividends. Just do what they signed on for."

"Because the client's here in town," he said. "Well, I could work around that if I knew his name. I could make sure he was out of it."

"Forget it," Dot said. "The client wants a long and happy life for everybody but the designated vic. Maybe the DV's close associates are near and dear to the client. That's just a guess, but all that really matters is that nobody else gets hurt. Capeesh?"

" 'Capeesh?' "

"It's Italian, it means—"

"I know what it means. It just sounded odd from your lips, that's all. But yes, I understand." He took a breath. "Whole thing may take a little time," he said.

"Then here comes the good news," she said. "Time's not of the essence. They don't care how long it takes, just so you get it right."

"I understand W.P. offered you a job," Vanessa said. "I know he hopes you'll take him up on it."

"I think he was just being generous," Keller told her. "I was in the right place at the right time, and he'd like to do me a favor, but I don't think he really expects me to come to work for him."

"He'd like it if you did," she said, "or he never would have made the offer. He'd have just given you money, or a car, or something like that. And as far as what he expects, well, W.P. generally expects to get whatever he wants. Because that's the way things usually work out."

And had she been saving up her pennies to get things to work out a little differently? You had to wonder. Was she truly under Garrity's spell, in awe of his power, as she seemed to be? Or was she only in it for the money, and was there a sharp edge of irony under her worshipful remarks?

Hard to say. Hard to tell about any of them. Was Hank the loyal son he appeared to be, content to live in the old man's shadow and take what got tossed his way? Or was he secretly resentful and ambitious?

What about the son-in-law, Doak? On the surface, he looked to be delighted with the aftermath of his college football career—his work for his father-in-law consisted largely of playing golf with business associates and drinking with them afterward. But did he seethe inside, sure he was fit for greater things?

How about Hank's wife, Ellie? She struck Keller as an unlikely Lady Macbeth. Keller could fabricate scenarios in which she or Rhonda Sue had a reason for wanting Wally dead, but they were the sort of thing you dreamed up while watching reruns of *Dallas* and trying to guess who shot J.R. Maybe one of their marriages was in trouble. Maybe Garrity had put the moves on his daughter-in-law, or maybe a little too much brandy had led him into his daughter's bedroom now and then. Maybe Doak or Hank was playing footsie with Vanessa. Maybe . . .

Pointless to speculate, he decided. You could go around and around like that and it didn't get you anywhere. Even if he managed to dope out which of them was the client, then what? Having saved young Timothy, and thus feeling obligated to spare his doting grandfather, what was he going to do? Kill the boy's father? Or mother or aunt or uncle?

Of course he could just go home. He could even explain the situation to the old man. Nobody loved it when you took yourself off a contract for personal reasons, but it wasn't something they could talk you out of, either. If you made a habit of that sort of thing, well, that was different, but that wasn't the case with Keller. He was a solid pro. Quirky perhaps, even whimsical, but a pro all the way. You told him what to do and he did it.

So, if he had a personal reason to bow out, you honored it. You let him come home and sit on the porch and drink iced tea with Dot.

And you picked up the phone and sent somebody else to Dallas.

Because either way the job was going to be done.

If a hit man had a change of heart, it would be followed in short order by a change of hit man. If Keller didn't pull the trigger, somebody else would.

His mistake, Keller thought savagely, was to jump in the goddam pool in the first place. All he'd had to do was look the other way and let the little bastard drown. A few days later he could have taken Garrity out, possibly making it look like suicide, a natural consequence of despondency over the boy's tragic accident.

But no, he thought, glaring at himself in the mirror. No, you had to go and get involved. You had to be a hero, for God's sake. Had to strip down to your skivvies and prove you deserved that junior lifesaving certificate the Red Cross gave you all those years ago.

He wondered whatever happened to that certificate.

It was gone, of course, like everything he'd ever owned in his childhood and youth. Gone like his high school diploma, like his Boy Scout merit badge sash, like his stamp collection and his sack of marbles and his stack of baseball cards. He didn't mind that these things were gone, didn't waste time wishing he had them any more than he wanted those years back.

But he wondered what physically became of them. The lifesaving certificate, for instance. Someone might have thrown out his baseball cards, or sold his stamp collection to a dealer. A certificate, though, wasn't something you threw out, nor was it something anyone else would want.

Maybe it was buried in a landfill, or in a stack of paper ephemera in the back of some thrift shop. Maybe some pack rat had rescued it, and maybe it was now part of an extensive collection of junior lifesaving certificates, housed in an album and cherished as living history, the pride and joy of a collector ten times as quirky and whimsical as Keller could ever dream of being.

He wondered how he felt about that. His certificate, his small achievement, living on in some eccentric's collection. On the one hand, it was a kind of immortality, wasn't it? On the other hand, well, whose certificate was it, anyway? He'd been the one to earn it, breaking the instructor's choke hold, spinning him and grabbing him in a cross-chest carry, towing the big lug to the side of the pool. It was his accomplishment and it had his name on it, so didn't it belong on his own wall or nowhere?

All in all, he couldn't say he felt strongly either way. The certificate, when all was said and done, was only a piece of paper. What was important was the skill itself, and what was truly remarkable was that he'd retained it.

Because of it, Timothy Butler was alive and well. Which was all well and good for the boy, and a great big headache for Keller.

Later, sitting with a cup of coffee, Keller thought some more about Wallace Penrose Garrity, a man who increasingly seemed to have not an enemy in the world.

Suppose Keller had let the kid drown. Suppose he just plain hadn't noticed the boy's disappearance beneath the water, just as everyone else had failed to notice it. Garrity would have been despondent. It was his party, his pool, his failure to provide supervision. He'd probably have blamed himself for the boy's death.

When Keller took him out, it would have been the kindest thing he could have done for him.

He caught the waiter's eye and signaled for more coffee. He'd just given himself something to think about.

"Mike," Garrity said, coming toward him with a hand outstretched. "Sorry to keep you waiting. Had a phone call from a fellow with a hankering to buy a little five-acre lot of mine on the south edge of town. Thing is, I don't want to sell it to him."

"I see."

"But there's ten acres on the other side of town I'd be perfectly happy to sell to him, but he'll only want it if he thinks of it himself. So that left me on the phone longer than I would have liked. Now what would you say to a glass of brandy?"

"Maybe a small one."

Garrity led the way to the den, poured drinks for both of them. "You should have come earlier," he said. "In time for dinner. I hope you know you don't need an invitation. There'll always be a place for you at our table."

"Well," Keller said.

"I know you can't talk about it," Garrity said, "but I hope your project here in town is shaping up nicely."

"Slow but sure," Keller said.

"Some things can't be hurried," Garrity allowed, and sipped brandy, and winced. If Keller hadn't been looking for it, he might have missed the shadow that crossed his host's face.

Gently he said, "Is the pain bad, Wally?"

"How's that, Mike?"

Keller put his glass on the table. "I spoke to Dr.

Jacklin," he said. "I know what you're going through."

"That son of a bitch," Garrity said, "was supposed to keep his mouth shut."

"Well, he thought it was all right to talk to me," Keller said. "He thought I was Dr. Edward Fishman from the Mayo Clinic."

"Calling for a consultation."

"Something like that."

"I did go to Mayo," Garrity said, "but they didn't need to call Harold Jacklin to double-check their results. They just confirmed his diagnosis and told me not to buy any long-playing records." He looked to one side. "They said they couldn't say for sure how much time I had left, but that the pain would be manageable for a while. And then it wouldn't."

"I see."

"And I'd have all my faculties for a while," he said. "And then I wouldn't."

Keller didn't say anything.

"Well, hell," Garrity said. "A man wants to take the bull by the horns, doesn't he? I decided I'd go out for a walk with a shotgun and have a little hunting accident. Or I'd be cleaning a handgun here at my desk and have it go off. But it turned out I just couldn't tolerate the idea of killing myself. Don't know why, can't explain it, but that seems to be the way I'm made."

He picked up his glass and looked at the brandy. "Funny how we hang on to life," he said. "Something else Sam Johnson said, said there wasn't a week of his life he'd voluntarily live through again. I've had more good times than bad, Mike, and even the bad times haven't been that godawful, but I think I know what he was getting at. I wouldn't want to repeat any of it, but that doesn't mean there's a minute of it I'd have been willing to miss. I don't want to miss whatever's coming next, either, and I don't guess Dr. Johnson did either. That's what keeps us going, isn't it? Wanting to find out what's around the next bend in the river."

"I guess so."

"I thought that would make the end easier to face," he said. "Not knowing when it was coming, or how or where. And I recalled that years ago a fellow told me to let him know if I ever needed to have somebody killed. 'You just let me know,' he said, and I laughed, and that was the last said on the subject. A month or so ago I looked up his number and called him, and he gave me another number to call."

"And you put out a contract."

"Is that the expression? Then that's what I did."

"Suicide by proxy," Keller said.

"And I guess you're holding my proxy," Garrity said, and drank some brandy. "You know, the thought flashed across my mind that first night, talking with you after you pulled my grandson out of the pool. I got this little glimmer, but I told myself I was being ridiculous. A hired killer doesn't turn up and save somebody's life."

"It's out of character," Keller agreed.

"Besides, what would you be doing at the party in the first place? Wouldn't you stay out of sight and wait until you could get me alone?"

"If I'd been thinking straight," Keller said. "I told myself it wouldn't hurt to have a look around. And this joker from the hotel bar assured me I had nothing to worry about. 'Half the town'll be at Wally's tonight,' he said."

"Half the town was. You wouldn't have tried anything that night, would you?"

"God, no."

"I remember thinking, I hope he's not here. I hope it's not tonight. Because I was enjoying the party and I didn't want to miss anything. But you *were* there, and a good thing, wasn't it?"

"Yes."

"Saved the boy from drowning. According to the Chinese, you save somebody's life, you're responsible for him for the rest of *your* life. Because you've interfered with the natural order of things. That make sense to you?"

"Not really."

"Or me either. You can't beat them for whipping up a meal or laundering a shirt, but they've got some queer ideas on other subjects. Of course they'd probably say the same for some of my notions."

"Probably."

Garrity looked at his glass. "You called my doctor," he said. "Must have been to confirm a suspicion you already had. What tipped you off? Is it starting to show in my face, or the way I move around?"

Keller shook his head. "I couldn't find anybody else with a motive," he said, "or a grudge against you. You were the only one left. And then I remembered seeing you wince once or twice, and try to hide it. I barely noticed it at the time, but then I started to think about it."

"I thought it would be easier than doing it myself," Garrity said. "I thought I'd just let a professional take me by surprise. I'd be like an old bull elk on a hillside, never expecting the bullet that takes him out in his prime."

"It makes sense."

"No, it doesn't. Because the elk didn't arrange for the hunter to be there. Far as the elk knows, he's all alone there. He's not wondering every damn day if today's the day. He's not bracing himself, trying to sense the crosshairs centering on his shoulder."

"I never thought of that."

"Neither did I," said Garrity. "Or I never would have called that fellow in the first place. Mike, what the hell are you doing here tonight? Don't tell me you came over to kill me."

"I came to tell you I can't."

"Because we've come to know each other."

Keller nodded.

"I grew up on a farm," Garrity said. "One of those vanishing family farms you hear about, and of course it's vanished, and I say good riddance. But we raised our own beef and pork, you know, and we kept a milk cow and a flock of laying hens. And we never named the animals we were going to wind up eating. The milk cow had a name, but not the bull calf she dropped. The breeder sow's name was Elsie, but we never named her piglets."

"Makes sense," Keller said.

"I guess it doesn't take a Chinaman to see how you can't kill me once you've hauled Timmy out of the drink. Let alone after you've sat at my table and smoked my cigars. Reminds me, you care for a cigar?"

"No, thank you."

"Well, where do we go from here, Mike? I have to say I'm relieved. I feel like I've been bracing myself for a bullet for weeks now. All of a sudden I've got a new lease on life. I'd say this calls for a drink except we're already having one, and you've scarcely touched yours."

"There is one thing," Keller said.

* * *

He left the den while Garrity made his phone call. Timothy was in the living room, puzzling over a chessboard. Keller played a game with him and lost badly. "Can't win 'em all," he said, and tipped over his king.

"I was going to checkmate you," the boy said. "In a few more moves."

"I could see it coming," Keller told him.

He went back to the den. Garrity was selecting a cigar from his humidor. "Sit down," he said. "I'm fixing to smoke one of these things. If you won't kill me, maybe it will."

"You never know."

"I made the call, Mike, and it's all taken care of. Be a while before the word filters up and down the chain of command, but sooner or later they'll call you up and tell you the client changed his mind. He paid in full and called off the job."

They talked some, then sat a while in silence. At length Keller said he ought to get going. "I should be at my hotel," he said, "in case they call."

"Be a couple of days, won't it?"

"Probably," he said, "but you never know. If everyone involved makes a phone call right away, the word could get to me in a couple of hours."

"Calling you off, telling you to come home. Be glad to get home, I bet."

"It's nice here," he said, "but yes, I'll be glad to get home."

"Wherever it is, they say there's no place like it." Garrity leaned back, then allowed himself to wince at the pain that came over him. "If it never hurts worse than this," he said, "then I can stand it. But of course it will get worse. And I'll decide I can stand *that*, and then it'll get worse again."

There was nothing to say to that.

"I guess I'll know when it's time to do something," Garrity said. "And who knows? Maybe my heart'll cut out on me out of the blue. Or I'll get hit by a bus, or I don't know what. Struck by lightning?"

"It could happen."

"Anything can happen," Garrity agreed. He got to his feet. "Mike," he said, "I guess we won't be seeing any more of each other, and I have to say I'm a little bit sorry about that. I've truly enjoyed our time together."

"So have I, Wally."

"I wondered, you know, what he'd be like. The man they'd send to do this kind of work. I don't know what I expected, but you're not it."

He stuck out his hand, and Keller gripped it. "Take care," Garrity said. "Be well, Mike."

Back at his hotel, Keller took a hot bath and got a good night's sleep. In the morning he went out for breakfast, and when he got back there was a message at the desk for him: *Mr. Soderholm—please call your office.*

He called from a pay phone, even though it didn't matter, and he was careful not to overreact when Dot told him to come home, the mission was aborted.

"You told me I had all the time in the world," he said. "If I'd known the guy was in such a rush—"

"Keller," she said, "it's a good thing you waited. What he did, he changed his mind."

"He changed his mind?"

"It used to be a woman's prerogative," Dot said, "but now we've got equality between the sexes, so that means anyone can do it. It works out fine because we're getting paid in full. So kick the dust of Texas off your feet and come on home."

"I'll do that," he said, "but I may hang out here for a few more days."

"Oh?"

"Or even a week," he said. "It's a pretty nice town."

"Don't tell me you're itching to move there, Keller. We've been through this before."

"Nothing like that," he said, "but there's this girl I met."

"Oh, Keller."

"Well, she's nice," he said. "And if I'm off the job there's no reason not to have a date or two with her, is there?"

"As long as you don't decide to move in."

"She's not that nice," he said, and Dot laughed and told him not to change.

He hung up and drove around and found a movie he'd been meaning to see. The next morning he packed and checked out of his hotel.

He drove across town and got a room on the motel strip, paying cash for four nights in advance and registering as J. D. Smith from Los Angeles.

There was no girl he'd met, no girl he wanted to meet. But it wasn't time to go home yet.

He had unfinished business, and four days should give him time to do it. Time for Wallace Garrity to get used to the idea of not feeling those imaginary crosshairs on his shoulder blades.

But not so much time that the pain would be too much to bear.

And, sometime in those four days, Keller would give him a gift. If he could, he'd make it look natural—a heart attack, say, or an accident. In any event it would be swift and without warning, and as close as he could make it to painless.

And it would be unexpected. Garrity would never see it coming.

Keller frowned, trying to figure out how he would manage it. It would be a lot trickier than the task that had drawn him to town originally, but he'd brought it on himself. Getting involved, fishing the boy out of the pool. He'd interfered with the natural order of things. He was under an obligation.

It was the least he could do.

9

Keller's Last Refuge

Keller, reaching for a red carnation, paused to finger one of the green ones. Kelly green it was, and vivid. Maybe it was an autumnal phenomenon, he thought. The leaves turned red and gold, the flowers turned green.

"It's dyed," said the florist, reading his mind. "They started dyeing them for St. Patrick's Day, and that's when I sell the most of them, but they caught on in a small way year-round. Would you like to wear one?"

Would he? Keller found himself weighing the move, then reminded himself it wasn't an option. "No," he said. "It has to be red."

"I quite agree," the little man said, selecting one of the blood-red blooms. "I'm a traditionalist myself. Green flowers. Why, how could the bees tell the blooms from the foliage?"

Keller said it was a good question.

"And here's another. Shall we lay it *across* the buttonhole and pin it to the lapel, or shall we insert it *into* the buttonhole?"

It was a poser, all right. Keller asked the man for his recommendation.

"It's controversial," the florist said. "But I look at

it this way. Why *have* a buttonhole if you're not going to *use* it?''

Keller, suit pressed and shoes shined and a red carnation in his lapel, boarded the Metroliner at Penn Station. He'd picked up a copy of *GQ* at a newsstand in the station, and he made it last all the way to Washington. Now and then his eyes strayed from the page to his boutonniere.

It would have been nice to know where the magazine stood on the buttonhole issue, but they had nothing to say on the subject. According to the florist, who admittedly had a small stake in the matter, Keller had nothing to worry about.

"Not every man can wear a flower," the man had told him. "On one it will look frivolous, on another foppish. But with you—"

"It looks okay?"

"More than okay," the man said. "You wear it with a certain flair. Or dare I say panache?"

Panache, Keller thought.

Panache had not been the object. Keller was just following directions. Wear a particular flower, board a particular train, stand in front of the B. Dalton bookstore in Union Station with a particular magazine until the client—a particular man himself, from the sound of it—took the opportunity to make contact.

It struck Keller as a pretty Mickey Mouse way to do things, and in the old days the old man would have shot it down. But the old man wasn't himself these days, and something like this, with props and recognition signals, was the least of it.

"Wear the flower," Dot had told him in the kitchen

of the big old house in White Plains. "Wear the flower, carry the magazine—"

"Tote the barge, lift the bale . . ."

"—and do the job, Keller. At least he's not turning everything down. What's wrong with a flower, anyway? Don't tell me you've got Thoreau on the brain."

"Thoreau?"

"He said to beware of enterprises that require new clothes. He never said a thing about carnations."

At ten past noon Keller was at his post, wearing the flower, brandishing the magazine. He stood there like a tin soldier for half an hour, then left his post to find a men's room. He returned feeling like a deserter, but took a minute to scan the area, looking for someone who was looking for him. He didn't find anybody, so he planted himself where he'd been standing earlier and just went on standing there.

At a quarter after one he went to a fast-food counter for a hamburger. At ten minutes of two he found a phone and called White Plains. Dot answered, and before he could get out a full sentence she told him to come home.

"Job's been canceled," she said. "The guy phoned up and called it off. But you must have been halfway to D.C. by then."

"I've been standing around since noon," Keller said. "I hate just standing around."

"Everybody does, Keller. At least you'll make a couple of dollars. It should have been half in advance . . ."

"*Should* have been?"

"He wanted to meet you first and find out if you thought the job was doable. *Then* he'd pay the first half, with the balance due and payable upon execution."

Execution was the word for it. He said, "But he aborted before he met me. Doesn't he like panache?"

"Panache?"

"The flower. Maybe he didn't like the way I was wearing it."

"Keller," she said, "he never even saw you. He called here around ten-thirty. You were still on the train. Anyway, how many ways are there to wear a flower?"

"Don't get me started," he said. "If he didn't pay anything in advance—"

"He paid. But not half."

"What did he pay?"

"It's not a fortune. He sent us a thousand dollars. Your end of that's nothing to retire on, but all you had to do besides stand around was sit around, and there are people in this world who work harder and get less for it."

"And I'll bet it makes *them* happy," he said, "to hear how much better off they are than the poor bastards starving in Somalia."

"Poor Keller. What are you going to do now?"

"Get on a train and come home."

"Keller," she said, "you're in our nation's capital. Go to the Smithsonian. Take a citizen's tour of the White House. Slow down and smell the flowers."

He rang off and caught the next train.

He went home and hung up his suit, but not before discarding the touch of panache from his lapel. He'd already gotten rid of the magazine.

That was on a Wednesday. Monday morning he was in a booth at one of his usual breakfast places, a Greek coffee shop on Second Avenue. He was reading the *Times* and eating a plate of salami and eggs when a fellow said, "Mind if I join you?" He didn't wait for an answer, either, but slid unbidden into the seat across from Keller.

Keller eyed him. The guy was around forty, wearing a dark suit and an unassertive tie. He was clean-shaven and his hair was combed. He didn't look like a nut.

"You ought to wear a boutonniere," the man said. "It adds, I don't know, a certain something."

"Panache," Keller suggested.

"You know," the man said, "that's just what I was going for. It was on the tip of my tongue. Panache."

Keller didn't say anything.

"You're probably wondering what this is all about."

Keller shook his head.

"You're not?"

"I figure more will be revealed."

That drew a smile. "A cool customer," the fellow said. "Well, I'm not surprised." His hand dipped into the front of his suit jacket, and Keller braced himself with both hands on the edge of the table, waiting to see the hand come out with a gun.

Instead the hand emerged clutching a flat leather wallet, which the man flipped open to disclose an ID. The photo matched the face across the table from Keller, and the accompanying card identified the face as that of one Roger Keith Bascomb, an operative of something called the National Security Resource.

Keller handed the ID back to its owner.

"Thanks," Bascomb said. "You were all set to flip the table on me, weren't you?"

"Why would I do that?"

"Never mind. You're alert, which is all to the good.

And I'm not surprised. I know who you are, and I know *what* you are."

"Just a man trying to eat his breakfast," Keller said.

"And a man who's evidently not put off by all that scary stuff about cholesterol. Salami and eggs! I have to say I admire you, Keller. I bet that's real coffee, too, isn't it?"

"It's not great," Keller said, "but it's the genuine article."

"My breakfast's an oat bran muffin," Bascomb said, "and I wash it down with decaf. But I didn't come here to put in a bid for sympathy."

Just as well, Keller thought.

"I don't want to make this overly dramatic," Bascomb said, "but it's hard to avoid. Mr. Keller, your country has need of your services."

"My country?"

"The United States of America. *That* country."

"My services?"

"The very sort of services you rode down to Washington prepared to perform. I think we both know what sort of services I'm talking about."

"I could argue the point," Keller said.

"You could."

"But I'll let it go."

"Good," Bascomb said, "and I in turn will apologize for the wild goose chase. We needed to get a line on you and find out a few things about you."

"So you picked me up in Union Station and tagged me back to New York."

"I'm afraid we did, yes."

"And learned who I was, and checked me out."

"Like a book from a library," Bascomb said. "Just

what we did. You see, Keller, your uncle would prefer to cut out the cutout man.''

''My uncle?''

''Sam. We don't want to run everything through
What's-his-name in White Plains. This is strictly
need-to-know, and he doesn't.''

''So you want to be able to work directly with me.''

''Right.''

''And you want me to . . .''

''To do what you do best, Keller.''

Keller ate some salami, ate some eggs, drank
some coffee.

''I don't think so,'' he said.

''I beg your pardon?''

''I'm not interested,'' Keller said. ''If I ever did
what you're implying, well, I don't do it anymore.''

''You've retired.''

''That's right. And, even if I hadn't, I wouldn't go
behind the old man's back, not to work for someone
who sent me off on a fool's errand with a flower in
my lapel.''

''You wore that flower,'' Bascomb said, ''with the
air of a man who never left home without one. I've
got to tell you, Keller, you were born to wear a red
carnation.''

''That's good to know,'' Keller said, ''but it doesn't
change anything.''

''Well, the same thing goes for your reluctance.''

''How's that?''

''It's good to know how you feel,'' Bascomb said.
''Good to get it all out in the open. But it doesn't
change anything. We need you, and you're in.''

He smiled, waiting for Keller to voice an objection.
Keller let him wait.

''Think it through,'' Bascomb suggested. ''Think

U.S. Attorney's Office. Think Internal Revenue Service. Think of all the resources of a powerful—some say too powerful—federal government, lined up against one essentially defenseless citizen.''

Keller, in spite of himself, found himself thinking it through.

"And now forget all that," said Bascomb, waving it all away like smoke. "And think of the opportunity you have to serve your nation. I don't know if you've ever thought of yourself as a patriot, Keller, but if you look deep within yourself I suspect you'll find wellsprings of patriotism you never knew existed. You're an American, Keller, and here you are with a chance to do something for America and save your own ass in the process.''

Keller's words surprised him. "My father was a soldier," he said.

> Breathes there the man, with soul so dead,
> Who never to himself hath said,
> This is my own, my native land!

Keller closed the book and set it aside. The lines of Sir Walter Scott's were quoted in a short story Keller had read in high school. The titular man without a country was Philip Nolan, doomed to wander the world all his life because he'd passed up his own chance to be a patriot.

Keller didn't have the story on hand, but he'd found the poetry in *Bartlett's Familiar Quotations*, and now he looked up *patriotism* in the index. The best thing he found was Samuel Johnson's word on the subject. "Patriotism," Dr. Johnson asserted, "is the last refuge of a scoundrel.''

The sentence had a nice ring to it, but he wasn't

sure he knew what Johnson was getting at. Wasn't a scoundrel the furthest thing from a patriot? In simplest terms, a patriot would seem unequivocally to be one of the good guys. At the very least he devoted himself to serving his nation and his fellow citizens, and often enough he wound up giving the last full measure of devotion, sacrificing himself, dying so that others might live in freedom.

Nathan Hale, say, regretting that he had but one life to give for his country. John Paul Jones, declaring that he had not yet begun to fight. David Farragut, damning the torpedoes, urging full speed ahead.

Good guys, Keller thought.

Whereas a scoundrel had to be a bad guy by definition. So how could he be a patriot, or take refuge in patriotism?

Keller thought about it, and decided the scoundrel might take refuge in the *appearance* of patriotism, wrapping selfish acts in the cloak of selflessness. A sort of false patriotism, to cloak his base motives.

But a true scoundrel couldn't be a genuine patriot. Or could he?

If you looked at it objectively, he had to admit, then he was probably a scoundrel himself. He didn't much feel like a scoundrel. He felt like your basic New York single guy, living alone, eating out or bringing home takeout, schlepping his wash to the laundromat, doing the *Times* crossword with his morning coffee. Working out at the gym, starting doomed relationships with women, going to the movies by himself. There were eight million stories in the naked city, most of them not very interesting, and his was one of them.

Except that every once in a while he got a phone

call from a man in White Plains. And packed a bag and caught a plane and killed somebody.

Hard to argue the point. Man behaves like that, he's a scoundrel. Case closed.

Now he had a chance to be a patriot.

Not to seem like one, because no one would know about this, not even Dot and the old man. Bascomb had made himself very clear on the point. "Not a word to anyone, and if anything goes wrong, it's the same system as *Mission: Impossible*. We never heard of you. You're on your own, and if you try to tell anybody you're working for the government, they'll just laugh in your face. If you give them my name, they'll say they never heard of me. Because they never did."

"Because it's not your name."

"And you might have trouble finding the National Security Resource in the phone book. Or anywhere else, like the *Congressional Record*, say. We keep a pretty low profile. You ever hear of us before? Well, neither did anybody else."

There'd be no glory in it for Keller, and plenty of risk. That was how it worked when he did the old man's bidding, but for those efforts he was well compensated. All he'd get working for NSR was an allowance for expenses, and not a very generous one at that.

So he wasn't doing it for the glory, or for the cash. Bascomb had implied that he had no choice, but you always had a choice, and he'd chosen to go along. For what?

For his country, he thought.

"It's peacetime," Bascomb had said, "and the old Soviet threat dried up and blew away, but don't let that fool you, Keller. Your country exists in a permanent state of war. She has enemies within and without her borders. And sometimes we have to do it to them before they can do it to us."

Keller, knotting his necktie, buttoning his suit jacket, didn't figure he looked much like a soldier. But he felt like one. A soldier in his own idiosyncratic uniform, off to serve his country.

Howard Ramsgate was a big man, broad-shouldered, with a ready smile on his guileless square-jawed face. He was wearing a white shirt and a striped tie, and the pleated trousers of a gray sharkskin suit. The jacket hung on a clothes tree in the corner of the office.

He looked up at Keller's entrance. "Afternoon," he said. "Gorgeous day, isn't it? I'm Howard Ramsgate."

Keller supplied a name, not his own. Not that Ramsgate would be around to repeat it, but suppose he had a tape recorder running? He wouldn't be the first man in Washington to bug his own office.

"Good to met you," Ramsgate said, and stood up to shake hands. He was wearing suspenders, and Keller noticed that they had cats on them, different breeds of cats.

When you pictured a traitor, he thought, you pictured a furtive little man in a soiled raincoat, skulking around a basement or lurking in a shabby café. The last thing you expected to run into was a pair of suspenders with cats on them.

"Well, now," Ramsgate was saying. "Did we have an appointment? I don't see it on my calendar."

"I just took a chance and dropped by."

"Fair enough. How'd you manage to get past Janeane?"

The secretary. Keller had timed her break, slipping in when she ducked out for a quick cigarette.

"I don't know," he said. "I didn't notice anybody out there."

"Well, you're here," Ramsgate said. "That's what counts, right?"

"Right."

"So," he said. "Let's see your mousetrap."

Keller stared at him. Once, during a brief spate of psychotherapy, he had had a particularly vivid dream about mice. He could still remember it. But what on earth did this spy, this traitor—

"That's more or less a generic term for me," Ramsgate said. "That old saw—create a better mousetrap and the world will beat a path to your door. Emerson, wasn't it?"

Keller had no idea. "Emerson," he agreed.

"With that sort of line," Ramsgate said, "it was almost always Emerson, except when it was Benjamin Franklin. Solid American common sense, that's what you could count on from both of them."

"Right."

"As it happens," Ramsgate said, "Americans have registered more patents for mousetraps than for any other single device. You wouldn't believe the variety of schemes men have come up with for snaring and slaughtering the little rodents. Of course"—he plucked his suspenders—"the best mousetrap of all's not patentable. It's got four legs and it says meow."

Keller managed a chuckle.

"I've seen my share of mousetraps," Ramsgate went on. "Like every other patent attorney. And every single day I see something new. A lot of the inventions brought to this office aren't any more patentable than a cat is. Some have already been invented by somebody else. Not all of them do what they're supposed to do, and not all of the things they're supposed to do are worth doing. But some of them work, and some of them are useful, and every now and then one of them comes along and adds to the quality of life in this wonderful country of ours."

Solid American common sense, Keller thought. This great country of ours. The man was a traitor and he had the gall to sound like a politician on the stump.

"So I get stirred up every time somebody walks in here," Ramsgate said. "What have you brought for me?"

"Well, let me just show you," Keller said, and came around the desk. He opened his briefcase and placed a yellow legal pad on the desktop.

" 'Please forgive me,' " Ramsgate read aloud. "Forgive you for what?"

Keller answered him with a choke hold, maintaining it long enough to guarantee unconsciousness. Then he let go and tore the top sheet from the legal pad, crumpled it into a ball, dropped it into the wastebasket. The sheet beneath it, the new top sheet, already held a similar message: "I'm sorry. Please forgive me."

It wouldn't stand up to a detailed forensic investigation, but Keller figured it would make it easy for them to call it suicide if they wanted to.

He went to the window, opened it. He rolled Ramsgate's desk chair over to the window, took hold of the man under the arms, hauled him to his feet, then heaved him out the window.

He put the chair back, tore the second sheet off the pad, crumpled it, tossed it at the basket. That was better, he decided—no note, just a pad on the desk, and then, when they look in the basket, they can come up with two drafts of a note he decided not to leave after all.

Nice touch. They'd pay more attention to a note if they had to hunt for it.

Janeane was back at her desk when he left, chatting on the phone. She didn't even look up.

Keller, back in New York, started each of the next five days with a copy of the *Washington Post* from a newsstand across the street from the UN building. There was nothing in it the first morning, but the next day he found a story on the obituary page about an established Washington patent attorney, an apparent suicide. Keller learned where Howard Ramsgate had gone to college and law school and read about a couple of inventions he'd helped steer through the patent process. The names of his survivors were given as well—a wife, two children, a brother in Lake Forest, Illinois.

What it didn't say was that he was a spy, a traitor. Didn't say he'd had help getting out the window. Keller, perched on a stool in a coffee shop, wondered how much more they knew than they were letting on.

The next three days he didn't find one more word about Ramsgate. This wasn't suspicious in and of itself—how often was there a follow-up to the suicide of a not-too-prominent attorney?—but Keller found himself trying to read between the lines of other stories, trying to find some subtle connection to Ramsgate's death. This lobbyist charged with illegal campaign contributions, that Japanese tourist caught in the crossfire of a drug-related shootout, a key vote on a close bill in Congress—any such item might somehow link up to the defenestration of Howard Ramsgate. And he, the man who'd made it happen, would never know.

On the fifth morning, as he found himself frowning over a minor scandal in the mayor's office, it occurred to Keller to wonder if he was being watched. Had anyone observed him in the days since Ramsgate's death? Had it been noted that he was starting each day, not around the corner from his apartment with the *New York Times* but five blocks away with the *Washington Post*?

He thought it over and decided he was being silly. But then was he being any less silly buying the *Post* each morning? He'd tossed a pebble into a pond days ago, and now he kept returning, trying to detect the shadow of a ripple on the pond's smooth surface.

He got out of there and left the paper behind. Later, thinking about it, he realized what had him acting this way.

He was looking for closure, for some sense of completion. Whenever he did a job for the old man, he made a phone call, got a pat on the back, bantered a bit with Dot, and, in the ordinary course of things, collected his money. That last was the most important, of course, but the acknowledgment was important, too, along with the mutual recognition that the job was done and done satisfactorily.

With Ramsgate he got none of that. There was no report to make, nobody to banter with, no one to tell him how well he'd done. Tight-lipped men in Washington offices might be talking about him, but he didn't get to hear what they were saying. Bascomb might be pleased with what he'd done, but he wasn't getting in touch, wasn't dispensing any pats on the back.

Well, Keller decided, that was okay.

Because, when all was said and done, wasn't that the soldier's lot? There would be no drums and bugles for him, no parades, no medals. He would get along without feedback or acknowledgment, and he would probably never know the real results of his actions, let alone the reason he'd drawn a particular assignment in the first place.

He could live with that. He could even take a special satisfaction in it. He didn't need drums or bugles, parades or medals. He had been leading the life of a scoundrel, and his country had called on him. And he had served her.

No one had given him a pat on the back. No one had called to say well done. No one would, and that was fine. The deed he had done, the service he had performed, was its own reward.

He was a soldier.

Time passed, and Keller got used to the idea that he would never hear from Bascomb again. Then one afternoon he was standing on line at the half-price ticket booth in Times Square when someone tapped him on the shoulder. "Excuse me," a fellow said, handing him an envelope. "Think you dropped this."

Keller started to say he hadn't, then stopped when he recognized the man. Bascomb! Before he could say anything the man was gone, disappearing into the crowd.

Just a plain white envelope, the flap glued down and taped shut. Nothing written on it. From the heft of it, you'd put two stamps on it before putting it in the mail. But there were no stamps, and Bascomb had not entrusted it to the mails.

Keller put it in his pocket. When he got to the front of the line he bought a ticket to that night's performance of a fifties musical. He thought of buying two tickets and hiding one in a hollowed-out pumpkin. Then, when the curtain went up at eight o'clock, Bascomb would be in the seat beside him.

He went home and opened the envelope. There was a name, along with an address in Pompano Beach, Florida. There were two Polaroid shots, one of a man and woman, the other of the same man, alone this time, sitting down. There were nine hundred-dollar bills, used and out of sequence, and two fifties.

Keller looked at the photos. They'd evidently been taken several years apart. The fellow looked older in the photo that showed him unaccompanied, and was that a wheelchair he was sitting in? Keller thought it might be.

Poor bastard, Keller started to think, and then caught himself. The guy had no pity coming. The son of a bitch was a traitor.

The thousand in cash fell a ways short of covering Keller's expenses. He had to pay full coach fare on the flight to West Palm Beach, had to rent a car, had to stay three nights in a hotel room before he could get the job done and another night afterward, before he could catch a morning flight home. The five hundred dollars he'd received as expenses for the Howard Ramsgate incident had paid for the Metroliner and his room and a good dinner, with a couple of dollars left over. But he had to dip into his own pocket to get the job done in Pompano Beach.

Not that it really mattered. What did he care about a few dollars one way or the other?

He might have cut corners by getting in and out faster, but the operation turned out to be a tricky one. The traitor—his name was Drucker, Louis Drucker, but it was simpler for Keller to think of him as "the traitor"—lived in a beachfront condo on Briny Avenue, right in the middle of Pompano Beach. The residents, predictably enough, had a median age well into the golden years, and the traitor was by no means the only one there with wheels on his chair. There were others who got around with aluminum walkers, while the more athletic codgers strutted around with canes.

This was the first time Keller's work had taken him to such a venue, so he didn't know if security was as much of a priority at every senior citizens' residence, but this one was harder to sneak into than the Pentagon. There was an attendant posted in the lobby at all hours, and there was closed-circuit surveillance of the elevators and stairwells.

The traitor left the building twice a day, morning and evening, for a turn along the beach. He was always accompanied by a woman half his age who pushed his chair on the hard-packed sand, then read a Spanish magazine and smoked a cigarette or two while he took the sun.

Keller considered and rejected elaborate schemes for getting into the building. They'd work, but then what? The woman lived in the traitor's apartment, so he'd have to take her out, too. He had no compunctions about this, recognizing that civilian casualties were inevitable in modern warfare, and who was to say she was an entirely unwitting pawn? No, if the only way to nullify the traitor led through her, Keller would take her out without a second thought.

But a double homicide made for a high-profile incident, and why draw unnecessary attention? With an aged and infirm quarry, it was so much simpler to make it look like natural causes.

Could he lure the woman off the premises? Could he gain access during her absence? And could he get out unobtrusively, his work completed, before she got back?

He was working it out, fumbling with a plan, when Fate dropped it all in his lap. It was mid-morning, with the sun climbing the eastern sky, and he'd dutifully dogged their footsteps (well, *her* footsteps, since the traitor's feet never touched the ground) a mile or so up the beach. Now the traitor sat in his chair facing the ocean, his head back, his eyes closed, his leathery skin soaking up the rays. A few yards away the woman lay on her side on a beach towel, smoking a cigarette, reading a magazine.

She put out the cigarette, burying it in the sand. And, moments later, the magazine slipped from her fingers as she dozed off.

Keller gave her a minute. He looked left, then right. There was nobody close by, and he was willing to take his chances with those who were fifty yards or more from the scene. Even if they were looking right at him, they'd never realize what was happening right before their eyes. Especially given the age of most of those eyes.

He came up behind the traitor, clapped a hand over his treacherous mouth, used the thumb and forefinger of his other hand to pinch the man's nostrils closed, and kept his air shut off while he counted, slowly, to a number that seemed high enough.

When he let go, the traitor's hand fell to one side. Keller propped it up and left him looking as though asleep, basking like a lizard in the warm embrace of the sun.

"Where've you been, Keller? I've been calling you for days."

"I was out of town," he said.

"Out of town?"

"Florida, actually."

"Florida? Disney World, by any chance? Do I get to shake the hand that shook the hand of Mickey Mouse?"

"I just wanted a little sun and sand," he said. "I went to the Gulf Coast. Sanibel Island."

"Did you bring me a seashell, Keller?"

"A seashell?"

"The shelling is supposed to be spectacular there," Dot said. "The island sticks out into the Gulf instead of stretching out parallel to the land, the way they're supposed to."

" 'The way they're supposed to'?"

"Well, the way they usually do. So the tides bring in shells by the carload and people come from all over the world to walk the beach and pick them up. But why am I telling you all this? You're the one who just got back from the damn place. You didn't bring me a shell, did you?"

"You have to get up early in the morning for the serious shelling," Keller said, wondering if it was true. "The shellers are out there at the crack of dawn, like locusts on a field of barley."

"Barley, huh?"

"Amber waves of grain," he said. "Anyway, what do I care about shells? I just wanted a break."

"You missed some work."

"Oh," he said.

"It couldn't wait, and who knew where you were or when you'd be back? You should really call in when you leave town."

"I didn't think of it."

"Well, why would you? You never leave town. When's the last time you had a vacation?"

"I'm on vacation most of my life," he said. "Right here in New York."

"Then I guess it was about time you went away for something besides work. I suppose you had company."

"Well . . ."

"Good for you, Keller. It's just as well I couldn't reach you. But next time . . ."

"Next time I'll keep you posted," he said. "Better than that, next time I'll bring home a seashell."

This time he didn't try to track the story in the papers. Even if Pompano Beach had a newspaper of its own, you couldn't expect to find it at the UN newsstand. They'd have the *Miami Herald* there, but somehow he didn't figure the *Herald* ran a story every time an old fellow drifted off in the sunshine. If they did, there'd be no room left in the paper for hurricanes and carjackings.

Besides, why did he want to read about it? He had carried out his mission and the traitor was dead. That was all he had to know.

It was almost two months before Bascomb got in touch again. This time there was no face-to-face contact, however fleeting.

Instead, Keller got a phone call. The voice was presumably Bascomb's, but he couldn't have sworn to it. The call was brief, and the voice never rose much above a low murmur.

"Stay home tomorrow," the voice said. "There'll be something delivered to you."

And in fact the FedEx guy came around the following morning, bringing a flat cardboard envelope that held a photograph, an index card with a name and address printed on it, and a sheaf of used hundreds.

There were ten of the bills, a thousand dollars again, although the address this time was in Aurora, Colorado, which involved quite a few more air miles than Pompano Beach. That rankled at first, but when he thought about it he decided there was something to be said for the low payment. If you lost money every time you did this sort of thing, it underscored your commitment to your role as a patriot. You never had to question your motives, because it was clear you weren't in it for the money.

He squared up the bills and put them in his wallet, then took a good long look at the photo of the latest traitor.

And the phone rang.

Dot said, "Keller, I'm lonesome and there's nothing on TV but Sally Jessy Raphaël. Come on out here and keep me company."

Keller took a train out to White Plains and another one back to New York. He packed a bag, called an airline, and took a cab to JFK. That night his plane landed in Seattle, where he was met by a lean young man in a double-breasted brown suit. The fellow wore a hat, too, a fedora that gave him a sort of retro look.

The young man—Jason, his name was—dropped

Keller at a hotel. In the morning they met in the lobby, and Jason drove him around and pointed out various points of interest, including the Kingdome and the Space Needle and the home and office of the man Keller was supposed to kill. And, barely visible in the distance, the snow-capped peak of Mount Rainier.

They ate lunch at a good downtown restaurant, and Jason put away an astonishing amount of food. Keller wondered where he put it. There wasn't a spare ounce on him.

The waitress was refilling the coffee when Jason said, "Well, I was starting to wonder if we missed him today. Just coming through the door? Gray suit, blue tie? Big red face on him? That's Cully Wilcox."

He looked just like his photo. It never hurt, though, to have somebody ID the guy in the flesh.

"He's a big man in this town," Jason said, his lips barely moving. "Harder they fall, right?"

"I beg your pardon?"

"Isn't that the expression? 'The bigger they are, the harder they fall'?"

"Oh, right," Keller said.

"I guess you don't feel like talking right now," Jason said. "I guess you got things to think about, details to work out."

"I guess so," Keller said.

"This may take a while," he told Dot. "The subject is locally prominent."

"Locally prominent, is he?"

"So they tell me. That means more security on the way in and more heat on the way out."

"Always the way when it's somebody big."

"On the other hand, the bigger they are, the harder they fall."

"Whatever that means," she said. "Well, take your time, Keller. Smell the flowers. Just don't let the grass grow under your feet."

Hell of a thing, Keller thought.

He muted the TV just in time to stop a cute young couple from advising him that Certs was two, two, two mints in one. He closed his eyes and adapted the dialogue to his own circumstances. *"Keller is a contract killer." "No, Keller is a traitor killer." "He's two, two, two killers in one. . . ."*

It was tough enough, he thought, to lead one life at a time. It was a lot trickier when they overlapped. He couldn't stall the old man, couldn't put off the trip to Seattle while he did his Uncle Sam's business in Colorado. But how long could he delay the mission? How urgent was it?

He couldn't call Bascomb to ask him. So he had to assume a high degree of urgency.

Which meant he had to find a way to do two, two, two jobs in one.

Just what he needed.

It was a Saturday morning, a week and a half after he'd flown to Seattle, when Keller flew home. This time he had to change planes in Chicago, and it was late by the time he got to his apartment. He'd already called White Plains the night before to tell them the job was done. He unpacked his bag, shucked his clothes, took a hot shower, and fell into bed.

The following afternoon the phone rang.

"No names, no pack drill," said Bascomb. "I just wanted to say *Well done.*"

"Oh," Keller said.

"Not our usual thing," Bascomb went on, "but even a seasoned professional can use the occasional pat on the back. You've done fine work, and you ought to know it's appreciated."

"That's nice to hear," Keller admitted.

"And I'm not just speaking for myself. Your efforts are appreciated on a much higher level."

"Really?"

"On the highest level, actually."

"The highest level?"

"No names, no pack drill," Bascomb said again, "but let's just say you've earned the profound gratitude of a man who never inhaled."

He called White Plains and told Dot he was bushed. "I'll come out tomorrow around lunchtime," he said. "How's that?"

"Oh, goody," she said. "I'll make sandwiches, Keller. We'll have a picnic."

He got off the phone and couldn't think what to do with himself. On a whim he took the subway to the Bronx and spent a few hours at the zoo. He hadn't been to a zoo in years, long enough for him to have forgotten that they always made him sad.

It still worked that way, and he couldn't say why. It's not that it bothered him to see animals caged. From what he understood, they led a better life in captivity than they did in the wild. They lived longer and stayed healthier. They didn't have to spend half their time trying to get enough food and the other half trying to keep from being food for somebody else. It was tempting to look at them and conclude that they were bored, but he didn't believe it. They didn't look bored to him.

He left unaccountably sad as always and returned to Manhattan. He ate at a new Afghan restaurant and went to a movie. It was a western, but not the sort of Hollywood classic he would have preferred. Even after the movie was over, you couldn't really tell which ones were the good guys.

Next day Keller caught an early train to White Plains and spent forty minutes upstairs with the old man. When he came downstairs Dot told him there was fresh coffee made, or iced tea.

He went for the coffee. She already had a tall glass of iced tea poured for herself. They sat at the kitchen table and she asked him how it had gone in Seattle. He said it went okay.

"And how'd you like Seattle, Keller? From what I hear it's everybody's city du jour these days. Used to be San Francisco and now it's Seattle."

"It was fine," he said.

"Get the urge to move there?"

He had found himself wondering what it might be like, living in one of those converted industrial buildings around Pioneer Square, say, and shopping for groceries at Pike Market, and judging the quality of the weather by the relative visibility of Mount Rainier. But he never went anywhere without having thoughts along those lines. That didn't mean he was ready to pull up stakes and move.

"Not really," he said.

"I understand it's a great place for a cup of coffee."

"They're serious about their coffee," he allowed. "Maybe too serious. Wine snobs are bad enough, but when all it is is coffee . . ."

"How's that coffee, by the way?"

"It's fine."

"I bet it can't hold a candle to the stuff in Seattle," she said. "But the weather's lousy there. Rains all the time, the way I hear it."

"There's a lot of rain," he said. "But it's gentle. It doesn't bowl you over."

"It rains but it never pours?"

"Something like that."

"I guess the rain got to you, huh?"

"How's that?"

"Rain, day after day. And all that coffee snobbery. You couldn't stand it."

Huh? "It didn't bother me," he said.

"No?"

"Not really. Why?"

"Well, I was wondering," she said, looking at him over the brim of her glass. "I was wondering what the hell you were doing in Denver."

The TV was on with the sound off, tuned to one of the home shopping channels. A woman with unconvincing red hair was modeling a dress. Keller thought it looked dowdy, but the number in the lower right corner kept advancing, indicating that viewers were calling in a steady stream to order the item.

"Of course I could probably *guess* what you were doing in Denver," Dot was saying, "and I could probably come up with the name of the person you were doing it to. I got somebody to send me a couple of issues of the *Denver Post*, and what did I find but a story about a woman in someplace called Aurora who came to a bad end, and I swear the whole thing had your fingerprints all over it. Don't look so alarmed, Keller. Not your actual fingerprints. I was speaking figuratively."

"Figuratively," he said.

"It did look like your work," she said, "and the timing was right. I'd say it might have lacked a little of your usual subtlety, but I figure that's because you were in a big hurry to get back to Seattle."

He pointed at the television set. He said, "Do you believe how many of those dresses they've sold?"

"Tons."

"Would you buy a dress like that?"

"Not in a million years. I'd look like a sack of potatoes in something cut like that."

"I mean any dress. Over the phone, without trying it on."

"I buy from catalogs all the time, Keller. It amounts to the same thing. If it doesn't look right you can always send it back."

"Do you ever do that? Send stuff back?"

"Sure."

"He doesn't know, does he, Dot? About Denver?"

"No."

He nodded, hesitated, then leaned forward. "Dot," he said, "can you keep a secret?"

She listened while he told her the whole thing, from Bascomb's first appearance in the coffee shop to the most recent phone call, relaying the good wishes of the man who never inhaled. When he was done he got up and poured himself more coffee. He came back and sat down and Dot said, "You know what gets me? 'Dot, can you keep a secret?' Can *I* keep a secret?"

"Well, I—"

"If I can't," she said, "then we're all in big trouble. Keller, I've been keeping *your* secrets just about as long as you've had secrets to keep. And you're asking me—"

"I wasn't exactly asking you. What do they call it when you don't really expect an answer?"

"Prayer," she said.

"Rhetorical," he said. "It was a rhetorical question. For God's sake, I know you can keep a secret."

"That's why you kept this one from me," she said. "For lo these many months."

"Well, I figured this was different."

"Because it was a state secret."

"That's right."

"Hush-hush, your eyes only, need-to-know basis. Matters of national security."

"Uh-huh."

"And what if I turned out to be a Commie rat?"

"Dot—"

"So how come I all of a sudden got a top-secret clearance? Or is it need-to-know? In other words, if I hadn't brought up Denver . . ."

"No," he said. "I was planning on telling you anyway."

"Sooner or later, you mean."

"Sooner. When I called yesterday and said I wanted to wait until today to come up, I was buying a little time to think it over."

"And?"

"And I decided I wanted to run the whole thing by you, and see what you think."

"What I think."

"Right."

"Well, you know what that tells me, Keller? It tells me what *you* think."

"And?"

"And I think it's about the same thing that I think."

"Spell it out, okay?"

"C-O-N," she said. "J-O-B. Total B-U-L-L-S-H—am I getting through?"

"Loud and clear."

"He must be pretty slick," she said, "to have a guy like you jumping through hoops. But I can see how it would work. First place, you want to believe it. 'Young man, your country has need of you.' Next thing you know, you're knocking off strangers for chump change."

"Expense money. It never covered the expenses, except the first time."

"The patent lawyer, caught in his own mousetrap. What do you figure he did to piss Bascomb off?"

"No idea."

"And the old fart in the wheelchair. It's a good thing you iced the son of a bitch, Keller, or our children and our children's children would grow up speaking Russian."

"Don't rub it in."

"I'm just making you pay for that rhetorical question. All said and done, do you think there's a chance in a million Bascomb's on the level?"

He made himself think it over, but the answer wasn't going to change. "No," he said.

"What was the tip-off? The approval from on high?"

"I guess so. You know, I got a hell of a rush."

"I can imagine."

"I mean, the man at the top. The big guy."

"Chomping doughnuts and thinking of you."

"But then you think about it afterward, and there's just no way. Even if he said something like that, would Bascomb pass it on? And then when I started to look at the whole picture . . ."

"Tilt."

"Uh-huh."

"Well," she said. "What kind of a line have we got on Bascomb? We don't know his name or his address or how to get hold of him. What does that leave us?"

"Damn little."

"Oh, I don't know. We don't need a whole hell of a lot, Keller. And we do know something."

"What?"

"We know three people he wanted killed," she said. "That's a start."

Keller, dressed in a suit and tie and sporting a red carnation in his buttonhole, sat in what he supposed you would call the den of a sprawling ranch house in Glen Burnie, Maryland. He had the TV on with the sound off, and he was beginning to think that was the best way to watch it. The silence lent a welcome air of mystery to everything, even the commercials.

He perked up at the sound of a car in the driveway, and, as soon as he heard a key in the lock, he triggered the remote to shut off the TV altogether. Then he sat and waited patiently while Paul Ernest Farrar hung his topcoat in the hall closet, carried a sack of groceries to the kitchen, and moved through the rooms of his house.

When he finally got to the den, Keller said, "Well, hello, Bascomb. Nice place you got here."

Keller, leading a scoundrel's life, had ended the lives of others in a great variety of ways. As far as he knew, though, he had never actually frightened anyone to death. For a moment, however, it looked as though Bascomb (né Farrar) might be the first. The man turned white as Wonder Bread, took an involuntary step backward, and clasped a hand to his chest. Keller hoped he wasn't going to need CPR.

"Easy," he said. "Grab a seat, why don't you? Sorry to startle you, but it seemed the best way. No names, no pack drill, right?"

"What do you think you're doing in my house?"

"The crossword puzzle, originally. Then when the light failed I had the TV on, and it's a lot better when you don't know what they're saying. Makes it more of an exercise for the imagination." He leaned back in his chair. "I'd have joined you for breakfast," he said, "but who knows if you even go out for it? Who's to say you don't have your oat bran muffin and decaf at the pine table in the kitchen? So I figured I'd come here."

"You're not supposed to get in touch with me at all," Farrar said sternly. "Under any circumstances."

"Give it up," Keller said. "It's not working."

Farrar didn't seem to hear him. "Since you're here," he said, "of course we'll talk. And there happens to be something I need to talk to you about, as a matter of fact. Just let me get my notes."

He slipped past Keller and was reaching into one of the desk drawers when Keller took him by the shoulders and turned him around. "Sit down," he said, "before you embarrass yourself. I already found the gun and took the bullets out. Wouldn't you feel silly, pulling the trigger and all it does is go *click*?"

"I wasn't reaching for a gun."

"Maybe you wanted this, then," Keller said, dipping into his breast pocket. "A passport in the name of Roger Keith Bascomb, issued by authority of the government of British Honduras. You know something? I looked on the map, and I couldn't *find* British Honduras."

"It's Belize now."

"But they kept the old name for the passports?"
He whistled soundlessly. "I found the firm's litera-
ture in the same drawer with the passport. An outfit
in the Caymans, and they offer what they call fantasy
passports. To protect yourself, in case you're ab-
ducted by terrorists who don't like Americans.
Would you believe it—the same folks offer other
kinds of fake ID as well. Send them a check and a
photo and they'll set you up as an agent of the National Security Resource. Wouldn't that be handy?"

"I don't know what you're talking about."

Keller sighed. "All right," he said. "Then I'll tell
you. Your name isn't Roger Bascomb, it's Paul Farrar.
You're not a government agent, you're some kind of
paper-pusher in the Social Security Administration."

"That's just a cover."

"You used to be married," Keller went on, "until
your wife left you for another man. His name was
Howard Ramsgate."

"Well," Farrar said.

"That was six years ago. So much for the heat of
the moment."

"I wanted to find the right way to do it."

"You found me," Keller said, "and got me to do
it for you. And it worked, and if you'd left it like
that you'd have been in the clear. But instead you
sent me to Florida to kill an old man in a wheelchair."

"Louis Drucker," Farrar said.

"Your uncle, your mother's brother. He didn't
have any children of his own, and who do you think
he left his money to?"

"What kind of a life did Uncle Lou have? Crippled,
immobile, living on painkillers . . ."

"I guess we did him a favor," Keller said. "The woman in Colorado used to live two doors down the street from you. I don't know what she did to get on your list. Maybe she jilted you or insulted you, or maybe her dog pooped on your lawn. But what's the difference? The point is you used me. You got me to chase around the country killing people."

"Isn't that what you do?"

"Right," Keller said, "and that's the part I don't understand. I don't know how you knew to call a certain number in White Plains, but you did, and that got me on the train with a flower in my lapel. Why the charade? Why not just pay the money and let out the contract?"

"I couldn't afford it."

Keller nodded. "I thought that might be it. Theft of services, that's what we're looking at here. You had me do all this for nickels and dimes."

"Look," Farrar said, "I want to apologize."

"You do?"

"I do, I honestly do. The first time, with that bastard Ramsgate, well, it was the only way to do it. The other two times I could have afforded to pay you a suitable sum, but we'd already established a relationship. You were working, you know, out of patriotism, and it seemed safer and simpler to leave it at that."

"Safer."

"And simpler."

"And cheaper," Keller said. "At the time, but where are you in the long run?"

"What do you mean?"

"Well," Keller said, "what do you figure happens now?"

"You're not going to kill me."

"What makes you so sure?"

"You'd have done it," Farrar said. "We wouldn't be having this conversation. You want something, and I think I know what it is."

"A pat on the back," Keller said, "from the man who never inhaled."

"Money," Farrar said. "You want what's rightfully yours, the money you would have been paid if I hadn't misrepresented myself. That's it, isn't it?"

"It's close."

"Close?"

"What I want," Keller said, "is that and a little more. If I were the IRS, I'd call the difference penalties and interest."

"How much?"

Keller named a figure, one large enough to make Farrar blink. He said it seemed high, and they kicked it around, and Keller found himself reducing the sum by a third.

"I can raise most of that," Farrar told him. "Not overnight. I'll have to sell some securities. I can have some cash by the end of the week, or the beginning of next week at the latest."

"That's good," Keller said.

"And I'll have some more work for you."

"More work?"

"That woman in Colorado," Farrar said. "You wondered what I had against her. There was something, a remark she made once, but that's not the point. I found a way to make myself a secondary beneficiary in an individual's government insurance policy. It's too complicated to explain but it ought to work like a charm."

"That's pretty slick," Keller said, getting to his feet. "I'll tell you, Farrar, I'm prepared to wait a week or so for the money, especially with the prospect of future work. But I'd like some cash tonight as a binder. You must have some money around the house."

"Let me see what I've got in the safe," Farrar said.

"Twenty-two thousand dollars," Keller said, slipping a rubber band around the bills and tucking them away. "That's what, fifty-five hundred dollars a pop?"

"You'll get the balance next week," Farrar assured him. "Or a substantial portion of it, at the very least."

"Great."

"Anyway, where do you get fifty-five hundred? There were three of them, and three into twenty-two is seven and a third. That makes it"—he frowned, calculating—"seven thousand, three hundred thirty-three dollars a head."

"Is that right?"

"And thirty-three cents," Farrar said.

Keller scratched his head. "Am I counting wrong? I make it four people."

"Who's the fourth?"

"You are," Keller told him.

"If I'd wanted to wait," he told Dot the next day, "I think he probably would have handed over a decent chunk of cash. But there was no way I was going to let him see the sun come up."

"Because who knows what the little shit is going to do next."

"That's it," Keller said. "He's an amateur and a nut case, and he already fooled me once."

"And once is enough."

"Once is plenty," Keller agreed. "He had it all worked out, you know. He'd manipulate Social Security records and get me to kill total strangers so that he could collect their benefits. Total strangers!''

"You generally kill total strangers, Keller."

"They're strangers to me," he said, "but not to the client. Anyway, I decided to take a bird in the hand, and the bird comes to twenty-two thousand. I guess that's better than nothing."

"It was," Dot said, "last time I checked. And none of it was work, anyway. You did it for love."

"Love?"

"Love of country. You're a patriot, Keller. After all, it's the thought that counts."

"If you say so."

"I say so. And I like the flower, Keller. I wouldn't think you'd be the type to wear one, but I have to say you can carry it off. It looks good. Adds a certain something."

"Panache," he said. "What else?"

10

Keller in Retirement

"*Retiring? You, Keller?*" Dot looked at him, frowned, shook her head. "Shy, maybe. But retiring? I don't think so."

"I'm thinking about it," he said.

"You're a city boy, Keller. What are you going to do, scoot off to Roseburg, Oregon? Buy yourself a little cabin of clay and wattles made?"

"Wattles?"

"Never mind."

"It was a nice enough town," he said. "Roseburg. But you're right, I'm a New Yorker. I'd stay right here."

"But you'd be retired."

He nodded. "I ran the numbers," he said. "I can afford it. I've squirreled some money away over the years, and my rent's reasonable. And I was never one to live high, Dot."

"You've had expenses, though. All the earrings you bought for that girl."

"Andria."

"I remember her name, Keller. I didn't want to say it because I thought it might be a sore point."

He shook his head. "She walked into my life," he said, "and she walked my dog, and she walked out."

"And took your dog along with her."

"Well, he pretty much walked in himself," he said, "so it figured he would walk out one day. For a while I missed both of them, and now I don't miss either of them, so I'd have to say I came out of it okay."

"Sounds like it."

"And I never spent serious money on earrings. What do earrings have to do with anything, anyway?"

"Beats me. More tea, Keller?"

He nodded and she filled both their cups. They were in a Chinese restaurant in White Plains, half a mile from the big old house on Taunton Place where she lived with the old man. Keller had suggested they meet for lunch, and she'd suggested this place, and the meal had been about what he'd expected. The food looked Chinese enough, but it tasted suburban.

"He's been slipping," he said. "He has his good days and his bad days."

"Not too many good days lately," Dot said.

"I know. And we've talked about it, how sooner or later we have to do something. And I got to thinking, and it seems to me all *I* have to do is retire."

"Throw in the towel," Dot said. "Cash in your chips. Walk away from the table."

"Something like that."

"And?"

"And what?"

"You're a young man, Keller. What are you going to do with the rest of your life?"

"The same as I do now," he said, "but without leaving town on a job eight or ten times a year. Except for those little interruptions, you could say I've been retired for years. I go to the movies, I read a book, I work out at the gym, I take a long walk, I see a play, I have the occasional beer, I meet the occasional lady . . ."

"Who takes your occasional dog for an occasional walk."

He gave her a look. "Point is," he said, "I keep on doing what I've been doing all along, except I don't take contracts anymore."

"Because you're retired."

"Right. What's wrong with that?"

She thought about it. "It almost works," she said.

"Almost? Why almost?"

"These things you do," she said, "aren't things you do."

"Huh?"

"What they are, they're things you keep busy with while you're waiting for the phone to ring. They're things you do between jobs. But if there weren't any jobs, if you finally got used to the idea that the phone wasn't going to ring, all that other stuff would have to be your whole life. And there's not enough there, Keller. You'd go nuts."

"You really think so?"

"Absolutely."

"I sort of see what you mean," he admitted. "The work is an interruption, and I'm usually irritated when the phone rings. But if it stopped ringing altogether . . ."

"Right."

"Well, *hell*," he said. "People retire all the time, some of them men who loved their work and put in sixty-hour weeks. What have they got that I don't?"

She answered without hesitation. "A hobby," she said.

"A hobby?"

"Something to be completely wrapped up in," she said, "and it doesn't much matter what it is. Whether you're scuba diving or fly-fishing or playing golf or making things out of macramé." She frowned. "Do you make stuff out of macramé?"

"I don't."

"I mean, what exactly *is* macramé, do you happen to know? It's not like papier-mâché, is it?"

"You're asking the wrong person, Dot."

"Or is it that crap you make by tying knots? You're right about me asking the wrong person, because whatever the hell macramé is, it's not *your* hobby. If it was you could make a cabin out of it, along with the clay and the wattles."

"We're back to wattles," he said, "and I still don't know what they are. The hell with them. If I had some sort of a hobby—"

"Any hobby, as long as you can really get caught up in it. Building model airplanes, racing slot cars, keeping bees . . ."

"The landlord would love that."

"Well, anything. Collecting stuff—coins, buttons, first editions. There are people who collect different kinds of barbed wire, can you believe it? Who even knew there *were* different kinds of barbed wire?"

"I had a stamp collection when I was a kid," Keller remembered. "I wonder whatever happened to it."

"I collected stamps when I was a boy," Keller told the stamp dealer. "I wonder whatever became of my collection."

"Might as well wonder where the years went," the man said. "You'd be about as likely to see them again."

"You're right about that. Still, I have to wonder what it would be worth, after all these years."

"Well, I can tell you that," the man said.

"You can?"

He nodded. "Be essentially worthless," he said. "Say five or ten dollars, album included."

Keller took a good look at the man. He was around seventy, with a full head of hair and unclouded blue eyes. He wore a white shirt with the sleeves rolled up, and a couple of pens shared his shirt pocket with some philatelic implements Keller recognized from decades ago—a pair of stamp tongs, a magnifier, a perforation gauge.

He said, "How do I know? Well, let's say I've seen a lot of boyhood stamp collections, and they don't vary much. You weren't a rich kid by any chance, were you?"

"Hardly."

"Didn't get a thousand dollars a month allowance and spend half of that on stamps? I've known a few like that. Spoiled little bastards, but they put together some nice collections. How did you get your stamps?"

"A friend of my mother's brought me stamps from the overseas mail that came to his office," Keller said, remembering the man, picturing him suddenly for what must have been the first time in twenty-five years. "And I bought some stamps, and I got some by trading my duplicates with other kids."

"What's the most you ever paid for a stamp?"

"I don't know."

"A dollar?"

"For one stamp? Probably less than that."

"Probably a lot less," the man agreed. "Most of the stamps you bought probably didn't run you more than a few cents apiece. That's all they were worth then, and that's all they'd be worth now."

"Even after all these years? I guess stamps aren't such a good investment, are they?"

"Not the ones you can buy for pennies apiece. See, it doesn't matter how old a stamp is. A common stamp is always common and a cheap stamp is always cheap. Rare stamps, on the other hand, stay rare, and valuable stamps become more valuable. A stamp that cost a dollar twenty or thirty years ago might be worth two or three times as much today. A five-dollar stamp might go for twenty or thirty or even fifty dollars. And a thousand-dollar stamp back then could change hands for ten or twenty thousand today, or even more."

"That's very interesting," Keller said.

"Is it? Because I'm an old fart who loves to talk, and I might be telling you more than you want to know."

"Not at all," Keller said, planting his elbows on the counter. "I'm definitely interested."

"Now if you want to collect," Wallens said, "there are a lot of ways to go about it. There are about as many ways to collect stamps as there are stamp collectors."

Douglas Wallens was the dealer's name, and his store was one of the last street-level stamp shops in New York, occupying the ground floor of a narrow three-story brick building on Twenty-eighth Street just east of Fifth Avenue. He could remember, Wallens said, when there were stamp stores on just about every block of midtown Manhattan, and when Nassau Street, way downtown, was *all* stamp dealers.

"The only reason I'm still here is I own the building," he said. "Otherwise I couldn't afford the rent. I do okay, don't get me wrong, but nowadays it's all mail-order. As for the walk-in trade, well, you can see for yourself. There's none to speak of."

But philately remained a wonderful pastime, the king of hobbies and the hobby of kings. Kids still mounted stamps in their beginner albums—though fewer of them, in this age of computers. And grown men, young and old, well-off and not so well-off, still devoted a substantial portion of their free time and discretionary income to the pursuit.

And there were innumerable ways to collect.

"Topical's very popular," Wallens said. "Animals on stamps, birds on stamps, flowers on stamps. Insects—there's series after series of butterflies, for example. Instead of running around with a net, you collect your butterflies on stamps." He thumbed a box of Pliofilm-fronted packets, pulling out examples. "Very attractive stamps, some of these. Railroads on stamps, cars on stamps, paintings on stamps—you can start your own little gallery, keep it in an album. Coins on stamps, even *stamps* on stamps. See? Modern stamps with pictures of classic nineteenth-century stamps on them. Nice-looking, aren't they?"

"And you just pick a category?"

"Or a topic, which is what they generally call it. And there's checklists available for the popular topics, and clubs you can join. You can design your own album, too, and you can even invent your own topic, like stamps relating to your own line of work."

Assassins on stamps, Keller thought. Murderers on stamps.

"Dogs," he said.

Wallens nodded. "Very popular topic," he said. "Dogs on stamps. All the different breeds, as you can imagine. . . . Here we go, twenty-four different dogs on stamps for eight dollars plus tax. You don't want to buy this."

"I don't?"

"This is for a kid's Christmas stocking. A serious collector wouldn't want it. Some of the stamps are the low values from complete sets, and sooner or later you'd have to buy the whole set anyway. And a lot of these packet stamps are garbage, from a philatelic point of view. Every country's issuing ridiculous stamps nowadays, printing up tons of colorful wallpaper to sell to collectors. But you've got certain countries, they probably don't mail a hundred letters a month from the damn place, and they're issuing hundreds of different stamps every year. The stamps are printed and sold here in the U.S., and they've never even seen the light of day in Dubai or Saint Vincent or Equatorial Guinea or whatever half-assed country authorized the issue in return for a cut of the profits. . . ."

By the time Keller got out of there his head was buzzing. Wallens had talked more or less nonstop for two full hours, and Keller had found himself hanging on every word. It was impossible to remember it all, but the funny thing was that he'd *wanted* to remember it all. It was interesting.

No, it was more than that. It was fascinating.

He hadn't parted with a penny, either, but he'd gone home with an armful of reading matter—three recent issues of a weekly stamp newspaper, two back numbers of a monthly magazine, along with a couple of catalogs for stamp auctions held in recent months.

In his apartment, Keller made a pot of coffee, poured himself a cup, and sat down with one of the weeklies. A front-page article discussed the proper method for mounting the new self-adhesive stamps. On the "Letters to the Editor" page, several collectors vented their anger at postal clerks who ruined collectible stamps by canceling them with pen and ink instead of a proper postmark.

When he took a sip of his coffee, it was cold. He looked at his watch and found out why. He'd been reading without pause for three straight hours.

"It's funny," he told Dot. "I don't remember spending that much time with my stamps when I was a kid. It seems to me I was outside a lot, and anyway, I had the kind of attention span a kid has."

"About the same as a fruit fly's."

"But I must have spent more time than I thought, and paid more attention. I keep seeing stamps I recognize. I'll look at a black-and-white photo of a stamp and right away I know what the real color is. Because I remember it."

"Good for you, Keller."

"I learned a lot from stamps, you know. I can name the presidents of the United States in order."

"In order to what?"

"There was this series," he said. "George Washington was our first president, and he was on the one-cent stamp. It was green. John Adams was on the pink two-cent stamp, and Thomas Jefferson was on the three-cent violet, and so on."

"Who was nineteenth, Keller?"

"Rutherford B. Hayes," he said without hesitation. "And I think the stamp was reddish-brown, but I can't swear to it."

"Well, you probably won't have to," Dot told him. "I'll be damned, Keller. It sounds for all the world as though you've got yourself a hobby. You're a whatchamacallit, a philatelist."

"It looks that way."

"I think that's great," she said. "How many stamps have you got in your collection so far?"

"None," he said.

"How's that?"

"You have to buy them," he said, "and before you do that you have to decide exactly what it is you want to buy. And I haven't done that yet."

"Oh," she said. "Well, all the same, it certainly sounds like you're off to a good start."

"I was thinking about collecting a topic," he told Wallens.

"You mentioned dogs, if I remember correctly."

"I thought about dogs," he said, "because I've always liked dogs. I had a dog named Soldier around the same time I had my stamp collection. And I thought about some other topics as well. But somehow topical collecting strikes me as a little, oh, what's the word I want?"

Wallens let him think about it.

"Frivolous," he said at length, pleased with the word and wondering if he'd ever had occasion to use it before. Not only did you learn the presidents in order, you wound up expanding your working vocabulary.

"I've known some topical collectors who were dedicated, serious philatelists," Wallens said. "Quite sophisticated, too. But all the same I have to say I agree with you. When you collect topically, you're not collecting stamps. You're collecting what they portray."

"That's it," Keller said.

"And there's nothing wrong with that, but it's not what you're interested in."

"No, it's not."

"So you probably want to collect a country, or a group of countries. Is there one in particular you're drawn to?"

"I'm open to suggestions," Keller said.

"Suggestions. Well, Western Europe's always good. France and colonies, Germany and German states. Benelux—that's Belgium, Netherlands, and Luxembourg."

"I know."

"British Empire's good—or at least it was when there was such a thing. Now all the former colonies are independent, and some of them are among the worst offenders when it comes to issuing meaningless stamps by the carload. Our own country's getting bad itself, printing stamps to honor dead rock stars, for God's sake."

"Reading the magazines," Keller said, "it made me want to collect everything, but most of the newer stamps . . ."

"Wallpaper."

"I mean, stamps with Walt Disney characters?"

"Say no more," said Wallens, rolling his eyes. He drummed the counter. "You know," he said, "I think I know where you're coming from, and I could tell you what I would do in your position."

"Please do."

"I'd collect worldwide," Wallens said, warming to the topic. "But with a cutoff."

"A cutoff?"

"They issued more stamps worldwide in the past three years than they did in the first hundred. Well, collect the first hundred years. Stamps of the world,

1840 to 1940. Those are your classic issues. They're real stamps, every one of them. They aren't pretty in a flashy way, they're engraved instead of photo-printed, and they're most of them a single color. But they're real stamps and not wallpaper."

"The first hundred years," Keller said.

"You know," Wallens said, "I'd be inclined to stretch that a dozen years. 1840 to 1952, and that way you're including the George the Sixth issues and stopping short of Elizabeth, which was about the time the British Empire quit amounting to anything. And that way you're also including all the wartime and postwar issues, all very interesting philateli-cally and a lot of fun to collect. A hundred years sounds like a nice round number, but 1952's really a better spot to draw the line."

Something clicked for Keller. "That's very appeal-ing," he said.

Wallens suggested he start by buying a collection. He'd save money that way and get off to a flying start. Two whole shelves in the dealer's back room held collections, general and specialized. Wallens showed him a three-volume collection, stamps of the world, 1840 to 1949. No great rarities, Wallens said as they paged through the albums, but plenty of good stamps, and the condition was decent throughout. The catalog value of the entire lot was just under $50,000, and Wallens had it priced at $5450.

"But I could trim that," he said. "Five thousand even. It's a pretty good deal, but on the other hand it's a major commitment for a man who never paid more than ten or twenty cents for a stamp, or thirty-two cents if he was getting ready to mail a letter. You'll want to take some time and think about it."

"It's just what I want," Keller said.

"It's nice, and priced very fair, but I'm not going to pretend it's unique. There are a lot of collections like this on the market, and it wouldn't be a bad idea for you to shop around."

Why? "I'll take it," Keller said.

Keller, at his desk, lifted a stamp with his tongs, affixed a folded glassine hinge to its back, then mounted the stamp in his new album. At Wallens's urging he had purchased a fine set of new albums and was systematically remounting all the stamps from the collection he had bought. The new albums were of much better quality, but that wasn't the only reason for the remounting operation.

"That way you'll come to know the stamps," Wallens had told him, "and they'll become yours. Otherwise you'd just be adding new stamps to another man's collection. This way you're creating a collection of your own."

And Wallens was right, of course. It took time and it absorbed you utterly, and you got to know the stamps. Sometimes the previous owner had mounted a stamp in the wrong space, and Keller took great satisfaction in correcting the error. And, as he finished transferring each country to the new album, he made himself a checklist, so he could tell at a glance what stamps he owned and what ones he needed.

He was up to Belgium now, and had gotten as far as Leopold II. The stamps he was working on had little tabs attached, stating in French and Flemish, the nation's two languages, that the letter was not to be delivered on a Sunday. (If you wanted Sunday delivery, you removed the tab before you licked the stamp and stuck it on the envelope.)

A couple of Keller's stamps lacked the Sunday tab,

which made them much less desirable, and Keller decided to replace them when he got the chance. He'd prepare his checklist accordingly, he thought, and the phone rang.

"Keller," Dot said, "I'll just bet you're playing with your stamps."

"Working with them," he said.

"I stand corrected. Speaking of work, why don't you come out and see me?"

"Now?"

"You're just a part-time philatelist," she pointed out. "You haven't retired yet. Duty calls."

Keller flew to New Orleans and took a cab to a hotel on the edge of the French Quarter. He unpacked and sat down with a city map and a photograph. The photo showed a middle-aged man with a full head of wavy hair, a deep tan, and a thirty-two-tooth smile. He was wearing a broad-brimmed Panama hat and holding a cigar. His name was Richard Wickwire, and he had killed at least one wife, and possibly two.

Six years previously, Wickwire had married Pam Shileen, daughter of a local businessman who'd done very nicely, thank you, in sulphur and natural gas. Several years into a stormy marriage, Pam Wickwire drowned in her swimming pool. After a brief mourning period, Richard Wickwire demonstrated his continuing enthusiasm for the Shileen family by marrying Pam's younger sister, Rachel.

The second marriage was, it seemed, also problematic. Rachel, a friend later testified, had feared for her life, and had reported that Wickwire had threatened to kill her. Straighten up and fly right, he'd told her, or he'd drown her the same as he'd drowned her sad-ass sister.

He didn't, though. He stabbed her instead, using the carving knife from the family barbecue set and sticking it straight into her heart. That at least was the prosecution's contention, and the evidence was pretty convincing, but the essential twelve persons were not unanimously convinced. The first trial ended in a hung jury, and on retrial the second jury voted to acquit.

So Jim Paul Shileen had a few drinks, loaded a six-gun, and went looking for his son-in-law. Found him, called him a son of a bitch, and emptied the gun at him, hitting him once in the shoulder and once in the hip, hitting a female companion of Wickwire's in the left buttock, and missing altogether with the three remaining bullets.

Shileen turned himself in, only to be charged with assault and attempted murder, acquitted of all charges, and given a stiff warning by the judge. "In other words," Dot had said, " 'You didn't do it. Now don't do it again.' So he's not going to do it again, Keller, and that's where you come in."

Wickwire, fully recovered from his wounds, was living in the same Garden District mansion he'd shared in turn with Pam and Rachel Shileen. He had married again, taking as his third bride not the young woman Shileen had wounded but a sweet young thing who'd been a juror, coincidentally enough, at his second trial. She'd visited him in the hospital after the shooting, and one thing led to another.

"The shooting evidently got his attention," Dot had said, "so he's got himself a couple of live-in bodyguards now, and you'd think they were his AmEx cards."

"Because he never leaves home without them."

"Apparently not. The client thought an explosive device might do the trick, and for all he cares the new wife and the bodyguards can come to the party, too. I figured you might not care for that."

"I don't."

"Too high tech, too noisy, and too much heat. Of course you'll do it your own way, Keller. You've got two weeks. The client wants to be out of the country when it happens, and that's how long he'll be gone. I figure if you can do it at all you can do it in two weeks."

Generally the case, he said. And what did the old man upstairs think about it?

"Unless he's telepathic," Dot said, "he's got no opinion. I took the call myself and headed the play on my own."

"I guess he was having a bad day."

"Actually," she said, "it was one of his better days, but I shortstopped the phone call anyway, and I figured, why give him a chance to screw this one up? You think I did the wrong thing?"

"Not at all," he said. "I've got no problem with that. My only problem is Wickwire."

"And you've got two weeks to solve him. Or until he murders wife number three, whichever comes first."

Keller studied the map, studied the photo. Wickwire's address looked to be within walking distance, and he felt capable of finding his way. And the weather was fine, and it would do him good to get out and stretch his legs.

He walked to Wickwire's residence and stopped

across the street for a look at the house. He was shooting for inconspicuous, but a woman pruning roses noted his interest and said, "That's where he lives. The wife-killer."

"Uh," he said.

"Just a matter of time before he goes for the hat trick," the woman said, savaging the air with her pruning shears. "That new wife's just playing moth to his flame, isn't she? Any girl that stupid, now you hate to see her hurt, but you wouldn't want her to produce young ones, either."

Keller said she had a point.

"The father-in-law? Not the dumbbell's daddy, I'm talking about Mr. Shileen. Now he's a gentleman, but he got excited and that's what threw his aim off."

"Maybe he'll do better next time," Keller said recklessly.

"What I hear," the woman said, "he's come to see there's things you can't do all by yourself. He went and hired some professional, flew him down here from Chicago to take care of things Mob-style."

Oh boy, Keller thought.

Keller had enjoyed walking to Wickwire's house, but enough was enough. He returned to his hotel on the St. Charles Avenue streetcar, and made his next visit to the Garden District the next morning in a rented Pontiac. He spent the better part of three days—or the worst part, if you asked him—trailing along after Wickwire's Lincoln. One of the bodyguards drove, the other rode shotgun, and Wickwire sat by himself in the rear seat.

If you were in fact from Chicago, Keller thought, there was an obvious Mob-style way to take care of things. All you had to do was pull up alongside the

Lincoln, zip your window down, and let go with a burst of auto fire at the rear side window. It was unlikely that Wickwire's car sported reinforced side panels and bulletproof glass, so that ought to do the trick. You could probably manage to spray the two bozos in the front seat while you were at it. Pow! Take that! Now you know how we handle things in the city with the big shoulders!

Not his style, Keller thought. He supposed it wouldn't be impossible to find someone local who could sell him the tools for the job, the gun and the ammunition, but it still wasn't his way of doing things. He was, after all, a New Yorker. He was inclined to be a little less obvious, a little more sophisticated.

Besides, no matter how airtight an alibi the client put together, the cops would figure he'd put out a contract. So the less professional the whole affair looked, the better it was for Jim Paul Shileen.

Keller walked around the Quarter. He passed bars offering genuine New Orleans jazz and restaurants boasting genuine New Orleans cuisine. If they had to keep insisting it was authentic, he thought, it probably wasn't. When a strip-club barker began his pitch, Keller waved him off; he didn't want to hear about genuine girls with genuine breasts.

Next thing he knew he was standing in front of an antique shop, studying the earrings in the window. He turned away, got his bearings, and headed for his hotel.

In his room he found himself changing channels as if determined to wear out the remote. He turned off the TV, picked up a magazine, flipped the pages, tossed it aside.

The thing was, he didn't want to be here. He wanted to be back in his own apartment, working on his stamps.

So what he had to do was figure out the right approach to Richard Wickwire and go ahead and do it and go home. Get out of New Orleans and get back to Belgium.

Let's see. Wickwire got out of the house a lot, and the bodyguards always went with him. But the new wife, for the most part, stayed home. So Keller could pay a call in Wickwire's absence.

Once inside the house, he could stuff the new wife in a coat closet and lay doggo, waiting for Wickwire to return, taking out him and his bodyguards before they had a clue. But that was heavy-handed, that was as Chicago as deep-dish pizza. There ought to be a subtler way . . . and just like that it came to him.

Get into the house. Arrange an accident for wife number three. Take her out back and drown her in the pool, say. Or break her neck and leave her at the foot of the stairs, as if she'd taken a header down the staircase. There was no end of ways to kill her, and how hard could any of them be? The woman obviously had the self-preservation instincts of a lemming.

Then let Wickwire explain.

It was poetic, and that part appealed to him. Wickwire, having murdered two wives with impunity, would get one of the state of Louisiana's special flu shots for a murder he hadn't committed, a wife he hadn't killed. Neat.

He went out and got something to eat, and by the time he got back to the room he had abandoned the scheme. There were a couple of things wrong with it, chief among them being the uncertainty of the enterprise. If they hadn't been able to convict him before, when everybody but the jury flat-out knew he was guilty, who was to say they could do it now? The bastard's luck might hold. You couldn't be positive it wouldn't.

Besides, the client had paid to have Wickwire killed, not framed. The client was getting on in years, and he didn't have all the time in the world. If Wickwire finally wound up convicted, and if he did indeed draw a sentence of death by lethal injection, he still had enough money to stretch out the appeal process for years on end. Revenge, Keller had heard, was a dish best enjoyed cold, but you didn't want it with mold growing on it. How sweet could it be if your victim outlived you?

Think of something else, Keller told himself, and let your subconscious take care of it. He picked up the stamp weekly he'd brought along—the current issue, he was a subscriber now—and flipped the pages until a story about precancels caught his eye. He read it, and half of another story. Then he straightened up in his chair and put the paper aside.

Gotcha, he thought.

He turned the idea over in his mind, and this time he couldn't find anything wrong with it. It would take special equipment, but nothing that would be too hard to come by. He'd obtained the same item once before, in a small city in the American heartland, and if you could find it in Muscatine, Iowa, how hard would it be to lay hands on it a few hundred miles downriver?

He checked the Yellow Pages and found a likely source within walking distance. He called, and they had what he wanted. He broke the connection and looked up motels in the Yellow Pages, then thought of another listing to check.

The dealer was a pudgy, round-shouldered fellow in his fifties. He wore a pale blue corduroy shirt with a button-down collar he hadn't troubled to button down. His suspenders had Roman coins on them, but the shop itself was exclusively devoted to stamps; there was a sign in the window, professionally lettered, asserting, WE DO NOT BUY OR SELL COINS.

"Nothing against them," said the man, whose name was Hildebrand. "But I don't happen to buy or sell chewing gum, either. Only difference is I don't have to put a sign in the window to keep the gum chewers away. I don't *know* anything about coins, I don't *understand* coins, I don't have a *feel* for coins, so why should I presume to traffic in the damned things?"

Keller's eyes went involuntarily to the suspenders. Hildebrand noticed, and rolled his eyes. "Women," he said.

That seemed to call for a reply, but Keller was stumped.

"My wife wanted to buy me suspenders," Hildebrand said, "and she thought suspenders with stamps would be nice, seeing that I've been a collector all my life, and a dealer *most* of my life. She bought me a tie with stamps on it a few years ago— U.S. classics, the Black Jack, the Jenny invert, the one-dollar Trans-Mississippi. Nice stamps, and it's a nice tie, and I wear it when I have to wear a necktie, which isn't often."

"I see," Keller said.

"So she couldn't *find* suspenders with stamps," Hildebrand said, "so she bought these, with *coins* on them, because according to her they amounted to the same thing. Can you imagine?"

"Wow," Keller said.

"All those years, and she thinks stamps and coins amount to the same thing. Well, what are you going to do, do you know what I mean?"

"Perfectly."

"Other hand, where would we be without 'em? Women, I mean. Or coins, for that matter, but—" He brought himself up short. "Enough of that. What can I do for you?"

"I'm in town on business," Keller said, "and I've got a little time to spare, and I thought I could look at some stamps."

"I'd say you came to the right place. What do you collect, if you don't mind my asking?"

"Worldwide. Before 1952."

"Oh, the good stuff," Hildebrand said, with what sounded like appreciation and respect. "The classics. Well, I've got plenty of stuff for you to look at. Any particular countries you'd like to see?"

"How about Austria? That's one of the checklists I happen to have with me."

"Austria," said Hildebrand. "You have a seat right here, why don't you? I've got a nice stock, mint and used. Including some of those early semipostals that get tougher to find every time you look for them. Do they have to be Never Hinged?"

"No," Keller said. "I hinge my stamps."

"Man after my own heart. You just make yourself comfortable. Here's a pair of tongs you can use, unless you brought your own?"

"I didn't think to pack them."

"What some folks do," Hildebrand said, "is keep an extra pair in their suitcase, and that way they've

always got tongs with 'em. Here's a stock book—
Austria—and here's a box of glassines, also Austria.
Enjoy yourself, and just give a holler if I can help
you with anything."

"Mr. Wickwire? My name is Sue Ellen? Sue Ellen
Bates?"

"Yes?"

"I guess you don't remember. In the restaurant? I
brought you your cocktails, and you smiled at me?"

"Rings a bell," Wickwire said.

"I said how I knew all along you were innocent,
and next time I came to the table you gave me a slip
of paper? With your name and number on it?"

"I did, did I? When was this, Sue Ellen?"

"Oh, it was a while ago. It took me this long to
get up my courage, and then I was out of town for
a while. I just got back, I'm staying at a motel until
I get my own place."

"Is that a fact?"

"And now you don't even remember me. Shoot, I
knew I should of called earlier!"

"Who says I don't remember you? Refresh my
memory, girl. What-all do you look like?"

"Well, I'm blond."

"You know, I kind of thought you might be."

"And I'm slim, except I'm what you call full-
figured."

"I think I'm beginning to remember you, child."

"And I'm twenty-four years old, and I stand five
foot seven, and my eyes are blue."

"Any tattoos or piercings I should know about?"

"No, I think they're tacky. Plus my mom'd about
kill me."

"Well, you sound good enough to eat."

"Why, Mr. Wickwire!"

"Just an expression. You know what'd be good? If I could meet you, that'd be the best way ever to refresh a man's memory."

"You want to meet me at a restaurant or something?"

"That's a little public, Sue Ellen. And in my position . . ."

"Oh, I see what you mean."

"Did you say you were staying at a motel, Sue Ellen? Where's it at?"

"Hello, this is Sue Ellen Bates calling?"

"Come again?"

"My name is like Sue Ellen Bates? I'm blond, and my eyes are like blue?"

"Oh, for God's sake," Dot said. "Keller, when are you going to grow up?"

"I've wondered that myself."

"You're using one of those telephone voice-changers, and I wish to God you'd disconnect it. You sound like a girl, and a stupid one at that."

"I don't know how you can say such a thing?"

"It's making every sentence sound like a question that does it," she said. "That's a nice touch, I've got to give you that. It makes you sound just like one of those teenage morons at the mall who can't remember where she parked her mother's car."

"Well," Keller said, "*he* likes me."

"Who? Oh, I get it."

"I'm meeting him the day after tomorrow. At my place."

"Not until then?"

"It's tough for him to get away."

"It's going to get even tougher. Well, at least

you're in a town with plenty to do. You shouldn't have trouble amusing yourself for the next couple of days."

"You're right about that," Keller said.

"Australia," the dealer said. He was a generation younger than Hildebrand, and his shop was on the second floor of an office building on Rampart Street. "I've got a good run of the early Kangaroos, if you'd like to see them. How about Australian States, while we're in that part of the world? Queensland, Victoria, Tasmania, New South Wales . . ."

"I haven't got my lists for those."

"Another time," the fellow said. "Here's tongs, here's a gauge if you want to check perfs. Let me know if there's anything else you need."

"I'll do that," Keller said.

The motel was in Metairie. Before his conversation with Richard Wickwire, Keller had called the motel and tried out the voice-changer on them, booking a room as Sue Ellen Bates. Then he drove over there, paid cash for a week in advance, and picked up the key. He let himself into the room, stowed some women's garments in the dresser and closet, and messed up the bed.

He didn't pay another visit to the room until an hour before Sue Ellen's date with Wickwire. He left the Pontiac a block away in a strip-mall parking lot, let himself into the room, and cracked the seal on a pint of bourbon. He poured an ounce of bourbon into each of two motel tumblers, made a lipstick mark on one of them, and placed them on the bedside table. He spilled a little bourbon on the rug, a little more on the chair, and left the pint standing open on the dresser.

Then he unlocked the door and left it very slightly ajar. He switched on the TV, tuned it to a talk show, lowered the volume. Next came the hard part—sitting and waiting. He should have brought the stamp weekly along. He'd read everything in it, but he could have read it again. You always picked up something you'd missed the first time.

Wickwire was due at two o'clock. At one-fifty, the phone on the bedside table rang. Keller frowned at it, then picked it up and said hello.

"Sue Ellen?"

"Mr. Wickwire?"

"I might be five or ten minutes late, sugar. Just wanted to let you know."

"I'll be waiting," Keller said. "You just come right on in."

He hung up and disconnected the voice-changer, wondering what he'd have done if he hadn't thought to hook it up earlier. Well, no sense trembling over unspilled milk.

At 2:10 Wickwire still hadn't shown. At 2:15 there was a knock at the door. "Sue Ellen?"

Keller didn't say anything.

"You here, Sue Ellen?"

Wickwire edged the door open. Keller, waiting behind it, let him get all the way inside. No telling who might be watching.

"Sue Ellen? Girl, where are you hiding yourself?"

Keller wrapped an arm around the big man's neck, got him in a choke hold, and applied the pressure, kicking the door shut while he was at it. Wickwire struggled at first, his shoulders bucking, then sagged in Keller's arms and slumped forward.

Keller let him go, stepped back, and kicked him three times in the face. Then he knelt down next to the unconscious Wickwire and broke his neck. He stripped the corpse to socks and underwear, heaved him onto the bed, and spilled most of the remaining bourbon into his open mouth. He took a chair and laid it on its side, took a pillow and flung it across the room, left dresser drawers half-open. He packed up the voice-changer, along with the clothing from the drawers and closet, and remembered to fetch Wickwire's wallet and money clip from his trousers.

He locked the door, fastened the chain bolt. The peephole in the door didn't afford much of a view, but he was able to see what looked like Wickwire's Lincoln Town Car parked at the very edge of his field of vision. It was odds-on the bodyguards were in it, listening to terrible music on the radio, waiting for their boss to knock off a cutie.

Or vice versa, Keller thought.

He wiped the surfaces where he might have left prints, then climbed out through the bathroom window and headed for the strip mall where he'd left the car.

Back in his own hotel, Keller packed his suitcase and checked flight schedules. There was, as far as he could tell, no point in sticking around. The job was done, and, if he said so himself, done rather neatly.

It would look for all the world like a badger game scam gone wrong. The woman who'd called herself Sue Ellen Bates had lured Wickwire to the motel room, and her male partner had turned up to extort money from him. There'd been a scuffle, with Wickwire sustaining injuries to the face and head before he had his neck broken, accidentally or on purpose.

Then the two con artists had had the presence of mind to try staging things, pouring bourbon on Wickwire, even though an autopsy would fail to show any of the stuff inside him. They hadn't troubled to straighten up after themselves, however, had stuck around only long enough to rob the corpse, then fled.

There were probably some loose ends and inconsistencies, but Keller didn't figure anybody would lose sleep over them. All in all, it was a death that looked like a logical consequence of the life Richard Wickwire had lately led, and both the New Orleans cops and the citizenry at large were apt to conclude that it couldn't have happened to a nicer guy. Which, come to think of it, was pretty much Keller's own view of the matter.

He'd stuffed Sue Ellen's clothes in one Dumpster, the telephone voice-changer in another. In the time-honored tradition of pickpockets and purse snatchers, he'd dropped Wickwire's wallet (minus the cash and credit cards) into a mailbox. The plastic, sliced into unidentifiable fragments, went down a storm drain. Wickwire's money clip—sterling silver, monogrammed—was identifiable, so he'd take it back to New York and manage to lose it there, where whoever found it would keep it or hock it or melt it or give it to a friend with the right initials.

Meanwhile it was full of cash, and the cash was now Keller's. He counted it, along with the bills from Wickwire's wallet, and was surprised by the total, which ran to just under fifteen hundred dollars.

He thought of Hildebrand, the man with the suspenders, and of the Austrian stamps he'd bought from him. There'd been a few more he'd have liked to buy, especially a mint copy of Austria's first stamp, Scott #1, the one kreuzer orange. It was an error, printed on both sides, and listed in the catalog at $1450. Hildebrand had tagged it $1000 and indicated he'd take $900 for it, but that struck Keller as an awful lot to pay for a stamp that his album didn't even have a space for. Besides, he could pick up a used copy for a tenth the price of a mint specimen.

Still, he hadn't been able to get the stamp out of his head. And now, with a windfall like this . . .

And it wasn't as if he were in that big a rush to get back to New York.

It was about a month later when the telephone rang in Keller's apartment. He was at his desk, working on his stamp collection. He still hadn't finished the task of remounting everything in his new albums, but he'd made good progress, having recently knocked off Sweden and started in on Switzerland.

He picked up the phone, and Dot said, "Keller, you work too goddam hard. I think you should take a vacation."

"A vacation," he said.

"That's the ticket. Haul your butt out of town and stay gone for a week."

"A week?"

"You know what? A week's not long enough to unwind, the way you go at it. Better make it ten days."

"Where do you want me to go?"

"Well, hell," she said. "It's your vacation, Keller. What do I care where you go?"

"I thought you might have a suggestion."

"Anyplace nice," she said. "So long as they've got a decent hotel, the kind where you'd be comfortable checking in under your own name."

"I see."

"Buy yourself a plane ticket."

"Under my own name," he said.

"Why not? Use your credit card, so you've got a good record for tax purposes."

Keller rang off and sat back, thinking. A vacation, for God's sake. He didn't take vacations, the kind that called for travel. His life in New York was a vacation, and when he traveled it was strictly business.

He had a good idea what this was about, and didn't really want to look at it too closely. Meanwhile, though, he had to pick a destination and get out of town. Where, though?

He reached for the latest stamp weekly, turned the pages. Then he picked up the phone and called the airlines.

Keller had been to Kansas City several times over the years. His work had always gone smoothly, and his memories of the town were good ones. They were crazy about fountains, he remembered. Every time you turned around you ran across another fountain. If a city had to have a theme, he supposed you could do a lot worse than fountains. They gladdened the heart a lot more than, say, nuclear reactor cones.

It was an unusual experience for him to travel under his own name and use his own credit cards. He sort of liked it, but felt exposed and vulnerable. Signing in at the restored downtown hotel, he wrote down not only his own name but his own address as well. Who ever heard of such a thing?

Of course, as a retiree he'd be doing that all the time. No reason not to. Assuming he ever went anyplace.

He unpacked and took a shower, then put on a tie and jacket and went to the third-floor suite to pick up an auction catalog.

There were half a dozen men in the room, two of them employees of the firm conducting the sale, the others potential bidders who'd come for an advance look at the lots that interested them. They sat at card tables, using tongs to extract stamps from glassine envelopes, squinting at them through pocket magnifiers, checking the perforations, jotting down notes in the margins of their catalogs.

Keller took the catalog to his room. He'd brought his checklists, a whole sheaf of them, and he sat down and got to work. The following day they were still offering lots for inspection, so he went down there again and examined some of the lots he'd checked off in the catalog. He had his own pair of tongs to lift the stamps with, his own pocket magnifier to squint through.

He got to talking with a fellow a few years older than himself, a man named McEwell who'd driven over from St. Louis for the sale. McEwell was interested exclusively in Germany and German states and colonies, and it seemed unlikely that the two of them would be butting heads during the sale, so they felt comfortable getting acquainted. Over dinner at a steakhouse they talked stamps far into the night, and Keller picked up some good pointers on auction strategy. He felt grateful, and tried to grab the check, but McEwell insisted on splitting it. "It's a three-day auction," he told Keller, "and you're a general collector with a ton of lots in there to tempt you. You save your money for the stamps."

It was indeed a three-day sale, and Keller was in his chair for all three days. The first session was all

U.S., so there was nothing for him to bid on, but the whole process was fascinating all the same. There were mail bids for all the lots, and floor action on the majority of them, and the auction moved along at a surprisingly brisk pace. It was good to have a session where he was just an observer; it gave him the chance to get the hang of it.

The next two days, he was a player.

He'd brought a lot of cash, more than he'd planned on spending, and he got more in the form of a cash advance on his Visa card. When it was all over he sat in his hotel room with his purchases on the desk in front of him, pleased with what he'd acquired and the bargain prices he'd paid, but a little bit anxious at having spent so much money.

He had dinner again that night with McEwell, and confided some of what he was feeling. "I know what you mean," McEwell said, "and I've been there myself. I remember the first time I paid over a thousand dollars for a single stamp."

"It's a milestone."

"Well, it was for me. And I said to the dealer, 'You know, that's a lot of money.' And he said, 'Well, it is, but you're only going to buy that stamp once.'"

"I never thought of it that way," Keller said.

He stayed on at the hotel after the sale was over, and every morning at breakfast he read the *New York Times*. On Thursday he found the article he'd been more or less waiting for. He read it several times through, and he would have liked to pick up a phone but decided he'd better not.

He stayed in Kansas City that day, and the next day, too. He walked around an art museum for a couple of hours without paying much attention to what he saw. He dropped in on a couple of stamp dealers, one of whom he'd seen at the auction, and he spent a few dollars, but his heart wasn't really in it.

The next day he packed his bag and flew back to New York. First thing the following morning he got on a train to White Plains.

In the kitchen, Dot poured him a glass of iced tea and muted the television set. How many times had he been here, sitting like this? But there was a difference. This time the two of them were all alone in the big old house.

"It's hard to believe he's gone," he said.

"Tell me about it," Dot said. "I keep thinking I should be bringing him his breakfast on a tray, taking the paper up to him. Then I remind myself I'll never get to do that again. He's gone."

"So many years . . ."

"For you and me both, Keller."

"The paper just said natural causes," he said. "It didn't go into detail."

"No."

"But I don't suppose it could have been all that natural. Or you wouldn't have sent me to Kansas City."

"That's where you went? Kansas City?"

He nodded. "Nice enough town."

"But you wouldn't want to live there."

"I'm a New Yorker," he said. "Remember?"

"Vividly."

"Natural causes," he prompted.

"Well, what could be more natural? You live too long, you got a mind that's starting to turn to pablum, you become erratic and unreliable, what's the natural thing for someone to do?"

"It was that bad, huh?"

"Keller," she said, "three weeks ago this reporter showed up. A kid barely old enough to shave, working his first job on the local paper. I'll tell you, I thought he was there to sell me a subscription, but no, he came to interview the old man."

"You'd think the editor would have sent somebody more experienced."

"It wasn't the editor's idea," she said, "or the kid's either, God help him. And who does that leave?"

"You mean . . ."

"He'd decided it was time to write his memoirs. Time to tell all the untold stories, time to tell where the bodies were buried. And I do mean bodies, Keller, and I do mean buried."

"Jesus."

"He saw this kid's byline on some high school basketball roundup and decided he was the perfect person to collaborate with."

"For God's sake."

"Need I say more? I'd already reached the point where I made sure all incoming calls got routed downstairs. Now I had to worry about the calls he made on his own. Keller, it's the hardest decision I ever had to make in my life."

"I can imagine."

"But what choice did I have? It had to be done."

"Sounds that way." He picked up his tea, put it down untasted. "Who'd you get for it, Dot?"

"Who do you think, Keller? You know the story about the little red hen?"

"No."

"Well, I'm not about to tell it to you, but she

couldn't find anyone to help her, so she did it all herself."

"You . . ."

"Right."

"Dot, for God's sake. I would have done it."

"I didn't even want you within five hundred miles, Keller. I wanted you to have an alibi that nobody could crack. Just in case somebody knew about the connection and decided to shake the box and see what fell out."

"I understand," he said, "but under the circumstances . . ."

"No," she said. "And I have to say it was easy for me, Keller. The hardest decision, but the easiest thing in the world. Something in his cocoa to make him sleep, and a pillow over his face to keep him from waking up."

"That's the kind of thing that shows up in an autopsy."

"Only if they hold one," she said. "His age, and then his regular doctor came over and signed the death certificate, and that's all you need. I had him cremated. It was his last wish."

"It was?"

"How do I know? I said it was, and they gave me the ashes in a tin can, and if some joker wants to do an autopsy now I'd say he's got his work cut out for him. I don't know what the hell to do with the ashes. Well, I'm sure I'll think of something. There's no hurry."

"No."

"It was something I never thought I'd have to do, something I never even figured I'd be capable of doing. Well, you never know, do you?"

"No."

"It's on my mind a lot, but I guess I'll get over that. This too shall pass, right?"

"You'll be fine," he said.

"I know. I'm fine now, as far as that goes. Now all I have to do is figure out what I'm going to do with the rest of my life."

"I was going to ask you about that."

She frowned. "What I suppose I'll do," she said, "is retire. I can afford it. I've put money aside myself, and he left me the house. I can sell it."

"Probably bring a good price."

"You would think so. And there's the cash on hand, which he didn't specifically leave me, but since I'm the only one who knows about it . . ."

"That makes it yours."

"You bet. So it's enough to live on. I can even afford to travel some. Go on cruises, put my feet up, see the world from the deck of a ship."

"You don't actually sound that enthusiastic, Dot."

"Well," she said, "it's probably because I'm not. What I'd rather do is keep on keeping on."

"Stay here, you mean?"

"Why not? And stay in the business. You know, I'm the one who's been pretty much running things lately."

"I know."

"But with you deciding to pack it in, it would mean finding other people to work with, and the ones I have access to are not people I'm crazy about. So I don't know."

"You can't work with people unless you feel a hundred percent about them."

"I know it. Look, I'm better off hanging it up. All I have to do is follow the same advice I gave you."

"And get a hobby."

"There you go. It really worked for you, didn't it? You're a full-fledged philatelist, and don't ask me to say that three times."

"I wouldn't dream of it. But that's me, all right."

"I'll bet you even found a stamp dealer in Kansas City. To pass the time while you were there."

"Actually," he said, "that's how I picked Kansas City." And he told her a little about the auction. "It's pretty amazing," he said. "You'll be sitting next to some rube in baggy pants and a dirty T-shirt, and he'll raise his index finger a few times and spend fifty or a hundred thousand dollars on postmasters' provisionals."

"Whatever they are," she said. "No, don't tell me. I have a feeling stamp collecting's not going to be my hobby, Keller, but I think it's great that it's yours. I guess we can say you're retired, can't we? And fully prepared to enjoy the Golden Years."

"Well," he said.

"Well what?"

"Well, not exactly."

"What's the matter?"

"Well, it's an expensive hobby," he said. "It doesn't have to be, you can buy thousands of stamps for two and three cents apiece, but if you really get serious about it . . ."

"It runs into money."

"It does," he agreed. "I'm afraid I've been dipping into my retirement fund the last month or so. I've spent more money than I expected to."

"No kidding."

"And the thing is I'm really enjoying it," he said, "and learning more and more about it as I go along. I'd like to keep on spending serious money on stamps."

She gave him a thoughtful look. "It doesn't sound as though you're quite ready to retire after all."

"I'm not in a position to," he said. "Not anymore. And I don't really want to, either. In fact I'd like to get as much work as I can, because I can use the money."

"To buy stamps."

"It sounds silly, I know, but . . ."

"No it doesn't," she said. "It sounds like the answer to a maiden's prayer. We always worked well together, didn't we, Keller?"

"Always."

"Some of the other jokers I was considering, I think they might have a hard time coming to terms with the idea of working for a woman. But I don't see that as a problem for you and me."

"Certainly not."

"Well," she said. "Thank God for stamp collecting is all that I can say. How about another glass of iced tea, Keller? And you can even tell me about postmasters' promotionals, if it makes you happy."

"Provisionals," he said. "And you don't have to hear about them. I'm happy already."

Please turn the page
for an exciting look at

HIT LIST

by
Lawrence Block

Now available from Avon Books

Keller, fresh off the plane from Newark, followed the signs marked Baggage Claim. He hadn't checked a bag, he never did, but the airport signage more or less assumed that everybody checked their luggage, because you got to the exit by heading for the baggage claim. You couldn't count on a series of signs that said *This is the way to get out of this goddamn place.*

There was a down escalator after you cleared security, and ten or a dozen men stood around at the foot of it, some in uniform, most holding hand-lettered signs. Keller found himself drawn to one man, a droopy guy in khakis and a leather jacket. He was the guy, Keller decided, and his eyes went to the sign the man was holding.

But you couldn't read the damn thing. Keller walked closer, squinting at it. Did it say Archibald? Keller couldn't tell.

He turned, and there was the name he was looking for, on a card held by another man, this one taller and heavier and wearing a suit and tie. Keller veered away from the man with the illegible sign—what was the point of a sign that nobody could read?—and walked up to the man with the Archibald sign. "I'm Mr. Archibald," he said.

"Mr. Richard Archibald?"

What possible difference could it make? He started to nod, then remembered the name Dot had given him. "Nathan Archibald," he said.

"That's the ticket," the man said. "Welcome to Louisville, Mr. Archibald. Carry that for you?"

"Never mind," Keller said, and held on to his carry-on bag. He followed the man out of the terminal and across a couple of lanes of traffic to the short-term parking lot.

"About the name," the man said. "What I figured, anybody can read a name off a card. Some clown's got to figure, why take a cab when I can say I'm Archibald and ride for free? I mean, it's not like they gave me a picture of you. Nobody here even knows what you look like."

"I don't come here often," Keller said.

"Well, it's a pretty nice town," the man said, "but that's beside the point. Which is, I want to make sure I'm driving the right person, so I throw out a first name, and it's a wrong first name. 'Richard Archibald?' Guy says yeah, that's me, Richard Archibald, right away I know he's full of crap."

"Unless that's his real name."

"Yeah, but what's the odds of that? Two men fresh off a plane and they both got the name Archibald?"

"Only one."

"How's that?"

"My name's not really Archibald," Keller said, figuring he wasn't exactly letting state secrets slip by the admission. "So it's only one man named Archibald, so how much of a long shot is it?"

The man set his jaw. "Guy claims to be Richard Archibald," he said, "he's not my guy. Whether it's his name or not."

"You're right about that."

"But you came up with Nathan, so we're in business. Case closed. It's the Toyota there, the blue one. Get in and we'll take a run over to long-term parking. Your car's there, full tank of gas, registration in the glove box. When you're done, just put her back in the same spot, tuck the keys and the claim check in the ashtray. Somebody'll pick it up."

The car turned out to be a mid-size Olds, dark green in color. The man unlocked it and handed Keller the keys and a cardboard claim check. "Cost you a few dollars," he said apologetically. "We brought her over last night. On the passenger seat there you got a street map of the area. Open it up, you'll see two spots marked, home and office. I don't know how much you been told."

"Name and address," Keller said.

"What was the name?"

"It wasn't Archibald."

"You don't want to say? I don't blame you. You seen a photo?"

Keller shook his head. The man drew a small envelope from his inside pocket, retrieved a card from it. The card's face displayed a family photograph, a man, a woman, two children and a dog. The humans were all smiling, and looked as though they'd been smiling for days, waiting for someone to figure out how to work the camera. The dog, a golden retriever, wasn't smiling, but he looked happy enough. "Season's Greetings . . ." it said below the photo.

Keller opened the card. He read: ". . . from the Hirschhorns—Walt, Betsy, Jason, Tamara, and Powhatan.

"I guess Powhatan's the dog," he said.

"Powhatan? What's that, an Indian name?"

"Pocahontas's father."

"Unusual name for a dog."

"It's a fairly unusual name for a human being," Keller said. "As far as I know it's only been used once. Was this the only picture they could come up with?"

"What's the matter with it? Nice clear shot, and I'm here to tell you it looks just like the man."

"Nice that you could get them to pose for you."

"It's from a Christmas card. Musta been taken during the summer, though. How they're dressed, and the background. You know where I bet this was taken? He's got a summer place out by McNeely Lake."

Wherever that was.

"So it woulda been taken in the summer, which'd made it what, fifteen months old? He still looks the same, so what's the problem?"

"It shows the whole family."

"Right," the man said. "Oh, I see where you're going. No, it's just him, Walter Hirschhorn. Just the man himself."

That was Keller's understanding, but it was good to have it confirmed. Still, he'd have been happier with a solo headshot of Hirschhorn, eyes narrowed and mouth set in a line. Not surrounded by his nearest and dearest, all of them with fixed smiles.

He didn't much like the way this felt. Hadn't liked it since he walked off the plane.

"I don't know if you'll want it," the man was saying, "but there's a piece in the glove box."

A piece of what, Keller wondered, and then realized what the man meant. "Along with the registration," he said.

"Except the piece ain't registered. It's a nice little

twenty-two auto with a spare clip, not that you're gonna need it. The clip, I mean. Whether you need the piece altogether is not for me to say."

"Well," Keller said.

"That's what you guys like, isn't it? A twenty-two?"

If you shot a man in the head with a .22, the slug would generally stay within the skull, bouncing around in there, doing no good to the skull's owner. The small-calibre weapon was supposed to be more accurate, and had less recoil, and would presumably be the weapon of choice for an assassin who prided himself in his artistry.

Keller didn't spend much time thinking about guns. When he had to use one, he chose whatever was at hand. Why make it complicated? It was like photography. You could learn all about f-stops and shutter speeds, or you could pick up a Japanese camera and just point and shoot.

"Just use it and lose it," the man was saying. "Or if you don't use it just leave it in the glove box. Otherwise it goes in a Dumpster or down a storm drain, but why am I telling you this? You're the man." He pursed his lips and whistled without making a sound. "I have to say I envy a man like you."

"Oh?"

"You ride into town, do what you do, and ride on out. Well, fly on out, but you get the picture. In and out with no hassles, no complications, no dealing with the same assholes day in and day out."

You dealt with different ones every time, Keller thought. Was that supposed to be better?

"But I couldn't do it. Could I pull a trigger? Maybe I could. Maybe I already done that, one time or another. But your way is different, isn't it?"

Was it?

The man didn't wait for an answer. "By the baggage claim," he said, "you didn't see me right away. You were headed for one of the other guys."

"I couldn't make out the sign he was holding," Keller said. "The letters were all jammed together. And I had the sense that he was waiting for somebody."

"They're all of them waiting for somebody. Point is, I was watching you, before you took notice of me. And I pictured myself living the life you lead. I mean, what do I know about your life? But based on my own ideas of it. And I realized something."

"Oh?"

"It's just not for me," the man said. "I couldn't do it."

It cost Keller eight dollars to get his car out of the long-term lot, which struck him as reasonable enough. He got on the interstate going south, got off at Eastern Parkway, and found a place to have coffee and a sandwich. It called itself a family restaurant, which was a term Keller had never entirely understood. It seemed to embody low prices, Middle American food, and a casual atmosphere, but where did family come into the picture? There were no families there this afternoon, just single diners.

Like Keller himself, sitting in a booth and studying his map. He had no trouble finding Hirschhorn's downtown office (on Fourth Street between Main and Jefferson, just a few blocks from the river) and his home in Norbourne Estates, a suburb a dozen miles to the east.

He could look for a hotel downtown, possibly within walking distance of the man's office. Or—he studied the map—he could continue east on Eastern Parkway, and there would almost certainly be a cluster of motels where it crossed I-64. That would give him easy access to the residence and, afterward, to the airport. He could get downtown from there as well, but he might not have to go there at all, because it would almost certainly be easier and simpler to deal with Hirschhorn at home.

Except for the damned picture.

Betsy, Jason, Tamara, and Powhatan. He'd have been happier not knowing their names, and happier still not knowing what they looked like. There were certain bare facts about the quarry it was useful to have, but everything else, all the personal stuff, just got in the way. It could be valuable to know that a man owned a dog—whether or not you chose to break into his home might hinge upon the knowledge—but you didn't have to know the breed, let alone the animal's name.

It made it personal, and it wasn't supposed to be personal. Suppose the best way to do it was in a room in the man's house, a home office in the basement, say. Well, somebody would find him there, and it would probably be a family member, and that was just the way it went. You couldn't go around killing people if you were going to agonize over the potential traumatic effect on whomever discovered the body.

But it was easier if you didn't know too much about the people. You could live easier with the prospect of a wife recoiling in horror if you didn't know her name, or that she had close-cropped blond hair and bright blue eyes and cute little chipmunk cheeks. It didn't take too much in the way of imagination to picture that face when she walked in on the death scene.

So it was unfortunate that the man with the Archibald sign had shown him that particular photograph. But it wouldn't keep him from doing the job at Hirschhorn's residence any more than it would lead him to abort the mission altogether. He might not care what calibre gun he used, and he didn't know that he took a craftsman's pride in his work, but he was a professional. He used what came to hand, and he got the job done.

"Now I can offer you a couple of choices," the desk clerk said. "Smoking or non, up or down, front or back."

The motel was a Super Eight. Keller went for non-smoking, rear of the building, first floor.

"No choice on beds," the clerk said. "All the units are the same. Two double beds."

"That still gives me a choice."

"How do you figure that?"

"I can choose which bed to sleep in."

"Clear-cut choice," the clerk said. "First thing you'll do is drop your suitcase on one of the beds."

"So?"

"So sleep in the other one. You'll have more room."

There were, as promised, two double beds in Room One-forty-seven. Keller considered them in turn before setting his bag on top of the dresser.

Keeping his options open, he thought.

From a pay phone, he called Dot in White Plains. He said, "Refresh my memory. Didn't you say something about an accident?"

"Or natural causes," she said, "though who's to say what's a natural cause in this day and age? Outside of choking to death on an organic carrot, I'd say you're about as natural a cause of death as there is."

"They provided a gun."

"Oh?"

"A twenty-two auto, because that's the kind guys like me prefer."

"That's a far cry from an organic carrot."

"Use it and lose it."

"Catchy," Dot said. "Sounds like a failure to communicate, doesn't it? Guy who furnished the gun didn't know it was supposed to be natural."

"Leaving us where? Does it still have to be natural?"

"It never *had* to, Keller. It was just a preference, but they gave you a gun, so I'd say they've got no kick coming if you use it."

"And lose it."

"In that order. Customer satisfaction's always a plus, so if you can arrange for him to have a heart attack or get his throat torn out by the family dog, I'd say go for it. On the other hand—"

"How did you know about the dog?"

"What dog?"

"The one you just mentioned."

"It was just an expression, Keller. I don't know if he has a dog. I don't know for sure if he's got a heart, but—"

"It's a golden retriever."

"Oh?"

"Named Powhatan."

"Well, it's all news to me, Keller, and not the most fascinating news I ever heard, either. Where is all of this coming from?"

He explained about the photo on the Christmas card.

"What a jerk," she said. "He couldn't find a head and shoulders shot, the kind the papers run when you get a promotion or they arrest you for embezzlement? My God, the people you have to work with. Be grateful you were spared the annual Christmas letter, or you'd know how Aunt Mary's doing great since she got her appendix transplant and little Tommy got his first tattoo."

"Little Jason."

"God, you know the kids' names? Well, they wouldn't put the dog's name on the card and leave the kids off, would they? What a mess."

"The guy was holding a sign. 'Archibald.' "

"At least they got that part right."

"And I said that's me, and he said, 'Richard Archibald?' "

"So."

"You told me they said Nathan."

"Come to think of it, they did. They screw that up too, huh?"

"Not exactly. It was a test, to make sure I wasn't some smartass looking for a free ride."

"So if you forgot the first name, or just didn't want to make waves . . ."

"He'd have figured me for a phony and told me to get lost."

"This gets better and better," she said. "Look, do you want to forget the whole thing? I can tell you're getting a bad feeling about it. Just come on home and we'll tell them to shit in their hat."

"Well, I'm already here," he said. "It could turn out to be easy. And I don't know about you, but I can use the money."

"I can always find a use for it," she said, "even if all I use it for is to hold on to. The dollars have to be someplace, and White Plains is as good a place as any for them."

"That sounds like something he would have said."

"He probably did."

They were referring to the old man, for whom they had both worked, Dot living with him and running his household, Keller doing what he did. The old man was gone now—his mind had gone first, little by little, and then his body went all at once—but things went on essentially unchanged. Dot took the phone calls, set the fees, made the arrangements, and disbursed the money. Keller went out there, checked out the territory, closed the sale, and came home.

"Thing is," Dot said, "they paid half in advance. I hate to send money back once I've got it in hand. It's the same money, but it feels different."

"I know what you mean. Dot, they're not in a hurry on this, are they?"

"Well, who knows? They didn't say so, but they also said natural causes and gave you a gun so you could get close to nature. To answer your question, no, I don't see why you can't take your time. Been to any stamp dealers, Keller?"

"I just got here."

"But you checked, right? In the Yellow Pages?"

"It passes the time," he said. "I don't think I've ever been in Louisville before."

"Well, make the most of it. Take the elevator up to the top of the Empire State building, catch a Broadway show. Ride the cable cars, take a boat ride on the Seine. Do all the usual tourist things. Because who knows when you'll get back there again."

"I'll have a look around."

"Do that," she said. "But don't even think about moving there, Keller. The pace, the traffic, the noise, the sheer human energy—it'd drive you nuts."

It was late afternoon when he spoke to Dot, and twilight by the time he followed the map to Winding Acres Drive, in Norbourne Estates. The street was every bit as suburban as it sounded, with good-sized one- and two-story homes set on spacious landscaped lots. The street had been developed long enough ago for the foundation plantings to have filled in and the trees to have gained some size. If you were going to raise a family, Keller thought, this was probably not a bad place to do it.

Hirschhorn's house was a two-story center-hall colonial with the front door flanked by a symmetrical planting of what looked to Keller like rhododendron. There was a clump of weeping birch on the left, a driveway on the right leading to a garage with a basketball hoop and a backboard centered over the door. It was, he noted, a two and a half car garage. Which was handy, he thought, if you happened to have two and a half cars.

There were lights on inside the house, but Keller couldn't see anybody, and that was fine with him. He drove around, familiarizing himself with the neighborhood, getting slightly lost in the tangle of winding streets, but getting straightened out without much trouble. He drove past the house another couple of times, then headed back to the Super Eight.

On the way back he stopped for dinner at a franchised steak house named for a recently deceased cowboy film star. There were probably better meals to be had in Louisville, but he didn't feel like hunting for them. He was back at the motel by nine o'clock, and he had his key in the door when he remembered the gun. Leave it in the glove compartment? He went back to the car for it.

The room was as he'd left it. He stowed the gun in his open suitcase and pulled up an armchair in front of the television set. The remote control was a little different from the one he had at home, but wasn't that one of the pleasures of travel? If everything was going to be exactly the same, why go anywhere?

A little before ten there was a knock on the door.

His reaction was immediate and dramatic. He snatched up the gun, chambered a round, flicked off the safety, and flattened himself against the wall alongside the door. He waited, his index finger on the trigger, until the knock came a second time.

He said, "Who is it?"

A man said, "Maybe I got the wrong room. Ralph, izzat you?"

"You've got the wrong room."

"Yeah, you sure don't sound nothin' like Ralph." The man's voice was thick, and some of his consonants were a little off-center. "Now where the hell's Ralph? Sorry to disturb you, mister."

"No problem," Keller said. He hadn't moved, and his finger was still on the trigger. He listened, and he could hear footsteps receding. Then they stopped, and he heard the man knocking on another door—Ralph's, one could but hope. Keller let out the breath he'd been holding and took in some fresh air.

He stared at the gun in his hand. That wasn't like him, grabbing a gun and pressing up against a wall. And he'd just gone and done it, he hadn't even stopped to think.

Very strange.

He ejected the chambered round, returned it to the clip, and turned the gun over in his hands. It was supposed to be the weapon of choice in his line of work, but it was more useful on offense than defense, handy for putting a bullet in the back of an unsuspecting head, but not nearly so handy when someone was coming at you with a gun of his own. In a situation like that you wanted something with stopping power, something that fired a big heavy slug that would knock a man down and keep him there.

On the other hand, when your biggest threat was some drunk looking for Ralph, anything beyond a rolled-up newspaper amounted to overkill.

But why the panic? Why the gun, why the held breath, why the racing pulse?

Why indeed? He waited until his heartbeat calmed down, then shucked his clothes and took a shower. Drying off, he realized how tired he was. Maybe that explained it.

He went right to sleep. But before he got into bed he made sure the door was locked, and he placed the little .22 on the beside table.

The first thing he saw when he woke up was the gun on the bedside table. Shaving, he tried to figure out what to do with it. He ruled out leaving it in the room, where the chambermaid could draw her own conclusions, but what were the alternatives? He didn't want to carry it on his person.

That left the glove compartment, and that's where he put it when he drove out to Winding Acres Drive. They gave you a free continental breakfast at the motel—a cup of coffee and a doughnut, and he wasn't sure what continent they had in mind—but he skipped it in order to get out to Hirschhorn's house as early as possible.

And was rewarded with the sight of the man himself, walking his dog.

Keller came up on them from the rear, and the man could have been anybody dressed for a day at the office, but the dog was unmistakably a golden retriever.

Keller had owned a dog for a while, an Australian cattle dog named Nelson. Nelson was long gone— the young woman whose job it was to walk him had, ultimately, walked off with him—and Keller had no intention of replacing either of them. But he was still a dog person. When February rolled around, he watched the American Kennel Club show on television, and figured one of these years he'd go over to Madison Square Garden and see it in person. He knew the different breeds, but even if he didn't, well, how tough was it to recognize a golden retriever?

Of course, a street like Winding Acres Drive could support more than one golden retriever. The breed, oafishly endearing and good with children, was deservedly popular, especially in suburban neighborhoods with large homes on ample lots. So just because this particular dog was a golden didn't mean it was necessarily Powhatan.

All this was going through Keller's mind even as he was overtaking man and dog from the rear. He passed them, and one glance as he did so was all it took. That was the man in the photograph, walking the dog in the photograph.

Keller circled the block, and so, eventually, did the man and the dog. Keller, parked a few houses away on the other side of the street, watched them head up the walk to the front door. Hirschhorn unlocked the door and let the dog in. He stayed outside himself, and a moment later he was joined by his children.

Jason and Tamara. Keller was too far away to recognize them, but he could put two and two together as well as the next man. The man and two children went to the garage, entering through the side door, and Keller keyed the ignition and timed things so that he passed the Hirschhorn driveway just as the garage door went up. There were two cars in the two and a half car garage, one a squareback sedan he couldn't identify and the other a Jeep Cherokee.

Hirschhorn left the Jeep for his wife and drove the

kids to school in the squareback, which turned out to be a Subaru. Keller stayed with the Subaru after Hirschhorn dropped off the kids, then let it go when Hirschhorn got on the interstate. Why follow the man to his office? Keller knew where the office was, and he didn't need to fight commuter traffic to go have a look at it now.

He found another family restaurant and ordered orange juice and a western omelet with hash browns and a cup of coffee. The orange juice was supposed to be fresh-squeezed, but one sip told you it wasn't. Keller thought about saying something, but what was the point?

"Bring your own catalog?"

"I use it as a checklist," Keller explained. "It's simpler than trying to carry around a lot of sheets of paper."

"Some use a notebook."

"I thought of that," he said, "but I figured it would be simpler to make a notation in the catalog every time I buy a stamp. The downside is it's heavy to carry around and it gets beat up."

"At least you've only got the one volume. That the Scott Classic? What do you collect?"

"Worldwide before 1952."

"That's ambitious," the man said. "Collecting the whole world."

The man was around fifty, with thin arms and legs and narrow shoulders and an enormous belly. He sat in an armchair on wheels, and a pair of high-tech aluminum crutches propped against the wall suggested that he only got out of the chair when he had to. Keller had found him in the Yellow Pages and had had no trouble locating his shop, in a strip mall on the Bardstown Road. His name was Hy Schaffner, and his place of business was Hy's Stamp Shoppe, and he was sure he could keep Keller busy looking at stamps. What countries would he like to start with?

"Maybe Portugal," Keller said. "Portugal and Colonies."

"Angra and Angola," Schaffner intoned. "Kionga. Madeira, Funchal. Hortha, Lourenco Marques. Tete and Timor. Macao and Quelimane." He cleared his throat, swung his chair around to the left, and took three small black looseleaf notebooks from a shelf, passing them over the counter to Keller. "Have a look," he said. "Tongs and a magnifier right there in front of you. Prices are marked, unless I didn't get around to it. They run around a third off catalog, more or less depending on condition, and the more you buy the more of a break I'll give you. You from around here?"

Keller shook his head. "New York."

"City or state?"

"Both."

"I guess if you're from the city you'd have to be from the state as well, wouldn't you? Here on business?"

"Just passing through," Keller said. That didn't really answer the question, but it seemed to be good enough for Schaffner.

"Well, take your time," the man said. "Relax and enjoy yourself."

Keller's mind darted around. Should he have said he was from someplace other than New York? Should he have invented a more specific reason for being in Louisville? Then he got caught up in what he was doing, and all of that mental chatter ceased

as he gave himself up entirely to the business of looking at stamps.

He had collected as a boy, and had scarcely
thought of his collection until one day when he
found himself considering retirement. The old man
in White Plains was still alive then, but he was
clearly losing his grip, and Keller had wondered if it
might be time to pack it in. He tried to imagine how
he'd pass the hours, and he thought of hobbies, and
that got him thinking about stamps.

His boyhood collection was long gone, of course,
with the rest of his youth. But the hobby was still
there, and it was remarkable how much he remembered. It struck him, too, that most of the miscellane-
ous information in his head had got there via
stamp collecting.

So he'd gone around and talked to dealers and
looked at some magazines, dipping a toe in the waters of philately, then held his breath and plunged
right in. He bought a collection and remounted it in
fancy new albums, which took hours each day for
months on end. And he bought stamps over the
counter from dealers in New York, and ordered them
from ads other dealers placed in Linn's Stamp News.
Other dealers sent him price lists, or selections on
approval. He went to stamp shows, where dozens of
dealers offered their wares at bourse tables, and he
bid in stamp auctions, by mail or in person.

It was funny how it worked out. Stamp collecting
was supposed to give him something to do in retirement, but he'd embraced it with such enthusiasm and
put so much money into it that retirement had ceased
to be an option. Then the old man had died while
Keller was at a stamp auction in Kansas City, and
Dot had decided to stay on and run the operation

out of the big house on Taunton Place. Keller took the jobs she found for him and spent a healthy share of the proceeds on stamps.

The philatelic winds blew hot and cold. There were weeks when he read every article in Linn's, others when he barely scanned the front page. But he never lost interest, and the pursuit—he no longer thought of it as a hobby—never failed to divert him.

Today was no exception. He went through the three notebooks of Portugal and colonies, then looked at some British Commonwealth issues, then moved on to Latin America. Whenever he found a stamp that was missing from his collection he noted the centering, examined the gum on the reverse, held it to the light to check for thins. He deliberated as intensely over a thirty-five cent stamp as over one priced at thirty-five dollars. Should he buy this used specimen or wait for a more costly mint one? Should he buy this complete set, even though he already had the two low values? He didn't have this stamp, but it was a minor variety, and his album didn't have a place for it. Should he buy it anyway?

Hours went by.

After he left Hy's Stamp Shoppe, Keller spent another couple of hours driving aimlessly around Greater Louisville. He thought about heading downtown for a look at Hirschhorn's office, but he decided he didn't feel like it. Why bother? Hirschhorn could wait.

Besides, he'd have to leave the car in a parking lot, and he'd have to make sure it was the kind where you parked it and locked it yourself. Otherwise the attendant would have the key, and suppose he opened the glove compartment just to see what it held? He might not be looking for a gun, but that's what he'd find, and Keller didn't figure that was the best thing that could happen.

It was a great comfort, having a gun. Took your mind off your troubles. You spent all your time trying to figure out where to keep it.

He'd missed lunch, so he had an early dinner and went back to his room at the Super Eight. He watched the news, then sat down at the desk with his catalog and the stamps he'd bought. He went through the book, circling the number of each stamp he'd acquired that day, keeping his inventory up to date.

He could have done this at home, at the same time that he mounted the stamps in his albums, but suppose he dropped in on another stamp dealer between now and then? If your records weren't right, it was all too easy to buy the same stamp twice.

Anyway, he welcomed the task, and took his time with it. There was something almost meditative about the process, and it wasn't as though he had anything better to do.

He was almost finished when the noise started overhead. God, who could it be, carrying on like that? And what could they be doing up there?

He stood it for a while, then reached for the phone, then changed his mind. He left the room and walked around the building to the lobby, where a young man with a wispy blond beard and wire-rimmed glasses was manning the desk. He looked up at Keller's approach, an apologetic expression on his face.

"I'm sorry to say we're full up," he said. "So are the folks across the road. The Clarion Inn at the next interchange going north still had rooms as of half an hour ago, and I'll be glad to call ahead for you if you want."

"I've already got a room," Keller said. "That's not the problem."

The young man's face showed relief, but only for a moment. *That's not the problem*—if it wasn't, something else was, and now he was going to hear about it, and be called upon to deal with it.

"Uh," he said.

"I'm in One-forty-seven," Keller said, "and whoever's in the room directly upstairs of me, which I guess would be Two-forty seven—"

"Yes, that's how it works."

"I think they're having a party," Keller said. "Or butchering a steer, or something."

"Butchering a steer?"

"Probably not that," Keller allowed, "but the point is they're being noisy about it, whatever it is they're doing. I mean really noisy."

"Oh." The clerk's gaze fell to the counter, where he seemed to find something fascinating on the few inches of Formica between his two hands. "There haven't been any other complaints," he said.

"Well, I hate to be first," Keller said, "but then I'm probably the only guest with a room directly under theirs, and that might have something to do with it."

The fellow was nodding. "The walls between the units are concrete block," he said, "and you never hear a peep through them. But I can't say the same for the floors. If you've got a noisy party upstairs, some sound does filter through."

"This is a noisy party, all right. It wouldn't be out of line to call it a riot."

"Oh."

"Or a civil disturbance, anyway. And filter's not

the word for it. It comes through unfiltered, loud and clear."

"Have you, uh, spoken to them about it?"

"I thought I'd speak to you."

"Oh."

"And you could speak to them."

The clerk swallowed, and his Adam's apple bobbed up and down. "Two-forty-seven," he said, and thumbed a box of file cards, and nodded, and swallowed again. "I thought so. They have a car."

"This is a motel," Keller said. "Who comes here on foot?"

"What I mean, I took one look at them and thought they were bikers. Like Hell's Angels? But they came in a car."

He was silent, and Keller could tell how much he wanted to ask a roomful of outlaw bikers to keep it down. "Look," he said, "nobody has to talk to them. Just put me in another room."

"Didn't I say, when you first walked in? We're full up. The No Vacancy sign's been lit for hours."

"Oh, right."

"So I don't know what to tell you. Unless . . ."

"Unless what?"

"Well, unless you wanted to call in a complaint to the police. Those guys might pay a little more attention to the cops than to you or me."

Just what he wanted. Officer, could you tell the Hell's Angels upstairs to pipe down? I've got urgent business in your town and I need my rest. My name? Well, it's different from the one I'm registered under. The nature of my business? Well, I'd rather not say. And the gun on the bedside table is unregistered, and that's why I didn't leave it in the car, and don't ask me whose car it is, but the registration's in the glove compartment.

"That's a little abrupt," he said. "Think how you'd feel if somebody called the cops on you without any warning."

"Oh."

"And if they figured out who called them—"

"I could call the Clarion," the clerk offered. "At the next interchange? But my guess is they're full up by now."

It was a little late to be driving around looking for a room. Keller told him not to bother. "Maybe they'll make it an early night," he said, "or maybe I'll get used to it. You wouldn't happen to have some ear plugs in one of those drawers, would you?"

The bikers didn't make it an early night, nor did Keller have much success getting used to the noise. The clerk hadn't had ear plugs, or known where they might be available. The nearest drugstore was closed for the night, and he didn't know where Keller might find one open. Would a 7-Eleven be likely to stock ear plugs? He didn't know, and neither did Keller.

After another hour of biker bedlam, Keller was about ready to find out for himself. He'd finished recording his new stamps in his catalog, but found the operation less diverting than usual. The noise from above kept intruding. With the job done and the stamps and catalog tucked away, he found a movie on television and kicked the volume up a notch. It didn't drown out the din from upstairs, but it did let him make out what William Holden was saying to Debra Paget.

There was no point, he found, in hitting the Mute button during the commercials, because he needed the TV sound to cancel out the bikers. And what good was TV if you couldn't mute the commercials?

He watched as much of the movie as he could bear, then got into bed. Eventually he got up, moistened scraps of toilet paper, made balls of them, and stuffed them in his ears. His ears felt strange—why wouldn't they, for God's sake? But he got used to it, and the near silence was almost thrilling.

Keller awoke to the faint sound of a phone ringing in the apartment next to his. Funny, he thought, because he couldn't usually hear anything next door. His was a pre-war building, and the walls were good and thick, and—

He sat up, shook off the mantle of sleep, and realized he wasn't in his apartment, and that the telephone ringing ever so faintly was right there on the bedside table, its little red bubble lighting up every time it rang. And just what, he wondered, was the point of that? So that deaf guests would be aware that the phone was ringing? What good would it do them? What could they do about it, pick up the receiver and wiggle their fingers at the mouthpiece?

He answered the phone and couldn't hear a thing. "Speak up," he said. "Is anybody there?" Then he realized he had little balls of toilet paper in his ears. "Hell," he said. "Just hold on a minute, will you?" He put the receiver down next to the gun and dug the wads of paper out of his ears. They had dried, of course, rather like papier mache, and it took some doing to get them out. He thought whoever it was would have hung up by then, but no, his caller was still there.

"Sorry to disturb you," she said, "but we've got you down for a room change. A second-floor unit? Housekeeping just finished with your new room, and I thought you might want to pick up the key and transfer your luggage."

He looked at his watch and was astonished to note that it was past ten. The noise had kept him up late and the toilet paper-induced silence had kept him sleeping. He showered and shaved, and it was eleven o'clock by the time he'd packed his things and moved to Room 210.

Once you were inside it with the door closed, the new room was indistinguishable from the one he'd just vacated. The same twin double beds, the same desk and dresser, the same two prints--a fisherman wading in a stream, a boy herding sheep—on the same concrete-block walls. Its second-floor front location, on the other hand, was the precise opposite of where he'd been.

Years ago a Cuban had told him always to room on the ground floor, in case he had to jump out the window. The Cuban, it turned out, was acting less on tradecraft than on a fairly severe case of acrophobia, so Keller had largely discounted the advice. Still, old habits died hard, and when offered a choice he usually took the ground floor.

Way his luck was running, this would be the time he had to go out the window.

After breakfast he drove into downtown Louisville and left the car on a parking ramp, the gun locked in the glove compartment. There was a security desk in the lobby of Hirschhorn's office building. Keller didn't figure it would be too much of a challenge, but he couldn't see the point. There would be other people in Hirschhorn's office, and then he'd have to ride down on the elevator and fetch the car from where he'd parked it. He exited the lobby, walked around for twenty minutes, then collected his car and drove over the bridge into Indiana. He rode around long enough to get lost and straightened out again, then stopped at a convenience store to top up the gas tank and use the phone.

"This fellow I've got to see," he said. "What do we know about him?"

"We know the name of his damn dog," Dot said. "How much more do you need to know about anybody?"

"I went looking for his office," he said, "and I didn't know what name to hunt for in the directory."

"Wasn't his name there?"

"I don't know," he said, "because I didn't go in for a close look, not knowing what to look for. Aside from his own name, I mean. Like if there's a company name listed, I wouldn't know what company."

"Unless it was the Hirschhorn Company."

"Well," he said.

"Does it matter, Keller?"

"Probably not," he said, "or I would have figured out a way to learn what I had to know. Anyway, I ruled out going to the office."

"So why are you calling me, Keller?"

"Well," he said.

"Not that I don't welcome the sound of your voice, but is there a point to all this?"

"Probably not. I had trouble getting to sleep, there were Hell's Angels partying upstairs."

"What kind of place are you staying at, Keller?"

"They gave me a new room. Dot, do we know anything about the guy?"

"If I know it, so do you. Where he lives, where he works—"

"Because he seems so white-bread suburban, and yet he's got enemies who give you a car with a gun in the glove compartment. And a spare clip."

"So you can shoot him over and over again. I don't know, Keller, and I'm not even sure the person who called me knows, but if I had to come up with one word it would be gambling."

"He owes money? They fly in a shooter over a gambling debt?"

"That's not where I was going. Are there casinos there?"

"There's a rack track," he said.

"No kidding, Keller. The Kentucky Derby, di dah di dah di dah, but that's in the spring. City's on a river, isn't it? Have they got one of those riverboat casinos?"

"Maybe. Why?"

"Well, maybe they've got casino gambling and he wants to get rid of it, or they want to have it and he's in the way."

"Oh."

"Or it's something entirely different, because this sort of thing's generally on a need-to-know basis, and I don't." She sighed. "And neither do you, all things considered."

"You're right," he said. "You want to know what it is, Dot? I'm out of synch."

"Out of synch."

"Ever since I got off the goddamn plane and walked up to the wrong guy. Tell me something. Why would anyone meet a plane carrying an unreadable sign?"

"Maybe they told him to pick up a dyslexic."

"It's the same as the little red light on the phone."

"Now you've lost me, Keller. What little red light on the phone?"

"Never mind. You know what I just decided? I'm going to cut through all this crap and just do the job and come home."

"Jesus," she said. "What a concept."